Dedication

To both my sons, Rodney Keith Ross and Randall Kirk Ross,
who gave me the idea of a cabin in the woods and deer hunters.
To Angela, my only daughter, who shares my love of books and of
writing.
Most of all, to my beloved husband J.W. Ross.
You have always been my number one fan, my friend and my soul
mate.
With your encouragement, your expertise, your patience and dedication
to my love of writing, you have helped me achieve my life-long desire
as a writer, that of publishing my first novel.
May I never forget to say "thank you"
and always remember to say
"I love you".

First Book Printing: October 2012

Self published by:
Patsy Kirksey Ross
208 Pitts Drive
Columbiana, Alabama 35051

HIDEAWAY

By
Patsy Kirksey Ross

***

The stench was coming from below. Amy wrinkled her nose as the unpleasant odor drifted upward to where she stood on the embankment. She scanned the bushes below for its source but could see nothing. She thought it was probably a wounded deer that had died in the bushes. She hated deer hunting season, hated the poachers that lay in wait for the beautiful, sleek animals that came to feed from the man-made feeders. She found the feeders on her land and had reported it to the game warden.

She started her descent, using a long stick to brace herself on the downhill climb. She slipped and fell to one knee. Getting up, she continued downward until she was on level ground. The odor was almost unbearable at this distance. She bent the weeds over with her stick, trying to spread them apart, looking for its source. Suddenly, she saw a flash of color, bright orange. Deer weren't bright orange. She had smelled a dead carcass before, yet this odor was worse than she remembered. She moved the brush aside with her hands and gasped at the sight before her. A man's body lay face down, with an arrow protruding from his back, between his shoulder blades. Dark, caked blood had plastered his shirt to his body. An orange knitted cap covered most of his blond hair. Flies swarmed his decomposing body.　Amy stumbled backward, her hand flying to her mouth.　She fell to the ground with a thud, and turning, she vomited once, then twice.　Slowly, she got to her feet, her limbs trembling.　She wished for her cell phone, but it was at the cabin.　She started to climb back up the embankment. It was harder going up. It took her forty-five minutes to get back to the cabin.　Relieved, she yanked the door open and almost fell inside in her haste.　A warm fire burned in the fireplace, as if to welcome her home.　The room smelled of hickory wood and roast coffee, but she noticed none of this. Her mind reeled, remembering the dead man's body lying in the brush.　With trembling hands, she opened her back-pack on the table and pulled out her cell phone.　She dialed 911 praying that it wasn't out of range.　After a click, an operator answered.

"There has been an accident....someone has been killed," she gasped.　She proceeded to tell the operator what she had found in the woods.　She started to give them directions and the lady asked her to stay on the line while the police and coroner were in route.　Amy knew that they would never find the cabin without directions, anyway.

It was half an hour later when the police and coroner arrived at the cabin.　The sun had begun to set and it was getting colder.　Amy was waiting for them in the yard, shivering.　She had forgotten to get her jacket.

Two officers, one in uniform and one in plain clothes got out of the car.

"Are you Amy Fontell?" one asked.

"Yes, Sir."

"I understand that you found a man's body."

"Yes.　It will take about forty-five minutes to hike down there.　It will be dark before then."

"We have lights.　Will you lead the way?"

"Let me get my jacket," she said, shivering.

Three men from the emergency vehicle followed with a wire basket to put the body in.　Amy walked at a fast pace and they kept up with her. She was feeling nauseous, the closer she got to the body. She did not want to look at it again.

"There has not been a report of a missing person in this area," one of the men was saying.

"May I ask, Miss Fontell, what you were doing way out here in these woods?" one of the men asked.

" I was hiking. I inherited a cabin and this property from my uncle. He died two years ago."

"You were hiking, alone?"

"Yes." she was startled by his question.

"This is hunting season. It's dangerous to be walking in the woods."

"You're probably right. I had to report poachers last year, although there aren't supposed to be hunters on my land."

Finally, they reached the embankment and Amy pointed downward.

"He's down there. You'll see him. I had rather not go down again."

"Fine, you stay here," he said, covering his nose. "Bring the lights," he called to those behind him.

Amy sat down on the cold ground, hugging her knees to warm herself. She watched as the men made their way to where the body lay. One of the men stretched a yellow 'crime scene' tape around the area. Surprised, Amy wondered if they thought it was a homicide instead of an accident. They made no attempt to move the body but were shining the lights all around the area. In a few minutes, the two men from the police car climbed back up to where Amy sat, shivering. She didn't know if it was from the cold, or nerves.

"We're getting somebody from forensics out here. That doesn't look like an accident," one of them said.

"Not an accident?" she repeated.

"From the angle and depth of the arrow, my guess is,

it was done at close range, with pre-meditation."

Amy felt chilled to the bone, thinking of such horror. She followed the two men back to the cabin. Once there, one began talking on his police radio, asking for additional men.

The other man said, "Thanks for your help, Miss Fontell. There's no need for you to stay out here in the cold. If we need another statement, we know where to find you. You will still be here, won't you?"

"Yes," she said weakly, still shaken by the ordeal.

"Before you go...., did you know the victim?"

"I didn't see his face because he was lying on his stomach. I ran to call you as soon as I saw him."

"Were you out here about two weeks ago, maybe two and a half weeks ago?"

"No, I wasn't at the cabin then," she answered, trembling. She wondered if they considered her a suspect. "I was here six weeks ago. Poachers had set out wooden food troughs for deer on my property. I reported it to the game warden. I didn't see anyone, just the troughs filled with corn and a lot of tracks."

"Did the game warden come out here?"

"Yes."

"Do you know his name? That would help."

"I have it inside. I'll get it for you," she answered.

Amy gave him the name and phone number of the game warden and he thanked her and said goodnight.

"Goodnight," she answered.

"Don't be frightened if you hear folks coming and going all night. There's a lot of investigating to be done before we can move him. Are you alone out here?"

"Yes, I am," she answered, wishing she weren't.

"Well, if you need anything else, there'll be plenty of policemen around for a while, anyway."

"Thank you. I'm sure I will be fine," she assured him, hoping she sounded more convincing than she felt.

When he had gone, she locked the door and put two more logs on the fire, poking it to make the sparks fly. She poured herself a cup of hot coffee and sitting before the fire, stared into the glowing flames. She kept seeing the man's body with the blood soaked shirt and the arrow. He had possibly been murdered. She wondered if there was a murderer lurking nearby. For the first time since she was a little girl, she was frightened. She wished she could go back to her apartment in the city but was afraid to leave. She had told the policeman that she would be here if they wanted to question her further. She sure didn't want them to think she was 'running away' for whatever reason.

Amy lay in her warm bed, unable to sleep. She kept hearing vehicles in the yard and the soft murmur of men's voices fading away into the distance. When she finally did fall asleep, she dreamed of murderers lurking in the bushes, with bow and arrow drawn.

When Amy awoke the next morning, it was quiet outside. She heard no automobiles coming or going. Hurrying to the window, she peered outside and saw nothing but woods. She sighed with relief, hoping that the police were gone and that they had removed the body. Freezing, she hurried to build the fire again. When she had it blazing she made coffee and fixed herself toast. She showered quickly, because the bathroom was still cold, and had just finished dressing when she heard a vehicle outside. Peering out the window, she saw a black sedan parked behind her car. She saw a tall man, dressed in a gray suit get out and walk toward the cabin. Her heart began to beat faster. She jumped as a loud knock sounded at the door, shattering the quietness.

"Who is it?" she asked, her heart racing. She did not recognize him from the night before.

"Lieutenant Barry Reeser, of the Montgomery County Sheriff's Department. I'd like to speak with Miss Fontell."

Amy unlocked the door and looked into the clearest,

blue eyes she had ever seen. He held up his badge for her to see.

"Are you Amy Fontell?"

When she nodded, he continued, "May I come in, Miss Fontell? I have a few questions I'd like to ask you."

"Please come in," she said, opening the door wider.

He glanced around the room, taking it all in.

"What can I do for you, Lieutenant?" she asked, nervously.

"May I sit down?"

"I'm sorry, please do." He sat in a chair before the fire.

Looking around again, he said, "This is a nice cabin. Have you had it long, Miss Fontell?"

"A couple of years. I inherited it from my uncle. I love the woods and wild things. It's peaceful out here," she rattled on.

He smiled, showing even, white teeth. His blue eyes seemed to twinkle at her.

"That's unusual for a female. Do you like hunting, also?" he asked, watching her closely.

She blushed, feeling uncomfortable.

"No. I wouldn't hunt wild animals. I like photographing them, not killing them."

"Do you keep any weapons here?" he asked suddenly.

She was caught off-guard. "I...yes, I keep a 38 revolver with me. I have a permit."

"May I see it?" he asked, watching her steadily.

"The revolver or the permit?"

"The permit."

"Of course." She fumbled through her backpack on the table until she found her wallet. She handed him the permit. Then, she pulled the revolver from the backpack and handed it to him butt first.

He grinned, his gaze meeting hers, and took it from her. He examined it closely, checking to see if it was loaded. She knew it wasn't. He handed it back to her.

"Did your uncle happen to own a bow?" he asked.

"I don't remember seeing one here when I cleaned the cabin. Do you want to look for one?" she felt her color rising.

"No, that's okay. Have you ever shot a bow, Miss Fontell?"

"Of course not, Lieutenant Reeser! Am I under suspicion for that man's murder?" she asked, shocked at his question. "I did not kill the man, I just happened to find his body!"

"I'm sorry. I have to ask these questions. Do you have any idea who the man is?"

"I've already told the other policeman, I couldn't see his face. I sure didn't stay there and look at him long, because it made me physically sick."

"That's understandable. It wasn't a pleasant sight. We'll have pictures by the end of the day. I'd like for you to look at them and see if you can identify him."

"Do I have to look at him again? I don't know anyone from around here."

"It could help. He might not be from around here, you know."

"Can't they take his fingerprints or something?" she asked, uneasily.

"Sure, that's being done already, but it would give us a lead to work on if you could identify him. Will you be here later this afternoon?"

"I was getting ready to go back to my apartment in the city. Is it all right if I do that?"

"Of course. But, I need your address and phone number, if you don't mind."

Amy blushed crimson. "Am I under investigation for his murder?"

"This is just routine questioning, Miss Fontell, I assure you," he answered, watching her closely.

Nervously, she wrote down her address and phone number and handed it to him.

He got up and walked to the door. "I will be by later this afternoon with the pictures, unless you had rather come to the Sheriff's Department to see them."

"No, my apartment is fine," Amy said, not wanting to go to the Sheriff's Department.

When he was gone, she trembled. She wished she had never come to the cabin this weekend and had never found the man's body in the woods. She was under suspicion for his murder and the real murderer had to be loose somewhere. She began to gather her belongings and set the cabin in order. She locked the doors and left.

***

At her apartment in the city, Amy told her roommate, Joan Caulfield, about everything that had happened at the cabin. Joan couldn't believe that they had questioned Amy as a suspect.

Sharply at three p.m., Lieutenant Reeser rang the doorbell. Amy escorted him to the living room and sat beside him on the sofa. Joan sat across the room, observing. He handed Amy a manila envelope.

"The man has been identified as 'Rodney Benson', Miss Fontell. Have you seen him before?"

She stared at a group of pictures, her fingers trembling. Surprisingly, they had been re-touched and weren't as gross as she had expected. Two of the pictures were of the man when he was alive.

"Where did you get those?" she asked, surprised.

"From his family. They have already been notified."

When she still hadn't answered his question, he asked again, " Do you know this man, Miss Fontell?"

"I've never seen him before," she answered.

"What about you, Miss. Caulfield?"

Joan sat beside Amy and examined the pictures. "No, I don't recognize him either."

"Didn't his family report him missing?" Amy asked. "That's what's strange. They said they thought he was still on a hunting trip."

"Where did he live?" Amy asked.

"Outside Lenox City; not very far away." He took the pictures and put them in the envelope. "I won't keep you any longer, Miss Fontell. If you happen to remember something you haven't told me, please give me a call." He handed her his card.

As she walked him to the door, he turned to her and said, "Be very careful if you stay at your cabin alone. Right now, we are considering this a homicide."

Her eyes wide, she asked, "Do you think the person who shot him could be someone from that area?"

"We won't rule out any possibility," he answered.

"You don't still consider me a suspect, do you, Lieutenant?"

His smile was disarming. "I don't believe that you have the strength to use the kind of bow it would take to penetrate an arrow that deeply into a man's back."

She shuddered, visibly, just imagining it. "Thank you, for that much, anyway. I understand that you are just doing your job, Lieutenant."

"Good evening, Miss Fontell, I will keep in touch."

She watched as he walked to his car before she closed the door. Joan was at her side, beaming.

"What a gorgeous hunk!" Joan sighed, dreamily.

"Joan!" Amy exclaimed, surprised. "Is that all that's on your mind? You just looked at pictures of a dead man!"

"Well, it was worth it, to get to look at him," Joan teased, "and he said he would 'keep in touch'. You're a lucky dog."

"I'm lucky, when I may be suspected of killing a man? When I am subjected to all this questioning?"

"Consider the source," Joan grinned, "enjoy it while you can."

"Well, I don't enjoy being questioned! It's scary."

"He wasn't wearing a wedding ring," Joan continued,

baiting her.

Amy drew in a sharp breath. "You're looking at a murdered man's pictures, but you notice that the lieutenant isn't wearing a wedding ring?" she scoffed.

"Lighten up, Amy. You're too serious! They'll find out who killed the guy. But, if I were you, I wouldn't go back to that cabin for a while. I don't know what it is that you like about that deserted place, anyway."

"It's peaceful and it's beautiful in the woods. I love it out there!" Amy retorted.

"What you need is a boyfriend, Amy, and then you could have some real fun out there!"

Amy had to laugh at her roommate. "You're terrible," she said.

Joan had fixed Amy up with several blind dates, but Amy had not cared for any of them. She had not met a man that she wanted to date the second time.

3

***

Two weeks had gone by. Amy was at work when Lieutenant Reeser called to ask her to meet him at the coffee shop nearby to update her on the homicide. She was surprised to hear from him, but agreed to meet him. He was waiting for her when she arrived.

"It's good to see you, Miss Fontell," he said, as he helped her with her chair. "I just ordered two coffees, would you like something else?"

"No thank you, coffee is fine, Lieutenant Reeser."

The waitress brought their coffee and Amy sipped hers slowly, wondering what he had to tell her.

"I thought you would like to know how the case is going," he began. "We're working closely with the game warden from that area. He has been very helpful. He told us that you had reported poachers on your land. He hasn't been able to catch them, but he has casts of different footprints found beside the feed boxes. One print was a match with the ones found beside the body. Now, we have to find out who that footprint belongs to."

"That's wonderful," Amy said, relieved. "Will it be difficult to find out who it belongs to?"

"About like looking for a needle in a haystack," he grinned.

"Oh, no," Amy said, disappointed.

"We'll get him, don't worry. They always slip up, eventually. I wanted to tell you, Miss Fontell, that we have men on stakeout near your cabin. You won't be able to see them, but they will be there for a while in case someone comes around. If you want to go back out there, you'd be safe now."

"I appreciate your telling me, Lieutenant. But, I think I will wait a while before I go back."

They finished their coffee and he walked her to her car.

"Thank you for the coffee, Lieutenant, and thank you for the information."

"It was my pleasure," he smiled and that smile warmed her heart. She thought he was very nice and she had enjoyed his company.

***

Amy was getting ready for work when the phone rang. Joan had already left for work.

"Hello," she answered.

"Are you Amy Fontell?" A woman's rough voice asked.

"Yes, this is Amy Fontell. Who is speaking?"

"Never mind who I am. I just wanna' know if you're the hussy that has the cabin close to Montgomery?"

"I beg your pardon?" Amy asked, her heart beating faster.

"You heard me, bitch! I'm wise to what goes on at that cabin, when the men are out there huntin'. You called the law on em' didn't you? My old man ain't happy about that, either. You better keep your mouth shut, if you know what's good for you!"

"I don't know what you're talking about!" Amy exclaimed. "Who are you?"

The receiver was slammed down hard, and the woman was gone. Amy was trembling. She found her wallet in her backpack and took out the card Lieutenant Reeser had given her. She dialed his work number.

"Montgomery County Sheriff's Department, how may I help you?" a lady's voice came over the line.

"May I speak with Lieutenant Reeser?"

"I am sorry, he is not in. Could someone else help you?"

Amy heard the 'beep' in the background and knew the call was automatically being recorded.

"I need to speak to him, personally. Would you please ask him to call me? My name is Amy Fontell and my number is 416-0276."

"I will see that he gets the message as soon as he comes in, Miss Fontell."

"Thank you." Amy said.

It was shortly after eight a.m. when Lieutenant Reeser called Amy. She told him about the phone call she had received that morning.

"It sounds like somebody is worried about something that you might tell us. Do you have any idea what she was talking about?" he asked.

"I don't have a clue, Lieutenant."

"Do you want me to have your phone monitored in case she calls back again?"

"Can I wait and see if she calls again, before you do that?"

"Yes, whatever you want to do," he said.

"I'm beginning to get worried, Lieutenant," she confessed.

"Would you feel safer if I put someone on stakeout outside your house for a while?"

"No, thank you. Let's just wait and see if she keeps harassing me."

"Okay. But, I want you to call me, if you get any more calls, no matter what time, day or night. Here's my home phone number: 416-6605. Write it down."

"I just did. Thank you, Lieutenant," she said, somehow feeling better since she talked to him.

Two weeks passed. Amy hadn't had any more harassing phone calls and she began to feel safe again. She had the urge to drive back to the cabin and wondered if there were policemen still on stakeout there. She decided to call Lieutenant Reeser to find out. He was in his office when she called.

"How are you, Miss Fontell?" he asked politely.

"I am fine, Lieutenant. But, I am getting bored here at the apartment and would like to go back to the cabin. Do you think it is safe?"

"We pulled our men off the stakeout. Nobody showed up out there." He paused a second and asked, "Would you feel better if I checked the place out for you?"

"I don't want to inconvenience you, Lieutenant," she said.

"When did you want to go?" he asked.

"In the morning."

"What if I meet you at your apartment at nine a.m. and follow you out there?" he asked.

"Are you sure you aren't too busy?"

"I'm sure," he answered. "I'll see you then."

When Amy hung up the phone she was excited at the prospect of seeing the lieutenant again. She told herself she was just bored; that was all there was to it. She suddenly decided to go to the supermarket to stock up on food for the cabin.

The next morning, Joan was incredulous. "I can't believe you are going back to that cabin!" she exclaimed.

"You just don't understand, Joan. Out there, I can write on my journal, or read. It's so peaceful."

"Was it peaceful the last time you were there?" she asked, making a point. "It was certainly peaceful for the guy you found with an arrow in his back!"

Amy blushed crimson. "You don't have to keep bringing that up," she pleaded. "Besides, I am not going alone. Lieutenant Reeser is going with me," she added, shyly.

Joan looked at her, disbelieving. "You don't say!" she grinned. "You're finally getting some smarts!"

"It's not what you think, Joan. He offered to check it out for me, to make sure no one is around."

"Uh-huh," Joan teased.

"That's the truth!" Amy said, embarrassed.

"I wondered why you bought so many groceries," Joan teased.

"Just hush, Joan. You'll believe what you want to, anyway."

"You bet I will," she grinned. "When are you coming back?"

"Sunday night, like always," Amy answered.

"Okay, have fun."

At that moment, the doorbell rang. It was Lieutenant Reeser. He helped her load the groceries into her car and followed her in his dark sedan. Amy watched him in her rear-view mirror and wondered if this was really 'in the line of duty' for him, or if he was doing this because he wanted to. He was a very attractive man. She wondered if he was married, even though he wasn't wearing a wedding ring.

"What am I thinking of?" she scolded herself and tried to keep her mind on the road ahead.

When Amy and Lieutenant Reeser arrived at the cabin everything looked normal. The lieutenant walked around in the yard and behind the cabin before he helped her unload the car. He checked every room when they went inside.

"It looks like everything is fine," he said, "unless someone is lurking in the woods," he teased.

"Do you have to say that?"

"I'm only kidding, Amy,…..Miss Fontell. Now, would you like for me to build you a fire? It's cold in here."

"I'm sure that is not part of your job description," she smiled. "I know how to build a fire."

He squatted down and began to shovel ashes into a bucket that he found beside the fireplace.

"I'll bring in some smaller pieces of wood," Amy said.

"If you'll wait, I'll do that," he offered.

"They're not heavy. They've already been split. I had a truck load delivered in the fall."

As she was getting the wood the lieutenant joined her, picking up twice as much as she did.

"Is the fireplace the only kind of heat you have here?" he asked as they piled the wood into the wood box beside the fireplace.

"Yes. My uncle used kerosene heaters. I don't like the smell of the fumes. It gives me a headache."

"You have to be careful with them sometime. The fireplace probably heats the cabin well enough, doesn't it?" he asked.

"Yes. The bedrooms are cool, but I have plenty of warm blankets." Her cheeks flushed pink as she felt his gaze on her. He grinned charmingly and chuckled.

"What?" she asked, puzzled.

"You are an unusual young lady, Miss Fontell. Most ladies I know would never leave the comforts of their home for the rustic enjoyment of your cabin."

"You may call me 'Amy' if you'd like, Lieutenant. I believe you will find that I am not like most 'ladies'," she added with a warm smile.

"Please call me 'Barry'," he grinned. He finished building the fire as she made a pot of coffee and put up the groceries.

"I have plenty of food, if you care to join me for lunch," she ventured.

"Thank you, I'd enjoy that. May I help?"

"Sure. If you'd like to grill the steaks on this little portable grill, I will make a salad."

As they were both busy with lunch, the lieutenant teased, "do you eat this well every day, or is this a special occasion, Amy?"

She felt herself blush and wondered why he had that affect on her.

"You are in luck today. I have sandwiches most of the time, but I just brought a lot of groceries this time."

"I did come at the right time," he smiled, charmingly.

As they were eating, Amy encouraged him to tell her about his family.

"There's not much to tell. My parents live a hundred miles from here. I have a younger brother still at home."

"No 'wife', Barry?" she ventured.

A shadow crossed his face for an instant. "I had a wife. She died of cancer two years ago. We had only been married a little over a year."

"Oh! I am so sorry. I didn't know."

"She was a great person. You remind me of her, Amy," he said, watching her reaction.

Amy didn't know what to say, so she said nothing. Finally, she got up to get cookies for dessert and the spell was broken.

Later, Amy and Barry walked in the woods. They discussed the case of the murdered man. He informed her that they still had no suspects.

"I'm hoping that the woman who called you will call again and give us a clue. There's something that is going on that we haven't figured out yet."

"I haven't even thought about her lately," Amy said.

"Be sure to call me if you hear from anyone," he said.

"I will." She noticed him scanning the woods and ground as they walked.

"Do you see something?" she asked.

"There are a lot of deer tracks here. Where is the food troughs you found baited?"

"They're farther down this way. Do you want to see them?"

"Sure."

She led him to the troughs. They were empty now.

"Didn't you say that the police got some footprints from around here?" she asked.

"Yes, all around the troughs and the man's body too. You know, it is pretty low-down to bait deer and shoot them when they come to feed," he said absently.

"Do you hunt, Barry?" she asked.

"Not any more. I hunted when I was growing up. I guess I've been too busy since I finished college and got a job."

"Is that when you started working for the Sheriff's Department?" she asked.

"Yes, it has been ten years."

"You must like that type of work to stay there so long."

"I love it. The only thing that I think would be more exciting is working in the forensic lab. That fascinates me. I've thought of going into that field later on."

Amy shuddered. "I don't think I could stomach that," she confessed.

"It's amazing what they can find. Even a hair or a thread or a drop of blood can lead to a conviction," he said.

"Maybe they can help find Rodney Benson's murderer," she said, absently.

"It may take a while, but we'll find him, eventually."

Suddenly Barry froze. He pulled Amy behind him, roughly. Caught off guard, she almost fell to the ground. He drew a weapon from his vest and whispered, "Get on the ground and don't move!"

She obeyed, feeling the dirt clods and rocks through her pants. She watched as he advanced, half crouched, toward the brush. Suddenly, he yanked the brush aside to reveal a man.

"Don't move!" Barry ordered.

"Hold on there, feller'," the old man shouted as he lumbered out of the brush, rifle in hand.

"Drop that weapon!" Barry ordered, with his gun

aimed at the man's chest.

"Wait just a minnit'! I'm a puttin' it down, rite' now. Don't go a-shootin'."

"Nice and easy," Barry ordered, advancing to take the rifle.

"You 'bout scairt' me to death, feller'," the old man wheezed, his arms raised in the air.

"Who are you, old man? What are you doing out here?"

"I wuz huntin' deer, afore you scairt' the livin' day-lights oughten' me!" he stammered.

"You can lower your hands now. What's your name, Sir?"

"My name's Homer Rafferty. I live a couple mile back through them woods there," he said, motioning north-east. "Who are you to be standin' there pointin' a gun at my vitals?"

Barry lowered his weapon. "I'm Lieutenant Reeser, Montgomery County Sheriff's Department."

Amy got to her feet, still trembling.

"Do you know this lady, Mr. Rafferty?" Barry asked.

The old man squinted his eyes at Amy, and then shook his head. "Can't say as I do. Howdy, Maam." He touched his hat politely.

"She's your neighbor, Mr. Rafferty, if you live across the woods. This is Amy Fontell; Amy, this is Mr. Rafferty."

"Hello," she said, nervously.

"Mr. Rafferty, are you aware that there is a murder investigation being conducted in this area?" Barry asked.

The old man was slow to answer. Finally, he said, "Yessir', there wuz some other fellows that come to my house to talk to me about it a while back; asked me a bunch of questions, they did."

"Were they policemen?" Barry asked.

"Yessir', they said they wuz."

"I'm sorry I scared you, Sir. But, you have to understand our predicament here."

"Yessir', I understand. But, could we go somewhere else to do our talkin'? I'm a-freezin' out here."

"Yes, Sir. We can go to Miss Fontell's cabin, if she doesn't mind." He gave her an inquiring look.

"Of course, that's fine," she agreed. She felt that the old man was harmless.

"I'll carry your rifle, Mr. Rafferty," Barry informed him, still holding it.

"You take good care of it, young feller'. I've had that there rifle fer' many a year."

"I'll take good care of it, Sir," Barry grinned.

At the cabin, Amy fixed a cup of coffee for each of them and sat down quietly to listen as Barry questioned Mr. Rafferty about anything that he might have seen or heard.

"I been a livin' out here for thirty five year. I knowed a Curtis Fontell that lived out here at this cabin. Wuz he kin to you, Missy?"

"He was my uncle; my father's brother."

"He wuz a good man, he wuz. I hunted with him sometime. He always gave me the meat, though, said he didn't like the taste of venison. You want some venison, Missy? I got a bunch in the freezer."

"No, thank you, Mr. Rafferty. I appreciate your offer, but I don't care for the taste of venison, either."

"Mighty good eatin', Missy. Mighty good eatin'!"

Barry interrupted their chatting. "Mr. Rafferty, are you responsible for the corn troughs on Miss. Fontell's property?"

"Nosir', not me, nosir'. Ain't no challenge to baitin' deer. I can kill plenty a-stalkin' em'. Ain't never baited no deer. I seen where somebody's been a-baitin' em' though."

"Have you run across other hunters in the woods, Mr. Rafferty?" Barry asked.

"Yeah, I seen other hunters at times, but I steer clear

of em'. Don't want no city slicker a-shootin' me fer' a deer."

"Would you recognize any of the hunters you've seen?" Barry asked.

"Nope, don't think I could. It's gettin' nigh on to dark, Lieutenant. Iffen' yer' finished askin' me questions, I need to be moseying on home."

"Certainly, Mr. Rafferty. Here's your rifle, Sir. Take care."

"It was nice meeting you, Mr. Rafferty," Amy said, as she walked him to the door.

"Same here, Missy. Iffen' you need anything, me and the Missus are just across the holler'. Ain't got no phone, but ye can yell real loud," he chuckled.

"I don't have a phone either, just my cell phone," Amy said.

When Mr. Rafferty was gone, Amy asked Barry, "Do you think he was telling the truth?"

"Could be, but he may not be telling everything he knows. He's a shrewd old man, I believe." He looked at his watch. "I've taken up your whole day, Amy, I'm sorry." He rose to leave.

"I've enjoyed your being here. Thank you so much for coming out."

"Would you mind giving me your cell phone number? I can call and make sure you're okay," he said.

She gave it to him, and asked, "Was I foolish to come out here, Barry? Do you think it's safe here?"

"I respect your wishes, Amy. But, you do need to be cautious. Don't go walking in the woods alone."

"Don't worry, I won't be doing that. I will stay close to the cabin if I go outside."

"Good. If anything out of the ordinary happens, call me. You've got my number."

"Thank you, I will."

For a moment they stood at the door, his blue eyes

gazing into hers. Finally, he took a deep breath while she seemed to be holding hers.

"I'll be in touch. Lock the door behind me." He opened the door and was gone.

Slowly Amy took a deep breath, her heart beating fast. Her knees were weak. No man had ever had this affect on her before.

When Amy went to bed that night she lay under the warm covers thinking of Lieutenant Reeser. She wondered if he had thought of her since he left. He was just doing his job. Was she making too much of his warm friendliness?

When Amy awoke the next morning she was cold. She looked at the clock and realized that she had slept later than usual. It was eight-thirty. She tip-toed across the cold floor and slipped on her slippers and robe. Then, she proceeded to build another fire in the fireplace. She remembered the last time a fire was built there; Lieutenant Reeser had built it. She wondered why everything reminded her of him. She saw their coffee cups still on the table. For the first time in years she was lonely. She hadn't been lonely since both her parents died. She had always been a private person and enjoyed solitude as well as company. After she had a warm fire blazing she went to get dressed and then fixed herself breakfast. Her cell phone rang suddenly, startling her.

"Hello," she said, hoping to hear Barry's voice.

"Hey girl," Joan's voice came across the line, "What's going on?"

"Hi, Joan. Nothing's going on. I'm just puttering around. I just built a warm fire."

"You just built a fire? Why didn't that handsome lieutenant of yours build it for you, Honey?" Joan teased.

"Joan, Lieutenant Reeser is not here. I told you why he came yesterday."

"Oh, rats! I thought you'd have something exciting to tell me by now."

"Sorry to disappoint you, Joan."

"Okay, when are you coming home?"

"I'll be there before you go to bed tonight.

"Good. Don't stay out there by yourself too late. See you in a little while."

As soon as Amy put the phone down it rang again. She wondered what Joan had forgotten.

"Hello again," she said.

"Hello to you, too." Barry chuckled. " Were you expecting me to call just now?"

Amy's pulse quickened at the sound of his voice. "Barry, hello. I'm sorry, I thought you were Joan calling back."

"How are things out there?" he asked.

She almost said 'lonely' but caught herself in time.

"Very quiet; nothing at all going on this morning."

"Good. I wanted to make sure you didn't have a burglar last night."

"No burglars," she laughed. "Thank you for being concerned, though."

"Any time I can be of service," he teased. After a long pause, he said, "Okay, I'll let you go now. Take care, Amy."

"I will. Thank you, Barry. Goodbye."

"Goodbye," he answered. She heard the click on the other end.

Now, Amy felt lonelier than before. She tried to get interested in a book, but her mind kept wandering. Finally, she decided to close the cabin and go back to her apartment. As she was going to her car a man in a pickup truck drove noisily into the yard and came to a stop within two feet of where she was standing. A dark-headed, bearded man glared at her through the dirty windshield before he opened the door and got out. Nervously, she glanced at her backpack on the seat where her revolver was hidden.

"Are you the Gal that lives here part of the time?" he

asked, his voice rumbling.

"Yes, who are you?" she answered nervously.

"Never mind who I am. I came to talk to you."

"I was just leaving; if you will excuse me." Her heart was hammering.

The big man walked around the truck and grabbed Amy's arm, roughly.

"I said, we're going to talk!"

"Take your hands off me! What do you want with me?" Amy tried to sound braver than she felt.

He jerked her around until his face was close to hers. He smelled of alcohol and stale tobacco.

"You're hurting me! Let me go!"

"Not 'till I find out what I came here for."

"What are you talking about? Are you crazy?"

His black eyes narrowed. Amy took a step back, cold with fear.

"The law's been snoopin' around, asking questions. You turned us in, didn't you?"

Amy began to tremble. Barry had said that they had no suspects.

"Who has been questioning you?" she asked, barely above a whisper.

"The game warden! Who do you think? All because of a damn nosey bitch! Ain't none of your business if we put corn troughs out to feed the deer!"

"It is my business! This is my property! You have no right to bait my deer and kill them on my property!"

"City slickers pay big bucks to hunt deer out here. They ain't your deer just because they run across your land! You're ignorant, Gal!" he snarled.

"I don't even know you," she stammered.

"What's to know? Just keep your nose out of everybody's business, if you know what's good for you!" He turned her loose and she fell against her car.

"Do you know about the man who was murdered?"

she asked, angrily, hating him for having touched her.

He swung back around, his dark eyes snapping.

"I don't know nothin' about no killin'. Do you understand?" he grated through his teeth.

She nodded, backing toward her car door.

"Now, git!" he yelled at her.

Her temper flared, overriding her caution.

"Don't you dare tell me what to do! This is my property and you are trespassing! You get off my property or I will call the police!"

"I ain't scared of you, Gal. I could break you in half, if I had a mind to."

Amy opened the car door and cautiously slipped inside, grabbing her backpack. Her hands were trembling so much that she could hardly open it. She felt the cold steel of the revolver and pulled it out. Her heart sank when she remembered that is was not loaded. But, he didn't know that. Amy brought the barrel up and pointed it at his chest.

His yellow, tobacco stained teeth showed in his sneer.

"Well, how about that? The little Gal is totin' a rod!" He didn't seem the least bit worried.

"Get in your truck, and get out of here," she shouted, trying to keep her hand from shaking.

"I'm goin', but it's because I'm ready to leave. You ain't scarin' me none. Just remember what I said; keep your mouth shut."

Amy watched as he got into his truck and scratched off, sending dirt and pebbles flying. She slammed her door and locked it, but had to calm herself before she could start the motor. She thought of calling Barry on the cell phone but decided to wait until she got to her apartment.

***

When Amy got back to her apartment she told Joan about the trespasser at the cabin.

"You're crazy, Amy! Don't go back out there! Have you told the lieutenant?"

"Not yet."

"Call him, now!"

Amy found his home phone number and dialed the number. It rang a few times before he answered, "Hello."

"Hi, this is Amy."

"Hello, Amy. Are you home?"

"Yes."

"Was everything okay when you left?"

"No."

"No? What happened?"

She began at the beginning and told him exactly what had happened.

"Are you sure you're all right? He didn't hurt you?" he asked, concerned.

"Not really. He just scared me to death."

"I'm sorry, Amy. I should have stayed. The next time you go, we will go in one vehicle and no one will know I am there. That is, if you want me to go. You're like a sitting duck there by yourself."

"I don't know if I want to go back," she said.

"It may be the only way to draw them out, if they think you're there; but don't go alone."

"He thinks I know something, Barry. I don't know anything! What do they think I know?"

"They may think that you saw or heard something."

"About the murder?"

"That's possible."

"Oh, no! Have the police figured out how long the man had been dead?"

"Between fourteen and sixteen days when you found him."

"I wasn't even at the cabin at that time!"

"They don't know that, Amy."

"You're scaring me, Barry," she confessed.

"I don't mean to. I'll get somebody out there to check for tire tracks. You say he came in a truck?"

"Yes, a four-wheel drive. It had mud all over it."

"Do you want to plan to go Friday or Saturday?" he asked. Then, he added softly, "You didn't say whether or not you wanted me to go with you."

"Of course I do. I sure don't want to go by myself."

"How about Friday after work? Can you be ready by five?" he asked.

"I'll be ready."

When Amy hung up the phone, she found Joan staring at her.

"You're not going back out there, are you?"

"The lieutenant is going with me this time," Amy answered shyly.

"He went with you the last time!" Joan exclaimed.

"But, he's staying this time," Amy explained, blushing, "just in case someone shows up again."

"Amy, you're getting in over your head. You're crazy to go back out there!"

"How can I keep from getting involved? I found a dead man, Joan! Now look what's happening!"

"By the way, Amy, some woman called you again. She sounded like a hick. She said she'd call you back later."

Later that night when Amy was sleeping, the phone woke her. She answered it, her nerves on edge from being awakened.

An unfamiliar, woman's voice asked, "Is this Amy Fontell?"

"Yes, who is this?"

"This is Sara Benson. You don't know me, but I heard about you. You found my husband's body in the woods."

"Mrs. Benson, I am so sorry," Amy said.

"It ain't your fault. I knew it would happen one day."

"Why?" Amy asked, surprised.

"Rodney was always pokin' his nose in places he had no business."

"Why did you call me, Mrs. Benson? How have you heard of me?"

"From Rodney's friends he hunted with. They seen you out there at the cabin sometime, but you may not have seen them. I want to know if you seen anything before Rodney was killed?"

"I wasn't out there at that time, Mrs. Benson."

"I thought maybe you'd seen or heard some of them arguing or something."

"I never saw any hunters. I only saw their baited troughs! Why won't people believe me?"

"Has somebody else been askin' you questions?" Mrs. Benson asked.

"Yes, a very rude woman called me and a heavy-set man with dark hair and beard harassed me when I was leaving my cabin." She hoped she had not revealed too much.

"That sounds like one of the hunters I seen Rodney with."

"Do you know his name?" Amy asked.

"No."

"Mrs. Benson, if you could come up with a name, you could help find the man who killed your husband."

"I'll see what I can find out," she said, reluctantly.

Amy decided not to tell Joan or Barry about the phone call until she found out more information.

Amy found herself looking forward to Friday. She refused to admit to herself that she was anxious to see Barry again. He phoned her during the week to make sure their plans were still on. She wondered how he felt about the prospect of spending the weekend alone with her at a deserted cabin. She felt both anxious and excited about the weekend. She hoped she did not feel awkward being alone with him.

Without realizing it, Amy spent extra time getting dressed and fixing her hair on Friday. After work she dressed in casual slacks and a beige sweater that enhanced her brown hair and brown eyes. She was waiting when Barry arrived.

He greeted her warmly, his smile enticing. "I see you're ready," he said, looking at her belongings beside the door.

"I hope I remembered everything we'll need," she said, shyly.

"I took the liberty of bringing a baked ham. I didn't want to eat all of your food," he grinned.

"You didn't have to do that. There is plenty of food."

"I am sure there is. But, at work we got hams for Christmas, so I have put mine to good use. I even baked it myself," he grinned.

"My, my! He even cooks, too!" Amy laughed.

Amy let Barry drive her car and she was completely relaxed and at ease with him on the way to the cabin. She had never felt exactly that way about any man before. She had dated several men but had not been interested enough to date them the second time.

Somehow, Barry Reeser was different; he was interesting

and exciting.

It was already dark when they arrived at the cabin. Barry began to build a fire in the fireplace while Amy put up the groceries. She put coffee on to brew and cut thick slices of ham for sandwiches. Barry helped when he had the fire blazing. He set trays before the fire and they ate there as the cabin began to warm. Later, he helped her wash the few dishes and then they settled down on the couch before the fire. It was only then, that she remembered to tell him about Mrs. Benson's call.

He was surprised, and said, "That is odd, don't you think?"

"I thought so too. She was civil, not like the other woman who called."

"Have you heard from that other woman?" he asked.

"No. I hope I never do."

"Let me know if you do."

They sat watching the flames, neither of them speaking for a moment.

"This is very nice," he said softly, the firelight reflecting in his blue eyes.

"Yes, you can forget all your troubles for a little while," Amy said, gazing into the fire.

"What troubles do you want to forget, Amy, other than this homicide case?" he asked.

"Oh, I don't know. I guess I don't really have any troubles. I have a good job; I get along well with my roommate. I guess I have a happy life."

"You guess?" he teased, watching her face in the firelight.

"I don't have any family. I guess that's a void in my life. My uncle was my closest relative after my parents died."

"I'm sorry to hear that. How long ago did your parents die?"

"It has been eight years. But, it still hurts." She had

never admitted that to anyone before.

"I understand. It has been two years since my wife died. Sometime it seems like yesterday, other times, like many years ago."

"Yes, exactly. I've never been able to figure out how it can seem both ways."

"Have you ever gotten serious with anyone?" he asked, suddenly. "A beautiful girl like you should have guys standing in line."

His question caught her off-guard. "I might ask you the same question," she answered.

"I haven't met anyone I was interested in.....until now," he said, softly. Slowly, he drew her into his arms. His fingers brushed a lock of her hair from her cheek. His touch caused a tingling sensation throughout her body and she shivered.

"Are you cold?" he asked.

She could only shake her head. She didn't trust her voice to speak.

Slowly, never taking his eyes from her face, he bent until his lips brushed hers, softly. She seemed to melt into his arms, her heartbeat quickening. He caressed her hair, and her cheek.

"Tell me if you want me to stop," he whispered.

Amy's eyes opened wide. "What did you say?" she asked nervously.

"I don't want to take advantage of you," he answered calmly. Yet, his heartbeat was keeping time with hers.

"I....I have never been intimate with a man, Barry. I don't believe in sex before marriage," she explained, embarrassed.

His eyes were shining. "What a priceless gift to give your husband," he whispered, as his lips touched hers again. His kiss was deeper, taking her breath away. She felt his tongue caress her lips and she couldn't get enough of being near him.

When she could draw a breath to speak, she asked, "Is this the way you work on all your cases, Lieutenant Reeser?"

"This is a first for me, Amy. Would you believe, I have only dated a few times since my wife died?"

"Why is that, Barry?" she asked, knowing the affect he must have on any female.

"Until that day I met you, I just wasn't interested. Somehow, I knew you were different."

"From whom?"

He grinned. "From the women who have tried to lasso me in the past two years."

"Tell me why you think I am different. We've only known one another for a few weeks."

"I like your spunk, for one thing; your independence. I don't know another woman who likes the woods and nature as you do. It's refreshing."

"You don't find me boring?" she teased.

"Hardly. You're very exciting." Once more his lips found hers as he pulled her even closer and then pulled her down beside him on the couch. Amy could feel his heartbeat keeping time with hers. She had never felt such sensations being near a man, as she felt now, lying beside Barry. She laid her head on his shoulder and she felt his lips on her hair.

"This is harder than I though it would be," he whispered.

"What?" she asked, innocently.

"Being this close, and not touching you."

"I'm sorry," she said, for lack of anything else to say.

He chuckled. "Don't be sorry, Sweetheart. Just let me hold you close like this for a while."

They lay together, watching the logs burn, the tiny sparks fly. He caressed her gently, until, finally, she fell asleep in his arms.

A long time later, Amy awoke. The fire had burned

low, but she felt the warmth of Barry's body as he lay sleeping beside her. She lay beside him, quietly basking in the feel of him beside her. How could she have gotten so involved with this man so quickly, she wondered. She wondered if this was the way it felt to love someone. She wondered if Barry could possibly feel the same way about her. She knew she should slip away and go to her own bed. But, she knew if she moved, he would awaken. Instead, she drew the afghan across both of them and snuggled closer to him. Soon, she was asleep again.

Amy woke when Barry eased off the couch and went to get more wood outside. The room had grown cold as the fire died down. She shivered as he left the door wide as he brought in more wood. He laid the wood down and started to close the door.

Suddenly, a man burst through the doorway with a rifle in his hands.

Barry didn't move, watching him.

"Well, well. What have we here? Ain't this real cozy?" the man drawled.

Amy jumped to her feet. She recognized him as the bearded man who had stopped her before.

"Get back, Amy!" Barry exclaimed, every muscle tensed.

"Naw,' let her come on over," the big man sneered, "maybe she'll be cozy with me too."

"Who are you? What are you doing here?" Barry demanded.

"Now, that ain't none of your damn business, feller'!" he sneered. "What are you doing here with this Gal, gettin' a little on the side?" he chuckled.

"Shut your filthy mouth!" Barry grated, and added, "Put that weapon down!"

The man's face turned beet red. "Who do you think you're giving orders to? I'm the one holdin' the gun!"

Amy realized Barry wasn't carrying his gun. She felt

sick to her stomach. She tried to draw the man's attention from Barry. Trembling, she asked, "What do you want?"

He grinned at her. "Well, now. I just wanted to have a little talk with you, Gal. But, I don't cotton to having no audience. Maybe you and me could go outside by ourselves."

"You're not taking her anywhere!" Barry retorted.

"Well, now. Is that a fact? Who's going to stop me?"

"I'll stop you," Barry answered, coldly.

"After I blow a hole through your belly?" the man sneered.

"No!" Amy screamed. "I'll go outside with you! Don't shoot him!"

"Amy, stay out of this!" Barry ordered.

"I won't!" she said, trembling. Ignoring Barry, she asked, "What could you possibly want with me?"

"I think you and me can have a real good talk about some pictures your old man had layin' around here."

"My father?" she asked, blankly.

"You're old man Fontell's kid, ain't you?" he snarled.

"Do you mean Curtis Fontell, her uncle?" Barry asked, suddenly.

The man looked confused. "How do I know? So, he was your uncle. He had some pictures made one time; I want them pictures!"

"I don't know anything about any pictures," Amy said, weakly.

"You're lyin'!" His eyes narrowed as he turned to face Amy. When he turned, Barry threw himself against the barrel of the rifle, pushing it from Amy's direction. The two men struggled fiercely, but the bearded man outweighed Barry by a hundred pounds. He knocked Barry down with a blow to the side of his head, and pointed the rifle at him.

"Stay down, you bastard, or I'll blow your brains out!" he grated.

"Please! Please, don't shoot him!" Amy pleaded weakly.

Barry was dazed but getting to his feet slowly when the blast of the rifle echoed throughout the room. Amy heard herself scream and fought to keep her knees from buckling beneath her. In a daze, she saw Barry slump to the floor, blood splattering his shirt.

"You've killed him!" she heard herself scream, "You crazy fool, you've killed him!"

Barry lay on the floor, not moving, blood seeping from his wound. In a panic, Amy rushed to his side, kneeling beside him.

"I told the bastard to stay out of it!" the man said, "I had no quarrel with him."

"You're a liar!" Amy said, coldly. She grabbed the afghan off the couch and pressed it to Barry's shoulder to try to stop the bleeding. He groaned, suddenly, and a flicker of hope ran through her.

"You can shoot me, too, if you want to, but I'm calling 911." She got to her feet, daring him to shoot her as she ran to get her cell phone.

He watched her silently, then glanced at Barry. Finally, he said, "Call them. But I ain't finished with you, Gal. We'll still have our little talk, I promise you."

With trembling fingers, Amy pressed 911. To her surprise, her voice was calm as she reported the shooting and requested a helicopter. She didn't know what time it was but knew it was still dark outside. She gave them directions to the cabin, realizing that she had given the police directions before. She turned to the bearded man.

"I have to get a flashlight and turn my car lights on, to help the helicopter pilot see where to land." She wondered if he would try to stop her. He didn't.

He said, "I'm gone," and disappeared through the doorway. She didn't hear his truck and wondered where he had left it. He didn't come back.

Amy hurried to Barry's side.

"Barry! Darling, please speak to me." She was trembling as she tried to cover his wound again. She saw that the blood was seeping from beneath his shoulder onto the floor. She lifted his shoulder, slightly, and saw that the bullet had gone through his shoulder and into the wooden floor.

"Dear God, please help him," she prayed, as tears flooded her eyes until she could hardly see. She folded the afghan over and beneath his shoulder, trying to staunch the bleeding. It slowed but didn't stop completely. He opened his eyes as she bent over him.

"Has he gone?" he asked, weakly.

Amy was so relieved to hear him speak, she sobbed. "Yes, Darling. He's gone."

"I didn't let him take you," he whispered.

"No, you certainly didn't!" she cried. She heard the sound of the helicopter in the distance and relief flooded her.

"The helicopter is almost here, Darling. I'll be right back. Please hold on....." She leaned over him, and careful not to hurt his shoulder, she kissed him on his cool lips. She thought of how warm and inviting his lips had been earlier and wondered how events could change so drastically and so quickly.

Outside, she waited for the helicopter to land. A paramedic, with his bag in hand, jumped out and followed her inside the cabin. In a moment, another paramedic joined him. Amy stood aside and watched as they tore Barry's shirt off his shoulder and began their work on him. He was conscious and responded to their questions. Amy knew that he had lost a lot of blood. He sounded weak when he tried to speak.

Amy was crying softly as she watched them work on Barry. When they had him lying on the stretcher and were about to carry him to the helicopter, he called to her, weakly.

"Wait, let me see Amy," he pleaded.

"You need to get to the hospital, Mr. Reeser. She can follow in her car. She'll see you there," the paramedic said. Amy was at his side, instantly, holding his hand. "I'm here, Darling. I'll be there with you soon."

He smiled, weakly and tried to nod his head. Then, he closed his eyes. Amy watched as they loaded him into the helicopter.

"We'll need to file a report as soon as you get to the hospital, Miss," the paramedic said. "They said Mr. Reeser is a police lieutenant. Is that right?"

"Yes, he is. Which hospital are you taking him to?"

"Chilton Memorial. You know where that is?"

"Yes, I will be there soon. Wait! Tell me how he is….."

"The bullet went clear through his shoulder and he's lost a lot of blood. Hopefully, the doctor can get him patched up. We gotta' go now!"

Amy watched as they lifted off. Then, she realized she was quite alone. Frightened, she hurried to lock up the cabin and gather her belongings. She was about to go out the door when she saw Barry's briefcase. She thought that he might need it later, so she grabbed it up. The weight of it made her hesitate and she opened it quickly. His revolver lay inside. She knew if he had carried it on his person, he might not be wounded now. Yet, she realized, he could possibly be dead. She shivered at the thought.

6

***

The drive to the hospital seemed to take forever. When Amy arrived she was directed to the emergency surgical waiting room. She slumped into one of the chairs, exhausted. She realized for the first time, that she had Barry's blood all over the front of her sweater and dried on her hands. A nurse passing by stared at her and hurried to her side.

"Are you okay?" she inquired.

"Yes, I am fine, thank you."

"Is that your blood, Dear?"

"No, it is someone else's blood. He was shot." Amy tried to explain.

She saw the nurse's brow rise slightly, and Amy added, "He's a police lieutenant."

"I see. Perhaps you need to come with me to file a report. It is required on all gunshot wounds."

When Amy finished the report she went back to the waiting room. She was there only a few minutes when a man entered. Seeing her, he came directly to where she was sitting and sat down beside her.

"Excuse me. Are you Amy Fontell," he asked.

"Yes, are you the doctor?"

"No," he said, drawing a badge from his vest pocket, "I am Captain Adams, Montgomery County Sheriff's Department."

"Then, you know about Lieutenant Reeser?" she asked, relieved to see someone.

"Yes, I was notified. He works for me, Miss Fontell. He is one of my best men on the force. I am aware of the homicide he is working on and the circumstances that led to his being shot tonight. Can you fill me in on the details?"

"Yes, Captain Adams." She began from the beginning and told him all that had transpired. She couldn't tell him the exact time but guessed. She realized that she and Barry must have slept on the couch most of the night. She blushed at this thought. The captain didn't seem to notice. When she finished telling him the details, she listened as he used his cell phone to call the Sheriff's Department and give orders to have forensic investigators and pathologists go to the cabin and retrieve the bullet and all the evidence that they could collect. She gave him the key to the cabin door, which another policeman came to the hospital to get. Captain Adams continued to sit with her.

"Miss Fontell, I will wait here in case there is word of Lieutenant Reeser, if you would like to freshen up," he offered, politely, glancing at her sweater with the dried blood.

"I guess I am a frightening sight," she exclaimed. "I suppose I can't let Barry….Lieutenant Reeser see me like this, can I?"

Captain Adams merely smiled at that.

"I have some clothes in my car. I'll just be a few minutes," Amy said and hurried outside.

When Amy returned Captain Adams was waiting for her.

"The doctor came and told me that Lieutenant Reeser is out of surgery and in recovery. We should be able to see him in an hour," he explained.

"Thank Goodness!" Amy exclaimed, tears filling her eyes. "He's going to be okay?"

"The doctor was optimistic but said it will take a

while for him to recover. It was a nasty wound at close range."

Amy shuddered, realizing what could have happened to Barry.

After a while the nurse told Amy and Captain Adams that they could go in to see the lieutenant. As she led them to his room, Amy spoke to the captain and said, "You go in and talk to him first." The captain agreed, so she waited just inside the door of his room. Barry was lying completely still with his eyes closed. The captain touched his arm lightly.

"Hey, Barry, are you awake? How are you doing, fellow?" he asked tenderly.

Barry opened his eyes and tried to focus on his visitor. "Captain?" he asked, groggily.

"Yeah, it's Captain Adams. I heard you had a visitor real early this morning."

Barry seemed to be trying to remember. "Yes, I guess I did. He wasn't too friendly, though," he said, his speech slurred. He moved and winced in pain.

"Don't be trying to move, Barry. You've had some repair work done on that shoulder. Do you remember who shot you?" the captain asked.

"I'm not likely to forget that face, Captain. He caught me off-guard without my weapon."

"It happens to the best of us, Barry. You can't always know ahead of time. I'm just thankful that you are all right."

A frown creased Barry's brow and he asked, "Did Miss Fontell arrive here safely?"

"As a matter of fact, she's waiting right here." The captain motioned her toward the bed.

Barry's blue eyes warmed at the sight of her. He reached his left hand toward her and she clasp it between both of hers. It was warm to her touch. Her eyes filled with unshed tears.

"I'm right here, Barry," she said, choking back the tears that threatened to escape. She thought he looked so pale and seemed so weak. He wasn't the Barry she was used to seeing.

"The guy didn't come back and bother you?" Barry asked, barely above a whisper.

"No, Darling, he didn't," she said, forgetting about the captain. Then, she added, "I am so sorry this happened to you! It is all my fault!" She couldn't stop the tears from flowing. The captain put his arm around her, to console her.

"Don't blame yourself, Miss Fontell," he said.

Before they could say more the nurse entered the room and said, "I am sorry, but Mr. Reeser needs to rest now."

"We'll come back later," Amy said, squeezing his hand in her own and blinking back her tears.

He nodded and then closed his eyes, obviously weak and tired.

In the waiting room the captain asked, "Do you think you could come down to the station later today to look at mug shots? Maybe we'll get lucky."

"Of course. I will do all I can to help."

"Good. I will check with you later to see how the lieutenant is doing." He rose to leave.

"Thank you, Captain Adams," she said.

When the captain left, Amy noticed other people in the waiting room for the first time. They sat, as preoccupied, as she. She remembered that this was Saturday, the day she should have spent at the cabin with Barry. She thought of herself as being strong and Barry had said she was independent. She didn't feel strong now. All she wanted to do was cry, but she fought back the tears. She thought of Joan and decided she needed her company. She called her on her cell phone and waited for her to arrive. When Joan arrived, she hugged Amy tightly.

"Have you been back in to see him?" Joan asked.

"No. I figured I'd better not press my luck, so soon."

"Which room is his?"

"Room 404." Amy answered.

Joan grinned wickedly and taking her by the hand, led Amy down the hall to Barry's room. They disappeared inside. Barry lay sleeping, hooked up to an IV and monitor. Joan stared at him for a moment.

"Lord, he looks bad," she whispered.

Alarmed, Amy hurried to his side. She watched as he breathed steadily and realized that he looked the same as before.

"He looks better than he did on the floor of the cabin, after he was shot," she whispered to Joan.

Joan shuddered, "I guess he would." Then, she added, "Let him know you are here."

Amy hesitated only a second. Then, bending over him, she placed her lips on his, softly.

Surprised at this, Joan watched as Barry opened his eyes and saw Amy. There was a twinkle in his blue eyes as he recognized her. He reached over with his left arm and encircled her waist, drawing her closer to him.

"Am I dreaming, or is this the real thing?" he asked, gruffly.

"I'm the real thing, Darling," Amy teased, swallowing the lump in her throat.

"Just what the doctor ordered," he said, weakly.

"Joan's here," Amy told him. "We sneaked in without the nurses knowing."

"Hello, Lieutenant," Joan said.

"Hello, Joan. Are you taking good care of my girl here?" he asked, his voice slurred.

"I sure am; teaching her all the tricks," she teased.

"She's got a mind of her own, my little wife," he said.

Surprised, Amy said, "I think you're doped up, Darling. I'm not your wife."

"My wife-to-be," he corrected.

Amy blushed. She wondered if he thought that she was his wife who had died.

"Are congratulations in order?" Joan teased.

"You two stop that!" Amy said, wanting to change the subject. She didn't understand what he was saying. "We'd better leave you alone before the nurse throws us out," she continued.

"She's right," Joan said, grinning. "She'll have that monitor of yours doing double-time. They'll think you are having a heart attack."

"Come back soon," he said. Then, he asked, "One more kiss?"

Amy kissed him softly on the lips. "I have to go now. I'll be back later."

"Uh huh," he sighed deeply and closed his eyes again.

Outside in the hall, Joan turned to Amy. "What was all that about?"

"I have no idea." Amy answered.

"Has he proposed to you?" Joan asked.

"No, he has not. I think he was talking out of his head because of the medicine."

"He said you were 'his wife'. Does he have a wife?"

"Not any more. She died two years ago. Maybe he thought I was her just now," Amy said, reluctantly.

"You're right. It was probably the medicine causing it," Joan assured her. "I think he really likes you, though. I can see it in his eyes, the way he looks at you. Did something happen between you two?"

"Not really. We kissed a few times, that's all," she confessed, blushing.

"That's good....for starters," Joan grinned. "After all, he is 'drop-dead-gorgeous'! Too bad he only has eyes for you!"

Amy wondered if he would even remember talking to her just now.

***

When Amy went to the Sheriff's Department she looked through stacks of mug shots but didn't recognize any of them. Captain Adams informed her that they had put out an A.P.B. with the bearded man's description and would be charging him with attempted murder of Lieutenant Reeser. Whether he was guilty of the murder of Rodney Benson remained to be seen. Amy remembered Sara Benson's call and hoped that she would call back with more information.

When Amy drove back to the hospital, she went directly to Barry's room without asking the nurses. She was surprised to find three people in his room, an older couple and a younger version of Barry, himself. She realized that this could only be his parents and brother.

"Hello," she said, shyly. "I'm Amy Fontell. You must be Barry's family. I can see the resemblance."

The tall, older gentleman shook her hand warmly. Amy knew, instantly, from whom Barry had inherited his blue eyes.

"I'm glad to meet you, Miss Fontell. I am David Reeser. This is my wife, Becky and my younger son, Joey. Barry has spoken of you."

Amy saw the concern on their faces. "How is he?" she asked, her gaze resting on Barry.

"He's asleep now," his father answered. "We have worn him out since we got here. We came as soon as we could, after his captain called us.

Amy wondered if they knew about her involvement with their son and wondered if they blamed her for his being shot. She noticed that Joey was watching her closely. The nurse came in at that moment to check on Barry and she frowned, slightly.

"I'm sorry, but only two visitors are allowed in the rooms at one time," she said.

"I'll go back to the waiting room," Amy offered, quickly.

"So will I," Joey volunteered. "Dad, you and Mom can stay."

Amy and Joey sat down in the waiting room. She felt uncomfortable because of the way he kept watching her. Finally, he broke the silence.

"How long have you known my brother?" he asked.

"Several weeks," she admitted.

"Do you know how he got shot?"

"Didn't the police explain it to you?" she asked.

"Not much. Do you know how it happened?"

"He is working on a homicide case and one of the suspects threatened him; there was a fight." She had no intention of telling this young boy all the details.

"That's about all we were told. There has to be more to it than that. Do you work with him?"

He was full of questions, Amy thought. "I am just a friend," she said.

"He told us you were with him when he was shot!" Joey exclaimed.

"He told you that?" she asked, surprised.

"Mom and Dad asked him what happened and he said 'Amy' called 911 and that a helicopter came to pick him up."

She tried to change his train of thought; "How did he

seem to you earlier, Joey?"

"He's real weak and in a lot of pain. I've never seen him sick before. It sort of scares me," he confessed.

Amy felt compassion for this younger brother and encouraged him to tell her about growing up with Barry to help him calm down. She began to enjoy talking with him. He reminded her of Barry; he had some of his mannerisms. They had been talking for over an hour when his parents joined them.

Mr. Reeser addressed Amy. "Barry is awake now. We told him you were out here and he asked to see you. We thought we would go to the cafeteria to eat while you visit with him."

"Thank you, Mr. Reeser."

Amy was glad to see Barry again. He was sitting, propped up against his pillows. When she entered the room, he smiled weakly. "Hello, Amy. It's good to see you."

"Barry! You're sitting up! Are you feeling better?" she asked, relieved.

"As long as I don't move," he teased.

She examined the bandages on his right shoulder. "That's really going to be sore for a while," she said, regretfully.

"The nurse said I have to get up and walk soon. They don't want me to get lazy." He closed his left hand around hers and asked, "Have you been here all day?"

"I went to the Sheriff's Department to look at mug shots earlier. I didn't recognize anybody."

"I won't forget that face," he said, frowning.

"Barry, he could have killed you!" she said, close to tears.

"But, he didn't. That's what is important, now." He lifted her hand to his lips and kissed it softly. He didn't take his gaze from her face. " I guess our plan worked," he added. "He showed up again."

"Unfortunately," she said.

"That wasn't exactly the way I had planned it," he chuckled.

Amy wasn't sure what he was referring to but didn't dare ask. She was remembering how wonderful it felt to be in his arms and so near him during the night.

"So, you met my parents and Joey?"

"Yes. They are very nice. Joey reminds me of you. He was full of questions about what happened."

"What did you tell him?"

"As little as I could get by with."

"Good. I try to keep my work a secret from them as much as I can. Mom and Dad worry too much."

"I can understand why," she said.

"When we catch the guy and you're no longer threatened, would you like to spend another weekend at the cabin?" he asked.

"Yes, I'd like that," she said, softly. But, she wondered if it would be wise.

The nurse interrupted them. She was coming to get Barry out of bed. Amy watched as he struggled to his feet. She saw the pain on his face each time he moved his right arm. Her heart went out to him. She followed behind them as the nurse walked him down the hallway and then back to the bed. He was sweating by the time he lay back on his pillows.

"You did very well, Mr. Reeser," the nurse said as she adjusted his IV and monitor. "Your dinner is on the way, so you will be fixed up for a while."

"Whew!" he exclaimed, weakly, after the nurse had gone. "I didn't realize it would be that hard to get out of bed and walk."

"You lost a lot of blood, Barry," Amy reminded him.

"They told me that they gave me a couple of units in surgery."

"See! You expect too much of yourself," she smiled.

"Maybe so."

The nurse brought his tray and left it.

"This ought to be fun, using my left hand to eat with."

"Would you like for me to feed you?" Amy offered.

He grinned. "Another time and place, maybe. But, right now, I'd better learn how."

Amy helped him get everything ready on his tray and watched, helplessly, as he tried to maneuver the fork with his left hand. He managed very well except for dropping a forkful of peas. She heard her stomach growl and realized that neither of them had eaten since the night before. Barry heard it too and he looked at her, inquisitively.

"You're hungry. You haven't eaten today, either. Here, eat some of this." He offered her a bite.

"No, thank you. I will eat when I leave here. Eat your dinner."

"I won't eat another bite, until you do," he challenged.

Laughing, she opened her mouth obediently, to receive a bite of roast. At that moment, the doctor walked into the room and observed this exchange."

"Well, well. Who is the patient here?" he grinned.

Amy blushed and moved away from the bed so that the doctor could examine Barry.

"I'm Dr. Bryant. I can see that you are feeling much better. I hear that you have been up already."

"Yes, Dr. Bryant." Barry answered.

"Keep up the good work and you'll be out of here in a couple of days."

"That long?"

"We have to keep you here to make sure that wound drains and doesn't get infected. We don't want you going home and having to come back." He wrote something on Barry's chart and left the room before they could ask any questions.

At that moment, Barry's brother, Joey came into the

room.

"Hey, Barry. I see you're eating, too. We had a good meal in the cafeteria. Mom and Dad are in the waiting room now."

"You finish your dinner, Barry," Amy said. I'll go home now. I'm leaving you in good hands. I'll tell your mom and dad to come back in." Their gaze met briefly, but she knew that Joey was watching. She patted his left shoulder and said, "I'll see you tomorrow."

"Good bye, Amy," he said and watched as she disappeared through the doorway.

***

When Amy got to her apartment, she fixed herself a sandwich and a glass of milk. After she had eaten she showered and dressed in her pajamas. She felt exhausted. Joan had left her a note to tell her she was on a date so Amy decided to go to bed early. Before she could, the phone rang. To her surprise, it was Barry.

"I wanted to make sure you made it home okay," he said, his voice sounding stronger.

"Don't you be worrying about me, Barry. You just concentrate on getting well. Are your mom and dad still there?"

"No, I gave them the key to my house and they've already gone over there to spend the night. I wanted to tell you, don't open your door unless you know who it is."

"I won't."

"Do you want me to have the captain send over a couple of guys from the department to watch your house?"

"No, don't do that. I don't think that man would be crazy enough to come here, with people all around."

"He could be crazy enough to try anything," he said. Then, he added, "The captain and sergeant came by to see me after you left. He may send someone out anyway, but you probably won't see them."

"Don't worry about me, Barry. I still have my gun."

"Do you know how to use it?"

"Hopefully. I took a training course when I first got it."

"Good. Keep it with you at all times and use it if you have to."

He was scaring her, but she didn't want him to worry.

"I'll be careful."

"Good."

"You need to rest, Darling," she said. "Good night."

"Good night, Sweetheart. I wish I were there and could hold you," he said, softly.

"I wish you were, too. I wish you hadn't been shot," she said, thinking that he would be hurting for a while. When she hung up the phone, she felt tired and lonely and afraid. She made sure the doors and windows were locked before she went to bed.

***

The next day was Sunday. Amy decided to go by the supermarket on her way to the hospital to get Barry a small fruit basket and balloons. When she was putting them inside her car, a woman suddenly appeared by her side. She shoved her aside and got in on the passenger's side of the car.

"Get in and don't make a scene!" she ordered.

Amy recognized the woman's voice as the one who had called and harassed her earlier. Her heart was pounding, but she didn't see a gun or anything threatening at the moment. The woman was tall, with red, frizzy hair and freckles. She was dressed in faded jeans and a jacket. Amy got inside her car, slowly. She tried to pull her backpack toward her, without the woman noticing. Amy knew her gun was inside and loaded this time.

"Who are you and what do you want?" Amy asked, nervously.

The woman motioned toward the balloons and fruit basket and said, "That guy that was shot, he ain't dead, is he?"

"How do you know about that?" Amy asked. "You know who shot him, don't you?"

"I don't have to tell you nothing! If you know what's good for you, you'll do what I say, and drive!"

"You think I'm crazy? I'm not going anywhere with you!"

Suddenly, the woman flicked a switchblade open. "Just in case you get any ideas," she snarled.

Amy almost panicked. She thought of screaming for help and trying to run.

"Just pull out of here and turn left at that next light," the woman instructed.

"Why? Where do you want me to go?" Amy asked, not moving.

"My old man's going to meet us somewhere."

Amy felt weak. "What does he look like?" she asked, remembering the man who shot Barry.

"What do you care what he looks like?" she snapped. "You've seen him! You know him. He's been to your cabin."

"I'm not going!" Amy exclaimed and tried to open the door.

The woman grabbed her wrist and twisted. "Start the car!" she grated and stuck the knife into Amy's coat sleeve. It cut the fabric and pricked her skin. Amy cried out.

"I said, start the car!" The woman let go of Amy's arm and held the knife to her side.

Trembling, Amy obeyed. She was more afraid of this woman than she was of the woman's husband.

Amy followed the woman's directions. They were just outside the city when she instructed Amy to stop at a deserted roadside park. At least it wasn't dark this time, Amy thought, it was still early in the morning.

"Pull over there," the woman said, pointing toward an old wooden picnic table.

Amy obeyed, looking around for other people, but there was no one. Then, she saw the man who had shot Barry coming from his truck that was parked under the trees. She noticed that he wasn't carrying a rifle this time.

The woman put her knife in her pocket and said, "Get

out. We're sitting at that table."

Amy noticed that the woman had put her backpack with her pistol on the floorboard on the passenger's side of the car. She wished she had it with her but knew it was impossible. She got out of the car and slipped the keys into her pocket. Reluctantly, she walked to where the man was waiting for her at the table. She sat down across from him, wanting to be as far away from him as possible.

"Did she give ye' any trouble?" he asked his wife, who sat down beside him.

"Not much. She knew better," she snarled.

"I told ye' we'd have our little talk," he grinned at Amy.

"I'm not saying a word to you, until you tell me who you are!" Amy said, frustrated. She was relieved that he was, at least, being civil to her.

"Why? So ye' can tell your 'boy friend' who I am?"

"I'm not speaking to you without some way to address you!"

He studied a moment and said, "Okay, call me Arthur. That'll do for now."

Amy wondered if that was his real name. "What is your wife's name?" Amy questioned.

"There ye' go askin' me questions, Gal! I'm here to ask the questions."

"What's her name?" Amy persisted.

"I can talk for myself! If you have to know, my name's Tammy," she retorted.

"Thank you," Amy said. At least she knew with whom she was dealing.

"Now, Girlie, like I was tellin' you the other day when we was interrupted; I'm lookin' fer' some pictures that your uncle took a few years ago."

"What does that have to do with you?" Amy asked.

"I knowed your uncle for years. Him and me, we did some business together."

"I don't believe you!" Amy exclaimed.

He leaned toward her, his eyes narrowing. "You callin' me a liar?"

"What sort of business are you talking about?" Amy asked, nervously.

"Never you mind about that. What'd you do with all his stuff when you moved into his cabin?"

Amy tried to remember. "I kept the furniture. I gave his clothes to a thrift store. The rest was just junk, so I burned it."

"Ye' burned it?" he asked, disbelieving. "Ye burned his pictures and stuff?"

"I didn't see any pictures! How many times do I have to tell you?" she asked, irritated."

"Don't get smart with me, Gal!" he snapped.

Amy's pulse quickened and she watched him, warily.

"I could search the cabin," he said, watching her closely.

"Yeah!" Tammy said, glaring at Amy.

"Shut yer' mouth! I'm handlin' this!" he snapped at his wife.

Amy wondered if he was as civil as she first thought.

"You tellin' me the truth, Gal? You ain't got no pictures?"

"I'm telling you, I have not seen any pictures that belonged to my uncle. Search the cabin if you don't believe me." She prayed that he would never set foot near the cabin again.

He stared at her for a long moment.

"You ain't believing her, are you, Arthur?" Tammy asked.

"Maybe I do. She ain't so dumb that she's playin' games with me, are you Gal?"

"I wouldn't be playing games with you, Arthur," she said, bravely.

He grinned. "You're right spunky. But, if I find out

ye' been lyin', ye'll be sorry."

"Can I go now?" Amy asked, cautiously.

"Not just yet. That feller' that jumped me, did he make it?"

"He's alive, if that's what you mean, no thanks to you."

"It was his own fault! He jumped me. I wasn't plannin' on shootin' nobody."

"You almost killed him!" Amy said, feeling weak, remembering.

"If you go runnin' to the law about this here, I can finish the job, savvy?" he snarled.

Amy shuddered. She believed he would, too. "I understand. I will keep my mouth shut. I don't want you hurting him again."

He grinned, showing tobacco-stained teeth. "Yer' sweet on him, ain't ye', Gal? I seen the way ye' was lookin' at him!"

Amy blushed and hated herself for it. "Maybe," she admitted, reluctantly. She was going along with him. She didn't want to antagonize him.

He laughed, aloud. "I busted up yer' cozy little hide-away, didn't I'"

Amy bit back the angry retort she was ready to give him. She told herself that she had to be cautious. "May I go now?" she asked, again."

"Let me rough her up a little. She's a smart ass!" Tammy jeered.

Before Tammy realized what was about to happen, Arthur slapped her across the face. She cowered away from him. Amy jumped, afraid that she would be next.

"I believe what ye' said, Gal. That's all that's savin' ye. I don't think ye' know anything about yer' uncle's affairs or his pictures." He chuckled and said, "If ye' did, ye'd high-tail it out of there and not come back."

"Thank you for believing me," Amy said.

"I tell you what; I'm still goin' to be lookin' around, in case them pictures turn up somewhere else. But, if yer' tellin' me the truth, Gal, ye' ain't got nothin' to worry about. Now, git!"

Amy almost fell in her haste to get up. They watched her as she nearly ran to her car. She tried to stay calm as she started the motor and backed out into the road. Inside, her nerves were screaming. When she was out of their sight, she began to tremble with fright and burst into uncontrollable tears. It took a long time for her to get control of herself. She had put up a good front with them. Actually, she was scared to death.

She thought about the things Arthur had said about her uncle. She wondered how he could have been involved with someone like Arthur. She tried to remember the last few times she had seen her uncle alive. Actually, she had known very little about him. Suddenly, she gasped, as she remembered what had completely slipped her mind before; she had kept a box of her uncle's personal belongings. She had stored the box in the attic in her apartment. She groaned aloud when she remembered Arthur's threat, if she were not telling him the truth. She wished she hadn't remembered the box.

Amy drove to the hospital and sat in the car, trying to figure out what to do. She did not want Barry to know that someone named Tammy had forced her to go with her to meet her husband, Arthur. Amy didn't want Barry to be upset or worry about her. She decided not to say anything for the present. As she started to get out of the car, she noticed her torn sleeve that Tammy had cut with her knife. She yanked the coat off and saw that her arm had bled slightly where it pricked her skin. She knew Barry was very perceptive. Looking around, she spotted her sweatshirt in the back seat. She grabbed it and pulled it on, covering her arm. Now, he wouldn't know.

Amy gathered up the almost forgotten fruit basket and

balloons to take to Barry. As she was passing the waiting room, she saw Mr. Reeser. She stopped and spoke to him, thinking that he looked tired this morning.

"Good morning, Miss Fontell. How are you?" he answered.

"I am fine, Sir. How is our patient?" she smiled.

Worry lines crossed his face. "Not very well, I am afraid. He has been running a temperature all night and this morning."

"Oh, no," Amy said, concerned. She had a sick feeling in the pit of her stomach. "Do you know why?" she asked.

"Could be 'post operative' they say; like it is a normal thing. But, I'm worried about him."

Amy felt concern for Mr. Reeser. He looked so depressed.

"I'm sure he will be all right, Mr. Reeser. This is a good hospital. They will take good care of him." She tried to sound more optimistic than she felt. She didn't want him to know how worried she really was. "Is your wife with him?"

"Yes, she's in there. Joey stayed at the house this morning."

"I'd like to take him these," she said, indicating the fruit and balloons. "Do you think he feels like having more company?"

He smiled, a replica of Barry's sweet smile. "I think he would enjoy that very much."

"Will you go in with me?" she asked.

"You go ahead. I will be in shortly."

When Amy entered Barry's room she found his mother sitting beside his bed. She noticed that Barry had his eyes closed. His face was flushed. She spoke to his mother and set his fruit basket down and tied his balloons to the end of his bed. At the sound of her voice, Barry opened his eyes and smiled weakly.

"Good morning," she said cheerfully. "I brought you something to cheer you."

"Mom, I'd like to talk to Audrey," he said, softly.

A startled expression crossed his mother's face. "Do you mean, Amy?"

He looked puzzled for a moment and then said, "Yes, Amy."

Mrs. Reeser got up quickly, motioning Amy to take her chair.

"I'll be back shortly," she said and left the room.

"Who is Audrey?" Amy teased, as she sat beside Barry and took his hand in hers. It was too warm, she thought, and his eyes were glassy from the fever.

An embarrassed expression crossed his face and he didn't respond.

"Well....?"she teased.

"Audrey was my wife," he said quietly.

"Oh," Amy said, shocked. She felt herself blush and was speechless.

"I'm sorry, Amy. I don't know why I said that." He squeezed her hand and caressed it with his thumb. Watching her closely, he added, "Thank you for the fruit basket and balloons. That was sweet of you."

Amy squeezed back the tears that threatened. She wondered if Barry was only interested in her because she reminded him of his deceased wife. She was grateful that the nurse interrupted them at that moment. It gave her the opportunity to excuse herself while the nurse took his vital signs.

"I will be back in a moment, when she is finished," Amy said. She went back to the waiting room where she found his parents. Mrs. Reeser looked at her, surprised.

"Are you leaving already?" she asked.

"No. The nurse is with him now," she explained. Amy sat down beside her and asked, bluntly, "Would you tell me about his wife?"

"Audrey? Has he told you about her dying of cancer?"

"That's all that he has told me."

"She died two years ago. They had only been married a little over a year. Barry was devastated; we all were. He hasn't been interested in anyone since, as far as I know. Of course, living so far away, we can't keep up with what is going on with him."

"He still loves her," Amy stated.

"I don't think you ever stop loving someone just because they pass away," his mother said.

"It would be hard to take her place," Amy said.

His mother looked at Amy and smiled, knowingly. "You wouldn't want to try to take her place. You would want to be yourself and make him forget that he misses her."

Amy looked into his mother's sweet, gentle face and said, "You are a wise lady, Mrs. Reeser. Thank you for your advice."

"Are you dating Barry?" she asked, simply.

Amy didn't know how to answer that. Had they actually had a date?

"I have been seeing him some. We are sort of working on a case together," she tried to explain.

"I didn't realize you were on the police force," she said, surprised.

"No, it's not like that, at all!" Amy laughed. "I could never do that!"

Amy and Mrs. Reeser chatted for a while longer while Mr. Reeser sat with Barry. Somehow, Amy felt better afterwards. Finally, Mrs. Reeser asked, "Wouldn't you like to go back and sit with him now?"

"Yes, I would, unless you want to."

"I'll be here all day. You go ahead. Run his father out when you go in," she said, with an understanding smile.

"I could never do that!" Amy laughed.

Amy didn't have to. As soon as she went in to see Barry his father slipped out, unnoticed.

When Barry saw her, he smiled, his blue eyes shining. "Hello, again," he said softly.

Amy felt of his brow. "You're not as warm as you were. Did the nurse give you something for your fever?"

"Yes, through the IV, along with the antibiotics."

"Good. Do you feel better, Darling?" she asked.

"I do now," he teased. "Can't you come a little closer?" he asked, as he pulled her nearer with his left hand.

She leaned over and planted a kiss on his brow. It was cooler now.

"Still not close enough," he teased.

She looked into his blue eyes and read the desire there. It matched her own. Slowly, she met his lips with her own and kissed him tenderly. She heard him draw his breath in sharply as he tried to pull her even closer.

"The nurse will throw me out of here for being in bed with you," she whispered, her heartbeat racing.

Ignoring her plea, he pulled her back down until their lips met again. When he finally released her, she was breathless.

"Wow! That must have been some kind of medicine that they gave you!" she teased, visibly shaken by his kiss.

"You're the only medicine I need," he said, softly.

A knock sounded at the door and Amy straightened up quickly. Captain Adams stuck his head inside.

"May I come in?" he greeted them warmly. "I saw your folks outside, Barry. They said you had company in here." He grinned, knowingly, at Amy.

"She's taking good care of me," Barry said.

"I bet she is," he teased. Pulling a package from his coat, he added, "Judy Mason said to give you this. You want Miss. Fontell to open it for you since your arm is out of commission right now?"

"Sure."

The captain handed the package to Amy and she began unwrapping it. She wondered who 'Judy Mason' was. She unwrapped a gold, Cross pen and a yellow legal pad.

"Read the note," the captain instructed.

Amy read, "Barry, this is for you to practice writing with your left hand while you are getting well. Take care, Love, Judy."

Both men laughed, but Amy wondered what they thought was so funny.

"Judy works in our office. You'd have to know her, to appreciate her," Captain Adams said.

"I'm sure," Amy replied, wondering how well Barry knew her.

When the men began to talk police business, Amy excused herself from the room. She thought of waiting for the captain to tell him about her abduction earlier. She wondered if he would keep it from Barry if she told him. When she saw the captain leaving, she excused herself from Barry's parents and caught up with him in the hallway.

"Miss. Fontell, you look concerned about something," he said, as they walked toward the main lobby. "Are you worried about the lieutenant?"

"I have been. But, I believe he is improving, don't you?"

"Yes, he definitely seems to be."

"There's something else I need to talk to you about," she ventured.

He stopped walking and looked at her closely. "What is bothering you, Miss. Fontell?"

"Could we talk in private somewhere?" she asked.

"How about the cafeteria? Is that private enough?"

"That's fine. I could use a cup of coffee," she agreed.

"It's lunch time. How about letting me buy your lunch? The food isn't bad here," he added.

"I'd enjoy that."

They got their trays and sat at a corner table away

from the crowd.

"Now, would you like to tell me what is bothering you?" he asked.

Amy began to tell him about what had happened to her earlier, concerning her abduction.

"That's kidnapping, Miss. Fontell!"

"Yes, I know. I was afraid of that woman, too, Captain."

"I wonder if that is their real name, or an alias?" he said.

Amy remembered Mrs. Benson's phone call and told him about that too.

"She is supposed to try to find out the man's name for me. I believe she said he was a hunting buddy of her late husband. Captain, do you think all of this ties together? What do you think my uncle had to do with that man?"

"It's hard to say, Miss. Fontell. I hate to mention this, since he was your uncle, but a lot of drug dealing goes on in that area."

"Oh, no!" she exclaimed. "Surely he wouldn't have been involved in drug dealing! I find that hard to believe!"

He was watching her closely and asked, "Did your uncle have a license to fly a small plane?"

She was puzzled. "You know, I believe my father did mention that Uncle Curtis did fly, at one time."

He nodded. "Some of the roughnecks from that county are dealers. We haven't been able to catch them."

"Where would my uncle have gotten a plane? I have never seen a plane of his."

"He could have chartered a plane. I'm just guessing, Miss. Fontell. He could have been perfectly innocent."

"What about the pictures that man, Arthur, was talking about? They might reveal something."

"Could be. But, you said you hadn't seen any pictures, didn't you?"

"I haven't. But, I remembered that I did keep a box

of Uncle Curtis' things. I put it in my attic."

"Don't tell anyone else about that box, Miss. Fontell," the captain said, concerned. "Can you get the box down and go through it?"

"Yes, I plan to."

"If you find any pictures that you think I need to see, call me."

"I certainly will, Captain. But, please don't tell Lieutenant Reeser."

She saw his brow rise in puzzlement. "Don't tell the lieutenant?"

She blushed. "I don't want him to worry, in his condition."

"I understand. But, I can't promise that, Miss. Fontell. I'm sorry. I will certainly use good judgment about waiting until I think he is able to handle all this. Will you be satisfied with that, at the moment?"

"Yes, Captain." Amy found that she liked the captain and she thought that he was very considerate and professional. She promised to keep in touch with him.

***

Amy decided to go home and look for her uncle's pictures. She was climbing up the ladder that pulled down from the attic when Joan came home and saw her.

"What on earth are you doing up there?" she asked.

"Looking for something that I stored up here," she answered.

"Have you lost your mind?" Joan called up to her.

"No, I have not lost my mind!" she answered as she climbed back down with a large box in her hands. "This is some of Uncle Curtis' things. I want to look through them."

"Have fun. I am going to fix lunch. Have you eaten?"

"Yes, thanks." Amy took the box to her bedroom for privacy. She didn't want to have to explain things to Joan. She took everything out of the box, piece by piece, examining each article. She found souvenirs from her uncle's war days and from his wedding and anniversaries. There was an album of family pictures. She put that aside to look at later. She found a small, manila envelope. Opening it, she saw that it contained several pictures. Her fingers trembling with anticipation, she leafed through each picture. In one picture, looking back at her was her uncle, clad in a leather jacket. He was standing beside a blue and white

Cessna. Another picture revealed her uncle and two men that she did not recognize, beside the same plane. The third picture made her gasp. It was of the man, 'Arthur' with her uncle and a deer that had been killed. Arthur was holding a hunting bow. Amy stared at the picture, remembering the man's body that she had found with the arrow protruding from his back. She shivered. The fourth picture was of her neighbor, Homer Rafferty and her uncle, near the cabin. Homer was holding his rifle. They were kneeling beside a deer. The fifth picture was of the plane with boxes and bundles stacked beside it. She thumbed through each picture once again. Then, she put them back into the envelope. She put the envelope in her backpack. She planned to give them to Captain Adams when she had the opportunity. She carefully put everything else back into the box and made room for it in her closet.

Amy heard the phone ring and then Joan called for her to get it. She picked up the phone near her bed.

"Hello," she said.

"Hello, Miss. Fontell?"

Amy recognized Sara Benson's voice. "Yes, Mrs. Benson. Have you found out anything?"

"Yes, I know who that man is that you asked me about. His name is Arthur Morgan. You want his address?"

"Of course!" Amy copied it as she repeated it.

"He may be the one who killed Rodney," Sara Benson said, "Why ain't they got him in jail?"

"It takes time for an investigation. I'm sure they are doing all they can. This information will help. Thank you so much for calling and giving it to me."

Amy glanced at her watch. It was two-thirty. She decided to call Captain Adams at his work. Luckily, he was there. She told him everything that Sara Benson had told her.

"Thanks to you, Miss. Fontell, we'll get on this right away. When we get him and his wife behind bars, then we'll tell the lieutenant. He'll be happy to hear it."

"I won't say a word yet, Captain. He may even be the one who killed Rodney Benson, as well as the one who shot Barry."

"We'll find out soon enough," the captain said.

Amy told him about the pictures and promised to take them to him later that day.

When she got off the phone she joined Joan in the kitchen. She decided to confide in her and sat down with a cup of coffee and told her everything that had happened.

Joan stared at her in disbelief. "Amy Fontell! You sit there, calmly telling me that you were kidnapped this morning, and that you are helping solve a murder case? I don't believe you! What are you going to do next? Until you met Lieutenant Reeser, you led such a dull life!"

"I hope this will be the end of it. I hope the case will be closed after the Morgan's arrest and conviction," Amy said.

After her talk with Joan, Amy took the pictures to Captain Adams. When she got back home, she was exhausted. She lay across her bed to rest and was soon sound asleep. She didn't awaken until after dark. She remembered that she had forgotten to call Barry. She decided to go see him, instead. She showered and dressed in black slacks and a gray sweater.

When Amy arrived at the hospital she found Barry walking down the hallway, a nurse following close behind. When he saw her, he smiled, making her heart melt.

"Look who's running around on his own," she teased. She hugged him gently, careful not to hurt him.

"It's good to see you," he said, softly. "You look great."

The nurse said, "If you will see that Mr. Reeser gets back to his room safely, I will let him walk with you."

"I believe I can do that," Amy smiled. She felt of his brow. "Your fever is gone. You're looking a lot better."

She let him walk a while longer and then escorted him back to his room. She could tell he was beginning to tire. She helped him get back into bed. He sighed as he lay down.

"That was hard work," she observed.

"A little," he confessed. Then, he reached for her and pulled her close. She kissed him once again.

"I wish I wasn't in this place," he teased.

"I wish you weren't either. Has the doctor said for sure when you can go home?"

"Maybe tomorrow or the next day, depending on how everything goes."

Amy visited with Barry until nine p.m.. She promised to call him in the morning and then went home.

Amy called Barry before she left for work. He had not had a temperature all night. He hoped to go home after seeing the doctor. She told him to call her if he did get to go home.

Captain Adams called Amy to tell her that the police had arrested Arthur and Tammy Morgan.

"I am so relieved to hear that!" she said.

"I am going to see Barry and I will tell him the good news," he continued.

"He may be going home today. You might want to call first." Amy informed him.

Before Amy left work that afternoon, Barry called to tell her that he was home. He gave her directions to his house.

"I won't come tonight, Barry. I will let you get settled in with your parents. I know all of you need some rest."

"I would enjoy seeing you again," he said.

"I would love to see you, too, Darling. You enjoy your family being there. I will see you tomorrow."

"They are planning to go home tomorrow, since they won't have to stay for my funeral," he joked.

"Don't even joke about that, Barry!" Amy exclaimed.

Suddenly, he was serious. "By the way, the captain told me about what happened to you. Why didn't you tell me?"

"I didn't want you worrying about me. You had enough to worry about."

"You could have been killed!"

"But, I wasn't. Don't think about it any more. They are both behind bars."

"For right now. But, they could get out on bail, you know."

She hadn't thought of that. "Maybe it will be too high and they can't afford it," she said.

"Maybe. It will still take a while for the case to go to court. You still need to be careful, Amy."

"I will, I promise. I'll come by to see you after work tomorrow. You take care of yourself, Barry."

The next afternoon after work, Amy drove to Barry's house. She was impressed when she saw it. It was a large, two-story brick house on a quiet street. She thought of his deceased wife living there with him. She rang the doorbell and waited. It took a couple of minutes for him to answer the door.

"I forgot to tell you to come to the side door. I don't use this part of the house much anymore," he said, as he opened the door and greeted her.

"You have a lovely house, Barry."

"Thanks. I'll show you around, if you'd like." He closed the door behind her and pulled her to him, gently.

"I've missed you," he said softly. His lips closed over hers, preventing her from answering. He kissed her softly at first, then passionately. She was trembling when he finally released her.

"You sure don't act like an invalid," she said, breathlessly.

"No?"

"You look like one, though," she teased. "How is

your shoulder?"

"Awfully darn sore. I've been wearing a sling most of the day. It seems to help."

"Where is it now?"

He grinned. "I can't put both my arms around you, with a sling on."

"What am I going to do with you?"

"How about......this?" he whispered as he bent to kiss her again.

Finally, she pulled away from him, trembling. "I think we'd better take that tour of your house now."

"You're right," he said, his blue eyes shinning. He led her through the house, showing her each room. It was spotlessly clean, even the rooms he said he no longer used. It was decorated beautifully and Amy wondered if his wife had done the decorating herself. He paused before the door to the master bedroom.

"This is my bedroom," he said, watching her closely. She felt shy about seeing where he slept and he sensed this. She didn't offer to cross the threshold but peered around the door.

"It's very nice. I love the bold colors." The walls were beige and the drapes and comforter were a mixture of gold, navy and forest green.

He hesitated a moment, still watching her closely. "My wife did the decorating. I can't claim any of the credit."

"She had very good taste," Amy said, softly. She could see a picture from that distance that looked like Barry and a beautiful woman. He had his arm around her.

"May I see a picture of her?" she asked.

He looked surprised for a second, and said, "Sure." Walking into the room, he went to the chest of drawers and got a different picture. He brought it to her. Taking it, Amy noticed that the woman looking back at her was, indeed, beautiful. She had dark hair and eyes, like her own.

"This was taken before we were married and before she found out she had cancer. She wouldn't let me take a picture of her after she got sick."

"I am so sorry that she died, Barry," Amy said, truthfully. However, she knew that if Audrey hadn't died, she would not be standing there now.

"I'm sorry too," he confessed. "We had a happy life together, even if it was for such a short time." He looked so sad that Amy had the urge to take him in her arms, but she didn't. Instead, she handed the picture back to him and he set it back down on the chest of drawers. Coming from the bedroom, he closed the door behind him.

"I need a picture of you, Amy," he said, hesitantly. "I guess you wonder why I still have all of these pictures of Audrey."

"I don't wonder that, Barry. She was your wife, and you loved her." She had to fight back the urge to cry for no reason at all.

He had a strange expression on his face as he watched her closely. He took both her hands in his but winced with pain as he pulled his shoulder the wrong way.

"I don't want to live in the past, Amy," he confided. "I want to look to the future...our future, yours and mine," he said, softly.

"Barry, we have only known one another for a few weeks," she said, her heartbeat quickening.

"Does that matter to you?" he asked, seriously.

She searched his beautiful, blue eyes, trying to see beyond their depth.

"I feel as though I have known you all my life, Darling. You are the one person I have been waiting for," she confessed.

He pulled her to him roughly and she heard him groan as his shoulder stopped him.

"Let's sit down and I'll try not to hurt your shoulder," she said, leading him to the living room.

When they were seated he turned to her, still holding her hands in his.

"I want you to know that I have not been interested in anyone since Audrey died. I think I told you that I have dated some. I have had plenty of opportunities, but I wasn't interested until now. With you, Amy, it's different. I want you, Sweetheart," he said softly, making her heart melt .

She could scarcely breathe as she looked at him, her desire matching his own. Tears slipped from between her dark lashes and slid down her cheeks.

He frowned, concerned. "What have I said to upset you, Sweetheart?"

She shook her head, unable to speak for a moment. "You have made me so happy!" she cried, kissing him on the cheek.

"Is that all?" he asked, grinning. He wiped the tears from her cheeks with his fingertips and kissed her on the nose, like a child. "How old are you, Sweetheart?" he teased.

Surprised, she answered, "I'm twenty three. Is that too old?"

He laughed aloud, his blue eyes dancing. "No, my Dear; that's too young! I am thirty-three! Do you want to get involved with 'an older man'?"

"What do you mean, 'involved'?" she asked, cautiously, trying to read his every expression.

"Well, first of all, I want to see you every day; I want us to go places together; I want to eat with you.....I want to sleep with you."

Her heartbeat was running away with her. She tried to calm herself before she spoke. "If you will remember, Barry, I told you once before...."

He didn't let her finish. "Sweetheart, I am not asking you to sleep with me now; I am asking you to marry me," he grinned.

Her dark eyes opened wider. "What did you say?"

she stammered.

"Will you marry me, Amy Fontell?" he whispered.

Tears, unbidden, filled her eyes again. "Oh, yes! Yes, my Darling!" she exclaimed, throwing her arms around him and kissing him repeatedly. He laughed with joy when he wasn't groaning from the pain in his shoulder. Suddenly, she sobered. Looking at him seriously, she said,

"There's one thing I have to know, Barry. I have to know that you are marrying me because you want 'me'...... not because I remind you of .....Audrey."

A pained expression crossed his face. "Why would you think that, Amy?" he asked quietly.

"I don't know why. But, I want you to tell me the truth...,please."

"I want to marry you, Amy, because I love you," he said softly. "Don't you believe me?"

"You haven't said you love me, before."

"Well, I practically just met you, Sweetheart."

"See, that's what I mean!"

"What are you trying to do, talk me out of it?" he chuckled.

"I don't know! I am scared," she confessed, "everything is happening so fast! All of a sudden I feel like a little girl again and I have been on my own for years."

"What are you scared of, Sweetheart?"

She hesitated and said softly, "I am afraid that I won't be able to take Audrey's place."

He was speechless for a moment. Then, he said, "I don't want you to 'take her place', Amy. That part of my life is over. I want to share the rest of my life with you. Don't you understand?"

"Your mother said the same thing," she confessed.

"What? You talked to my mother about us?"

"No, not about 'us'. We were discussing Audrey at the hospital that day. She basically said the same thing that you just said; that no one should try to take her place but make a new life with you."

He was still puzzled. "I had no idea that you and my mother talked about that, at the hospital."

Amy smiled. "Your mother and I will get along fine. She is a sweet lady. I like your father, too. He reminds me of you."

He shook his head at her, disbelieving. "You are full of surprises," he grinned. "I see that I am going to have my hands full with you."

11

***

Amy was happier than she had ever been. Barry was slowly getting stronger but wasn't able to go back to work yet. They were together every evening for as long as Amy dared. He respected her and always took her home before their emotions got out of control. They visited the cabin one Saturday but didn't spend the night. He surprised her by presenting her with an engagement ring. She had never been happier. She no longer thought of Arthur or Tammy Morgan nor of the dead body she had found.

Barry went to his office for a few hours and then went to see Amy at her apartment. As soon as she saw him, she knew that he was concerned about something.

"What's wrong, Darling? You haven't overdone it, have you?" Amy asked.

"What?" he asked, his thoughts obviously elsewhere.

She handed him a cup of coffee and sat down across from him. "You said you had been to your office for a few hours. Have you gone back too soon?"

"Not soon enough," he said seriously. He met her gaze steadily and added, "Arthur Morgan is not the man who killed Rodney Benson."

Amy almost dropped her cup. "What are you saying?"

"Captain Adams told me. The plaster casts of footprints that they found in the dried mud around the body don't match Morgan's. His shoe size is two sizes larger than those prints."

"Oh, no! What's going to happen now?"

"Morgan has turned state's evidence for a lesser sentence. He has promised to tell all he knows about the murdered man and drug trafficking."

"They're not going to let him go, are they, Barry? They just can't!" Amy exclaimed, remembering how ruthless he seemed.

"No, he will serve time. But, not long enough, unfortunately, because of the deal they made. He reached across the table and took both her hands in his. She noticed he did not wince with pain and knew his shoulder was healing. "Sweetheart, I hate to tell you this, but it looks like your uncle was involved in the drug deals."

Amy was stunned.

Barry continued, "According to Morgan, your uncle used the plane to fly drugs from a small airport outside Orville, about ten miles from the cabin. Morgan hasn't said where the drugs came from. Either he doesn't know, or he is keeping it to himself. The reason he was so worried about the pictures your uncle had, was because they can be evidence used against him. He said the boxes and packages stacked beside the plane in that one picture, contained drugs. I doubt you could prove that in court, though. He claims that one of the buyers they were selling to wanted proof of what they could deliver. Your uncle had those pictures taken and kept a copy of each one."

Amy was trying to comprehend it all. Finally, she said, "I hope you don't think that all my family was like Uncle Curtis."

Barry looked at her pained expression and chuckled. "Sweetheart, I don't think that for a moment. You have no control over what someone else does, even if it is someone in your family."

"That makes me feel better," she confessed.

Barry continued, "Morgan knew Rodney Benson. He was one of his hunting buddies. He also identified one of the other men as one who was being blackmailed by Benson. He said instead of paying off the guy, he got rid of him."

"Does he know that for a fact? Did he see him do it?" Amy asked, intrigued.

"I don't know the answer to that, Sweetheart. Maybe it will all come out in the trial."

"What about his wife, Tammy?" Amy asked.

"She's still in jail. Neither of them could afford the bail. Personally, I hope they both stay there," he added.

"Me too!" she said, shivering at the thought of their being loose.

"That is enough talk of criminals," he said, getting up. "I'm going back to work next week. The doctor has released me."

Amy slipped her arms around him. "Are you sure you are ready?"

He grinned at her, seductively. "I have certainly enjoyed being with you for the past few weeks, but I am ready to get back to work. It's not that you aren't exciting enough," he teased.

"I understand. You're ready to be with 'Judy' again," she said, mischievously.

"Judy?" he asked, puzzled.

"The 'Judy' who works with you. The one who sent you the gift to the hospital."

"Judy who?" he teased as he bent to kiss her softly.

12

***

Several weeks passed. Spring came with all its glory. Amy and Barry visited the cabin one weekend. The trees were leafed out and wildflowers were in bloom. Barry helped Amy do her spring-cleaning of the cabin, and then they walked in the woods and picked wildflowers. They had set their wedding date for early in June. Amy had never been happier.

When it grew dark, they went inside. Amy made sandwiches while Barry built a small fire in the fireplace.

"You know, this place really grows on you," Barry chuckled, stretching out on the couch and pulling Amy down beside him. "I could get used to this." He took her in his arms and kissed her tenderly.

"Hopefully, we don't have to worry about Arthur Morgan barging in on us again," she said shivering at the thought.

"Nope. He'll be behind bars for a while. I don't think I've told you, Sweetheart; we still haven't caught Rodney Benson's murderer yet. The guy Morgan identified as the blackmailer has disappeared."

"Hopefully you will, sooner or later," Amy said.

"Do you remember my telling you, Sweetheart, that I am interested in Forensics? I have decided to go into that field. I am going to start classes right away to learn all I can. I can work in the lab, hands-on, while I am learning."

She stared at him for a moment, wondering how anyone could enjoy such a thing.

"Do you have a problem with that?" he asked, concerned at her expression.

"Of course not, Barry. It's your career. Do whatever you enjoy. It just brought back memories of Rodney Benson's body. I can't imagine touching a dead body, much less examining it!"

He hugged her tight and kissed her on the cheek. "Don't think about it. Think about us; about our wedding; where we'll live," he said tenderly."

"That does sound exciting," she admitted.

"Would you like to go house-hunting one afternoon?" he asked.

Amy was surprised. "Won't we live in your house?"

"Do you want to? I thought you would want a new house that you could decorate yourself." He hesitated a moment, and then added, "I thought you might not want to live where there are so many memories of Audrey."

"You are so thoughtful, Darling. It would be fun to look at houses together."

"How about Monday after work? I'll call some realtors and get some houses lined up for us to see."

"That's perfect," she agreed.

He drew her closer and covered her lips with his. As they kissed, he pulled her down onto the couch until they were lying close. She could feel his heartbeat keeping time with hers.

"Why did we set the date for our wedding so far away?" he whispered into her ear as he brushed his lips against it, gently. He took her breath away as he kissed her cheek, her throat. Amy ached with the need for him. She had never had such feelings before. Her senses were reeling as he continued to caress her gently, whispering endearments in her ear. He drew a deep breath, and hugged her so tight she could barely breathe. He tucked her head beneath his chin and lay very still for a few moments, waiting for their heartbeats to slow.

"Will you sleep here with me tonight, Sweetheart?" he whispered huskily into her fragrant hair. "I just want to hold you like this."

Amy remembered the other time they had shared this couch. She snuggled even closer to him. "That would be wonderful," she whispered. She laid her head on his chest. Before long, she drifted off to sleep.

Birds chirping outside the window woke Amy. She found that she couldn't move. Barry had his arms around her and had her tucked firmly against his body as he lay sleeping. She took this opportunity to bask in the nearness of him. She had dreamed during the night; dreamed of his caressing her and kissing her tenderly. She wondered, now, if it had actually been a dream. She traced his strong jaw with her fingertip and felt the stubble of his beard beginning to grow. She ran her finger across his warm lips. He stirred, slightly, and sighed. Her love for him over-whelmed her. Bending, she kissed his lips, softly, waking him from his deep sleep. Opening his eyes, he groaned and pulled her over on top of himself. He returned her kiss, making her forget everything but the man in her arms.

Finally, he sighed, and said, "What a wonderful way to wake up."

"Good morning, Darling," Amy said, softly. "Did you sleep well?"
There was a mischievous gleam in his eyes as he said, "I dreamed I was lying beside a beautiful princess all night."

"Really?" Amy teased.

"Yes, really. She had dark brown hair that smelled of lilacs."

"How strange! I had a similar dream. I dreamed a gallant knight was lying beside me. When he kissed me, he stole my heart away."

Barry chuckled. "I love you so much, Sweetheart. I can hardly wait to make you mine."

"Me too. I love you more than I ever dreamed possible," she confessed.

"Just wait until our wedding night," he promised, as he kissed her again.

13

***

Barry began his schooling and training in the forensic lab. He didn't discuss much of his work with Amy, fearing it would upset her. She was interested in his work, but she didn't want to hear any gory details.

Amy was preparing dinner for Barry one evening when the phone rang. He answered it for her.

"Hello, is Miss. Fontell there?" a woman's voice asked.

"Yes, hold on, please." He handed Amy the phone.

"Hello," Amy said.

"Miss. Fontell, this is Sara Benson. You remember me, don't you?"

Amy was surprised to hear from her. "Of course, Mrs. Benson. How are you?"

"I'm okay, I reckon. I just wanted to know if you've heard any more from the police? I ain't heard anything for a long time."

"I'm sorry, Mrs. Benson. The last I heard, they still haven't caught the man whom they suspect killed your husband.

"That's what I was afraid of. It may be my fault," she said.

"How could it be your fault?" Amy asked.

"I know the man they're looking for. He used to come over here and pick up Rodney sometime. When I found out they suspected him, I went to his house and accused him to his face. I even told him the police was lookin' for him."

"Mrs. Benson, that was a dangerous thing to do!" Amy exclaimed.

"I know it, but I had to see him for myself. He tried to lie his way out of it, but I didn't believe a word he said. Now, he's run off, and it's probably my fault."

"If he has family here, he may come back sometime," Amy said.

"Maybe you're right," she agreed.

"Don't give up hope. The police will catch him one day, I'm sure," Amy encouraged.

"Well, 'bye. I just wanted to find out what was going on."

"Good bye, Mrs. Benson." Amy hung up the phone.

"Why does that woman keep calling you?" Barry asked.

"I have no idea. She could call the police department just as easily. It's strange, isn't it?"

"Very strange. I only heard your side of the conversation; what did she do that you thought 'was a dangerous thing to do'?" he asked.

Amy revealed the whole conversation to Barry.

"There's something here that does not ring true. She is saying that she knows the suspect. By the way, his name is Tommy Pinkerton. Then, she says she went to talk to him and 'warned' him that the police are looking for him. Does all of this sound logical to you, Sweetheart?"

"Not really. But, what could be going on?"

"It's possible she is calling you to find out how much the police know, not for her benefit but for Pinkerton's. She may be lying about the whole thing. According to Morgan, Rodney Benson was blackmailing Pinkerton. He claimed that he didn't know the reason; it could be drug related or something else."

"Do you think I need to be careful what I tell her, Barry? Have I told her too much already?"

"I don't think you have. You put her mind at ease if she's worried about his getting caught."

Amy stared at Barry, trying to comprehend it all.

He continued, "Pinkerton may be lying low, trying to find out if we're getting closer. Or, he could really be gone from here. I wish we could find out, somehow."

"Let me help," Amy said, excited. "I could contact her, or even go out there to talk to her and see if I could find out something more."

"Don't you even think of such a thing!" Barry exclaimed. "You remember what happened to me, or have you forgotten?"

"No, I haven't forgotten. I just want closure to this case so we can go on with our lives."

"I don't want you putting your life in danger, ever!" Barry said. "Let the police handle it."

After her discussion with Barry, Amy couldn't get her mind off Sara Benson. The more she thought of her, the more she was convinced that Sara knew more than she appeared to know. Amy wanted to know all she could about her uncle's involvement with the men in the pictures. She wondered if Sara knew about the pictures. She wondered if Tommy Pinkerton knew about the pictures. Her curiosity getting the better of her, she decided to call Sara to find out where she lived. Perhaps she would talk to her again and find some answers to her questions. She decided to call Sara one afternoon when she was alone at the apartment. Sara seemed surprised to hear from Amy and even more surprised when she wanted directions to her house. She gave her directions and Amy agreed to drive out to see her that same afternoon.

On her way to Sara Benson's house Amy considered

what she was actually doing. She knew Barry would not approve. She pushed that thought from her mind and concentrated on finding Sara's house. The directions led her to a rural area. It was similar to that of her cabin but was several miles closer. She passed a gray, wooden store building that had a sign out front that read 'Pinkerton's'. She caught her breath, sharply, as she recognized the name. The store was deserted, although there were dried mud tracks leading to and from the store. Sara had said to go two miles past the little store and that her house was the first one on the left, under the pine trees. Amy checked the speedometer but saw the house before it registered the mileage. Once a white house, it was now gray streaked from pine residue. There was a patch of green grass in the front yard, instead of the typical dirt yards she had passed. She had a sense of foreboding as she parked the car and walked to the door. Too late, she wondered if this was such a good idea, after all. Before she could knock on the door Sara Benson opened it and greeted her.

"You're Miss. Fontell, aren't you? Come on in," she said, hesitantly.

Amy entered a small room that was painted a dull blue.

"Take a seat," Sara said, moving clothes off the couch to make room for her.

Amy sat down on the couch, gingerly. Sara Benson was an attractive woman with bleached-blond hair. She was dressed in faded jeans and a western shirt.

"Did you find out somethin' about the murder?" Sara asked, cautiously.

"No, Sara. I was wondering if you could give me any more information," Amy said, watching her closely.

Sara appeared nervous and uncomfortable. "What do you mean?" she asked, quickly.

"The police know that the murder may be drug related. Were you aware of this, Mrs. Benson?"

Sara blushed. "No, I ain't heard nothin' about no drugs. Rodney wasn't mixed up in no drugs."

"Arthur Morgan was the one who told them that. He was harassing me, trying to get some pictures that my uncle had taken. One of those pictures included your husband and Tommy Pinkerton."

Sara blushed crimson. "You got them pictures now?" she asked, nervously.

"No, my uncle had them."

"Your uncle's dead, ain't he?" Sara asked.

"Yes, did you know him?"

Sara was evasive with her answer. "I seen him a time or two when I was workin' at the store down the road. He came in there a few times."

"The gray store down the road with the 'Pinkerton's' sign out front?" Amy asked pointedly, watching her reaction.

"I've worked there some but not for a while."

Amy tried to figure that out in her mind. "Is that Tommy Pinkerton's store?" she asked bluntly.

Sara was fidgety again, as she answered, "Yeah, so what?"

"You must know him very well."

"He didn't stay in the store much," Sara answered, evasively.

Amy knew now, that Sara had lied about how well she knew Tommy Pinkerton. She wondered what else she was lying about.

"I won't keep you, Mrs. Benson," Amy said as she got up and started to the door. " I have enjoyed our visit."

"Sure, anytime," Sara replied, obviously relieved that Amy was leaving.

On the way home, Amy wondered if Sara Benson and Tommy Pinkerton were having an affair. That would explain a lot of things. Her imagination running away, she imagined that Pinkerton killed Rodney in a fit of jealousy.

She was glad she had gone to talk to Sara. She had learned things she didn't know before. She decided not to mention the visit to Barry, however. She knew that he would not approve of her interfering.

The next time Amy saw Barry she asked him questions concerning Tommy Pinkerton when she brought up the subject of Rodney Benson's murder.

"What did Tommy Pinkerton do to make a living?" she asked casually.

"He probably made most of his money selling drugs," Barry answered. "He owns a dumpy little store out in the country. I haven't seen it, but Captain Adams has. I doubt he could have made a living by selling groceries to hunters a few months out of the year. I imagine the store is just a 'front' for his drug dealing. That's what Morgan has told, anyway." He looked at her curiously. "Are you still worrying about that case, Sweetheart?"

"I guess I will worry, until you catch the killer," she answered.

"We feel certain it's Pinkerton. We just need more evidence. We need to make a plaster cast of his tire tracks as well as his tennis shoes to see if they are a match with the ones the forensic pathologist have from the crime scene. Unfortunately, he can't be found, nor his truck."

"Can't you get a warrant to search his house?"

"We were going to do that. But, his wife gave us permission, without it. She had already left him and moved out. But, it was too late. He had cleaned the place out. He didn't even leave a pair of shoes."

"Where did he live?" Amy asked.

"Somewhere near his store. Why do you ask? I thought you didn't enjoy hearing about my work, Amy."

"I do enjoy hearing about your work. I am especially interested in this case, because of my uncle." She didn't want to tell him that she was still gathering information since talking to Sara Benson.

14

***

A week later, Amy and Barry drove out to the cabin for the weekend. As they drove into the yard it was obvious that there had been an intruder. Amy gasped when she saw the front door, which was splintered and hanging by only one hinge.

"Don't touch a thing!" Barry instructed her as he got his forensic equipment from the trunk of his car. "There may still be prints, if it hasn't been too long." They walked carefully around the splintered door and into the cabin.

"Oh my goodness!" Amy exclaimed, as she saw the mess around her. The furniture was overturned with cushions and drawers strewn everywhere.

"Has anything like this ever happened to you before?" Barry asked.

"No. Never!"

"Either it was pure vandalism, or someone was looking for something," Barry said. He hugged her to him, gently. "I'm sorry, Sweetheart. You've had a rough time. You don't deserve this."

Then, he said, "Look around and see if there's anything missing. But, try not to touch anything. I'm going to the car and call Captain Adams. I need some help out here."

Amy did as he instructed but didn't find anything missing. Nothing had been left unturned. Even the mattresses had been moved. A sick feeling crept into her stomach when she remembered what she had told Sara Benson about the pictures. She didn't believe Sara could have done all this. But, Tommy Pinkerton could have. She was in a dilemma. She didn't know whether to tell Barry what she feared, or not. She knew that he would be furious with her, especially now. Afraid to brave his wrath, she decided to keep quiet for the time being.

Amy watched as Barry and his colleagues did their work collecting evidence that the intruder left. As she watched Barry at work, she was impressed with all he had learned in such a short time. She was fascinated, watching them. She began to understand his love for forensic science. She heard them discussing the evidence. They were especially careful with the shattered door. There, they found threads from fabric on the splinters as well as an almost perfect shoe print where the door had been kicked in. Next, they found blood on a nail that was protruding from one of the boards. Amy could tell that the men were excited about finding all the evidence, especially, the blood. She knew that they would be able to do a DNA test on the blood. If Pinkerton was apprehended, they would know if this was a match with his blood.

When the investigators finished all their work and had gone, Barry went inside to take a break. Amy began straightening up the cabin as he sat, watching her.

"Amy, I think I'll try to find old Mr. Rafferty's house. I'll see if he has some wood I can borrow or buy, to build a new door facing and put up a make-shift door until I can get a new one. Do you feel okay about staying alone for a few minutes?"

"I'll be fine," she answered.

"Do you have your gun?" he asked, looking around for her backpack that she always carried with her.

"It's still in the car. I'll get it." She walked with him to his car.

"I haven't had much time to spend with you today, Sweetheart," he said, "I'm sorry."

"Don't apologize, Darling. You have done a lot for me today. I want you to know that I admired you today, watching you do your job so well."

He grinned. "That's good to know." Bending, he planted a kiss on her lips, lightly. "I'll be back in a few minutes. Be careful while I'm gone."

Soon, Barry was back at the cabin with Mr. Rafferty following in an old, rattling truck. Amy watched as Barry unloaded a large, wooden door from the back of Mr. Rafferty's truck. Mr. Rafferty carried several boards in his arms.

"Howdy, Maam," he said, cordially.

"Hello, Mr. Rafferty."

"Mr. Rafferty is a life saver!" Barry said, setting the door down at the opening.

"Well, I had this here extra door. I taken' it off of a shed a while back. Figured I'd have a use for it one day. I'm real sorry to hear about somebody breakin' in on ye'," he said to Amy.

"Thank you so much, Mr. Rafferty. We will gladly pay you for the door and wood and for bringing it over," she said.

He frowned at her. "Now, do I look like a gold digger, Missy? I done discussed that with your gentleman friend here. I ain't takin' no pay fer' helping out a neighbor. No, indeed!"

Amy watched as Barry made a new door facing, using Mr. Rafferty's tools he brought over. Then, they hung the door. He even had a pad lock to lock the door with, later. When they finished Amy invited Mr. Rafferty to eat a sandwich with them.

"I don't mind if I do. It's been a while since I et'."

Amy had the cabin in good order again. They sat at the table and ate and visited with Mr. Rafferty.

"I heard tell that Arthur Morgan's in jail and his wife too," he said, suddenly, shaking his head. "Heard he shot a policeman. Is that right?"

Amy's gaze met Barry's. She let him answer that.

"You heard right, Sir," Barry said.

"Heard that his wife kidnapped somebody," he continued.

"Correct. They will be away for a while," Barry answered, again. "Do you know Morgan well?"

"Well enough. I seen him in the woods a lot. He likes to hunt. He was a friend of your uncle, Missy."

"Really?" Amy said, feigning surprise.

"He had some business dealings with your uncle, I reckon."

"What kind of business dealings, Mr. Rafferty?" Barry asked, casually.

Mr. Rafferty hesitated a moment, his eyes twinkling. "Well, I can't rightly say. They was real secretive about what they was doing. This little lady's uncle, he taken' me over to Orville one day. They was carryin' boxes and stuff to a airplane he liked to fly. Tried to get me to go a-flyin' with him. I weren't about to get in no plane, not me. I'm a keepin' my feet on the ground!"

Barry's eyes narrowed. "Would you testify in court to what you saw at Orville, Mr. Rafferty?"

Mr. Rafferty's eyes grew wide. "Testify in court? Fer what? I ain't seen what was in them boxes."

"Arthur Morgan will tell us that. Your testimony could reinforce what he says."

"I'll have to think about that. Can't rightly say, just now."

"Good enough. It will be a while before he goes to trial," Barry stated.

It was dark when Mr. Rafferty left. Amy and Barry

cleaned the kitchen together and then sat down to relax. It had been a trying day for both of them.

"Sweetheart, we can't lock the door from the inside. Do you feel comfortable staying here tonight?" Barry asked.

"I hadn't thought of that," she said, a worried expression on her face."

"Whomever it was that broke in, probably won't be back," he continued. "They either found what they were looking for, or it's not here. What did you keep here that would be worth stealing?" he asked.

Amy's heartbeat quickened. She was afraid to tell him the truth but afraid not to.

He noticed her hesitation. "What is it?" he asked, watching her.

"I don't know how to tell you this...," she stammered.

"Tell me what? What are you keeping from me?"

"You will be angry with me, Barry," she confessed.

"Why would I be angry, Sweetheart?"

"Because, I did something that you told me not to do," she answered, cautiously.

"What did I tell you not to do?" he asked, puzzled.

Taking a deep breath, Amy proceeded to tell him about her visit with Sara Benson, ending with her statement to Sara concerning her uncle's pictures.

She watched as his expression changed. She had never seen him look as he did now. His blue eyes narrowed and seemed to change to a dull gray.

"I can't believe you were so ignorant!" he grated.

Amy's temper flared. "Ignorant? You call me ignorant when all I was trying to do was help?"

"I warned you because I knew it would be a dangerous thing to do! Now, see what it got you? This incident here at the cabin has to be related! Somebody had to be looking for those pictures!"

"Okay, so Sara Benson wanted the pictures!" she retorted.

"Sara Benson didn't do this wreckage. It's not physically possible! We're dealing with a male here!"

Amy felt sick to her stomach as well as angry. "You don't have to be so hateful!" she retorted, tears filling her eyes.

Barry stared at her, the muscles in his cheek twitching. Amy knew he was furious with her. He took a deep breath and got up quickly, without replying to her statement. He began to gather up their belongings.

"Get your things. I'm taking you home," he said.

"Fine!" she answered, snatching up her backpack.

On the way to her apartment neither Amy nor Barry spoke until they were almost there. Finally, Barry broke the silence.

"Amy, I'm sorry I yelled at you. You have to understand my concern; you could be dealing with a murderer here."

"What are you talking about?" she snapped.

"I'm talking about Pinkerton. He's still out there somewhere! Sara Benson may have gone straight to him with the information you gave her. It's likely he is lying low somewhere."

Amy had nothing to say. She couldn't speak for the lump in her throat. They said nothing else until they pulled into her driveway at the apartment.

Then, Barry spoke. "I'm going to send somebody out to watch your apartment for a while. For God's sake, don't do anything so foolish again!"

"Well! I'm sorry I am so foolish!" Suddenly, she yanked her engagement ring off her finger and threw it into his lap. "I'm sure that a fine detective like you can't afford to be married to such a foolish girl as I am! Don't bother to have my house watched!" She didn't give him a chance to reply but hurried to the door. He didn't follow her but waited until she was safely inside before he left.

Inside, Amy was glad to see that Joan wasn't home. She dropped her bags on the floor and hurried to her bedroom where she fell across the bed and cried. She couldn't erase Barry's angry face from her mind, nor his angry voice, accusing her. She cried until no more tears would come. She didn't think that he had a right to speak to her as he had. If that was the way he planned to talk to her after they were married, she wanted no part of it, she told herself.

Amy refused to tell Joan the reason she and Barry had quarreled. She knew that Joan's reaction would be the same as Barry's. She hadn't heard from Barry since they quarreled. She spotted an unmarked police car near the apartment during the week. She knew that Joan hadn't seen it or she would have mentioned it. She knew that Barry had done as he said he would. Her heart ached for him; for his charming smile and considerate manner. When she remembered their quarrel, she cried again.

15

***

Weeks later, Captain Adams called Amy. She was surprised and pleased to hear from him.

"How are you, Miss. Fontell?" he asked.

"I am fine, Captain, thank you."

" I have an update on the vandalism at your cabin, if you'd like to hear it," he said.

"Yes, please!"

"From all the evidence that the detectives and foren-sic pathologists gathered, it is clear that the man who kicked your door in has the same shoe size as the man who murdered Rodney Benson. We have a good match on the tread of his tennis shoe to the one found beside the body, although a little more worn. The real clincher, will be the DNA test. When we pick up Tommy Pinkerton one day, we'll be able to see if his blood is a match with the blood found on a nail and splinters on the cabin door."

A strange feeling ran through Amy. She realized that Barry had been right all along. She knew now, that he was justified in being so angry.

"Miss Fontell?" Captain Adams said, when she hadn't replied.

"Yes, Captain. I'm sorry. I was just re-living that day at the cabin. I really do appreciate your calling to tell me this. It was so thoughtful of you."

"I'm afraid I can't take credit for that. Actually, Barry asked me to call you and give you an update."

Amy was surprised and pleased. "Did he really?" she managed to say.

The captain cleared his throat. "I was sorry to hear that the two of you are no longer engaged. You make a fine couple, Miss. Fontell. Is there no chance for a reconciliation?"

She had to smile at this and asked, "Did Barry ask you to say that too?"

"Certainly not! That is my own question," he chuckled.

"What has he told you, Captain?"

"Only, that you are no longer engaged. That came as a shock to me. I understood that you two were in the process of buying a house."

Amy had a sinking feeling. "We were, at one time. I suppose Barry has cancelled that."

"I wouldn't know about that. He doesn't talk much about his personal life; only when he has to. Back to the subject of your cabin and Pinkerton; Barry and I both strongly urge you not to go back out there alone, Miss. Fontell, for your own safety."

"Don't worry, Captain. I don't plan to."

"Barry went out there and put up a new door for you; he did tell me that. Which reminds me; he said to tell you that he hid the new key under the flowerpot beside the steps."

Amy was astonished. "He did that for me?" she asked.

"Yes, he did. I may be out of line saying this; he still regards you very highly, Miss. Fontell.

"I appreciate everything you have told me, Captain," she managed to say, in spite of the lump in her throat.

"Any time. I will keep in touch. Think about what I

have said."

"Yes, Captain. Thank you." Amy hung up the phone. Tears filled her eyes when she thought of Barry being concerned for her. She wondered if he thought of her as she thought of him. She ached for him, for his smile, his touch and for the velvety sound of his voice. She loved him with all her being. She had no doubt about that. She wondered if he still loved her. She wondered if she should make the first move to see if he was still interested. After all, she reminded herself, she was the one who had thrown her engagement ring into his lap. Couldn't he at least have called her? She hadn't called him, either.

After work one evening Amy decided to drive by the house that she and Barry had picked out to buy. She was curious to see if someone else had bought it. It was a new, two-story brick with a pool in the back yard. Amy had looked at the pool and dreamed of moonlight swims with Barry. As she drove down Chandalar Court, she was disappointed to see that the 'For Sale' sign was gone from the front yard. She noticed that there were shades covering all the windows. She had a lonely, forlorn feeling. She would never live in her 'dream house' and have moonlight swims with the man she loved. Yet, she could not bring herself to call Barry.

Amy and Joan were shopping on Saturday. It was June and Amy was especially depressed. June 5th had been the date that she and Barry had set for their wedding day. She and Joan stopped at a deli in the mall and ordered pizza. They were sipping iced tea when Amy almost dropped her glass.

"What's wrong with you?" Joan asked, watching her closely.

Amy's cheeks flushed pink as she stared across the room. Joan followed her gaze and saw Barry Reeser enter the deli and sit down at an empty table.

"Now's your chance to talk to him!" Joan whispered

to Amy.

"You're crazy!" Amy exclaimed, "I'm not going to run over there."

The waitress brought their pizza and Amy tried to choke hers down. She was having a hard time. When she looked across the room again she found Barry's eyes on her. Her heartbeat was racing. He raised his hand in a greeting and she waved back, nervously.

"For Pete's sake, Amy! Go talk to him!" Joan encouraged.

"Hush, Joan!" Amy said, almost chocking on her food. She saw him get up and he was suddenly standing beside their table. Looking down at them, he smiled and said,

"Hello ladies."

Amy remembered that captivating smile. She remembered how his lips felt on hers.

"Hello, Barry," she managed to say.

"Hey, Barry. Will you excuse me a minute? I'll be back in a jiffy!" Joan said, as she hopped up from her chair and left the table.

"Did I scare her off?" Barry grinned.

"No, she'll be back," Amy answered. "How are you, Barry?" she asked.

"I'm okay. How about you?" he answered.

"The same," she said, knowingly. She saw that there was sadness in his eyes that she had never seen before.

"I came over to ask you and Joan to join me for coffee at my table," he said, watching her closely.

"That would be nice. I would enjoy that," she said, accepting his invitation.

At that moment, a petite, blond-headed lady descended upon Barry before he realized it.

"Barry! What a nice surprise! Are you having lunch? May I join you?" she asked, smiling sweetly at him and Amy.

"Hi, Judy. Actually, I am. I've just invited two other ladies to join me. Amy, this is Judy Mason. She works at the Sheriff's Department. Judy, this is Amy Fontell."

"Glad to meet you, Amy. Let me go order and I'll join you, Barry," Judy announced.

"I'm sorry about that, Amy," he apologized when Judy left the table. "Will you join me, anyway?"

"I'd rather not, now, Barry. Thank you for inviting us anyway. Maybe another time."

"Sure. It's good to see you, Amy," he added, hesitantly.

"It's good to see you too, Barry."

Barry went back to his table. Amy watched as Judy Mason joined him. She felt as though a knife were piercing her heart. She felt tears welling in her eyes. She tried to blink them away. She did not want to be seen crying in a public place.

Joan came back to their table. "Who is that?" she asked, glaring at Judy from across the room.

"She works with Barry, or used to, anyway."

"Why is she over there, instead of you?" Joan asked, angrily.

"She just popped in and invited herself. He had just asked us to join him, Joan," Amy explained.

"Do you want to join him?" Joan asked.

"Certainly not! Not with her over there!" Amy replied.

"Rats! This was a great opportunity for the two of you and she spoiled it!"

"Joan, forget it. It's over between us," Amy said, blinking back her tears.

"Yeah, sure. I saw the way you two looked at one another. It's written all over your faces. Why are you both wasting time? Life is too short!"

"I can't stay here any longer, Joan. I'm leaving," Amy said, getting up. She laid money on the table and said,

"Please pay my bill for me." She circled the room to avoid seeing Barry with Judy Mason again.

Amy was miserable after seeing Barry in the deli on Saturday. She longed to talk to him, to share things with him once again. But, she couldn't bring herself to call him; not unless she had a good reason. She was getting ready for bed when the phone rang.

"Miss Fontell, this is Sara Benson," the voice said, hesitantly.

Amy's heartbeat quickened. "Hello, Mrs. Benson. What can I do for you?" she asked, cautiously; she did not trust her anymore.

"I just wanted to invite you out to my house again. How about tomorrow?" Sara asked.

Amy was not going to make the same mistake, twice. "I'm sorry, Mrs. Benson, but I can't come tomorrow."

"When could you come? How about the next day?"

"I'll have to call you back to let you know," Amy stalled.

"All right. You call me, I'll be waitin'," she hung up the phone.

Amy was suspicious. She didn't dare go out there again. She believed that Sara Benson was responsible for her cabin being trashed. She automatically thought of Barry. She wanted to tell him about this call. She dialed his number before she could change her mind.

"Hello," Barry answered.

"Hello, Barry," Amy said, nervously.

"Amy, it's good to hear from you," he said, softly. "How have you been?"

"Okay, I suppose. How about you?"

"Keeping busy. There's a lot to learn about forensic science."

"I'm glad you're enjoying it. I wanted to tell you that Sara Benson just called me."

"What did she want?"

"She wanted me to come back out there for a visit."

"Amy, I hope you're not going back out there! She could be setting you up."

"I'm not going, Barry. Don't worry."

"Good! I'll talk to Captain Adams. I have a hunch it's time we started looking for Tommy Pinkerton around Sara Benson's place."

"Captain Adams told me that you put up a new door at the cabin. I appreciate that. You'll have to send me a bill for whatever you spent."

He hesitated a moment, and then said, "I won't be sending you a bill, Amy. It was something I wanted to do."

"Thank you, Barry," she said, a lump forming in her throat.

"Amy..., would you go out to dinner with me sometime?" he asked, softly.

"Do you still want me to?" she asked, blinking back the tears.

"Don't you know the answer to that?" he asked.

"I would love to," she said, glad that he couldn't see the tears flowing.

"How about tomorrow night at seven?" he asked.

"I'll be ready."

"I'll see you then. Thanks for calling, Amy. Good night."

"Good night, Barry." She heard him hang up the phone. She was trembling. She was too excited to sleep and decided to pick out what she would wear to dinner. She chose a navy skirt and jacket with a white, sleeveless blouse. When she finally went back to bed, she dreamed she was at the cabin with Barry.

Sharply at seven o'clock the next evening Barry rang the doorbell at Amy's apartment. She opened the door.

"Hello," he said, softly. "Are you ready to go?"

"Yes," she answered, trying not to sound as anxious as she felt.

As they were leaving he asked, "Is there a certain place you'd like to eat?"

"You choose," she said, taking in his handsome features.

"I hoped you'd say that," he grinned. "I took the liberty of reserving a table at Romano's. They have great prime rib."

"You know me pretty well, don't you?" she said, smiling.

"Not well enough," he answered, meeting her gaze for a moment before he had to watch the traffic.

Amy had been to Romano's only once before. It was an expensive and romantic restaurant. Inside, the waiter showed them to their table by a window that overlooked the lights of the city below. The room was dimly lit with candles that cast a romantic glow."

"It's lovely here," Amy said, looking around.

"You're lovely tonight," Barry stated. He reached across the table and took her hand in his. He caressed her hand with his thumb, as was his habit. He watched her face in the candlelight.

His touch sent tingling sensations through her body, reminding her of previous times.

"I've missed you, Amy," he said, softly.

She looked into his blue eyes, made darker by the candlelight. "I've missed you, too, Barry." After a moment, she added, "I'm sorry for acting the way I did that day. Please forgive me." She felt tears threatening.

"I already have, long ago," he answered.

She was surprised. "You have?"

He showed her his enchanting smile once again. "I couldn't stay mad at you," he said, softly. "I tried, but I kept remembering things...., the way you look...., how you felt in my arms."

"What are you saying?" she asked, her heartbeat racing.

"I'm saying, Sweetheart, that I love you."

She couldn't stop the tears that slid down her cheeks.

"I didn't think I would ever hear you say those words again. I'm not sure that I deserve to hear them, Darling."

"You deserve more than I can ever give you, Sweetheart."

"Why didn't you say something before? I have been so miserable!" she said, confused.

"I wanted you to want me. I didn't want to force myself on you," he answered.

"Oh, Barry! I've never stopped wanting you!"

The waiter bringing their food interrupted them.

Amy was so happy she could hardly concentrate on eating. Somehow, they finished their meal and had coffee before they left the restaurant. As they walked to his car, Barry slipped his arm around Amy. At the door, instead of getting inside, Amy turned to him. Looking up into his face in the moonlight, she said, "I love you, Barry."

He looked at her for a long moment, without saying a word. Then, he pulled her to him, roughly, his lips crushing hers. She returned his kiss, passionately. Finally, both trembling with passion, they got into the car and kissed again, more slowly.

"Will you come home with me for a little while?" he asked, huskily.

She nodded and laid her head on his shoulder as he started the car. When she became aware of where he was driving, she sat up, suddenly.

"This is not the way to your house," she said, confused. They had turned down Chandalar Court.

He grinned mischievously and pulled her to him with one arm. "Yes, it is. You'll see."

"What do you mean?" she asked, as they pulled into the driveway and came to a stop.

"Barry! Someone lives here!" she exclaimed as she

recognized their 'dream house' that they had chosen so long ago.

"I know," he grinned, watching her closely.

"We can't do this! We're trespassing!" she protested, seeing the lights on inside the house.

"Didn't you pick this house as your 'dream house', our dream house?" he teased.

"You know I did. But, someone lives here now. Can't you see?" she stated.

"Yes, I know," he said, gently.

"Then, what are we doing here?" she asked, confused.

"You'll see. Come on." He took her arm and led her to the front door. There, he took a key from his pocket and stuck it in the lock.

Amy gasped, finally realizing what he was trying to tell her. She pulled away from him, looking up into his face.

He was laughing at her, although he tried not to.

"Barry! You live here! You bought this house!" she exclaimed, amazed.

"I bought 'our' house, just for you," he added, softly.

She threw her arms around his neck and almost choked him with hugs and kisses.

"You're so wonderful! I've never met another man like you!"

"I certainly hope not," he teased. He bent and kissed her there in the doorway, taking her breath away.

"Everyone will see us!" she exclaimed, blushing. She hurried to close the door behind them. "Darling," she added, " are you saying that you still want to marry me? Even though I threw my engagement ring at you?"

"That's what I'm saying, Sweetheart. Will you take your ring back? Will you marry me, and live in this house with me, as my wife?" he asked, softly.

Tears filled her eyes. "There's nothing in this world that I had rather do. Darling, I love you so much," she whispered.

After kissing her again, he said, "Come, let me show you the house again. We'll get your ring when we tour the bedroom."

As they walked through the house Barry said, "Some pieces of furniture I got rid of. I thought you'd want to replace them, anyway."

When they got to the master bedroom, Amy exclaimed, "Barry! You bought the new king-size bed that we looked at!"

"You like it? You'll have to pick out your colors for the comforter and drapes," he grinned. "I don't know anything about that sort of thing."

"Barry, you did all of this for me, yet you never let me know, until now," she said, amazed. "What if we hadn't gotten back together?"

He shrugged. "I don't know. I guess I would still be waiting. I had faith in you," he grinned.

She threw her arms around him again, squeezing him tight.

He laughed at her. "For a girl who is somewhat reserved, you're certainly feisty tonight."

"Do you mind?" she teased.

"What do you think?" he answered, as his lips covered hers. He led her to the bed and pulled her down beside him. "We can try it out for the first time," he whispered. "Just for a little while," he assured her.

Her heart was pounding as he pulled her even closer, and his mouth founds hers again. She returned his deep, passionate kisses, her senses reeling.

Suddenly, looking into her eyes, he said, "Let's get married, Sweetheart; tonight..., tomorrow, as soon as we can."

"Darling, you're not serious?" she asked.

"Absolutely! We can, as soon as we get a blood test and license. How about it?" he whispered.

"I—I need time to get ready," she explained.

"Why? Couldn't we have a quiet ceremony by a Justice of the Peace? Or, would you really rather wait and have a formal wedding?" he asked, seriously.

She thought for a moment before answering. He had been so considerate of her, doing everything in his power to make her happy. Couldn't she do this one thing for him?

"Let's go tomorrow," she whispered.

"Wonderful!" he sighed. "But, that's too long to wait," he grinned, as he smothered her with kisses again.

A long time later, Amy traced Barry's jaw with her fingertips. When he opened his eyes, she said, "Darling, we aren't at the cabin, you know. We can't lie here all night," she giggled.

"Why not?" he groaned, holding her even tighter in his arms. "Maybe, by this time tomorrow, we can." He thought for a moment and added, "I can get a few days off. I'd like to take you some place special."

"Darling, this place is special. Can't we stay here?" she asked.

"Do you really want to?" he asked, surprised.

"We have all the privacy we could possibly want. We have our own private pool," she grinned. "What more could we possibly want?"

"That sounds great! You've convinced me. We'll stock up with food and drinks and hibernate here," he grinned.

"Now, you need to take me home. I only have a few hours to do a week's worth of preparing."

"Do you have to go?" he asked, reluctant to let her go.

"Yes, I have to go, Darling. I will arrange to be off a few days, too. When you get ready to go for the blood test, call me on my cell phone. I will meet you. I will be shopping before we go to the court house to see the Justice of the Peace."

"You have to go shopping?" he teased, knowingly.

She blushed. "Hush. I need some 'unmentionables'. Don't say another word."

He hugged her tight. "Just think, Sweetheart; you're soon going to be mine."

"I know," she said, seriously, "and you will be my husband. It doesn't seem real."

"It will….., I promise," he said, kissing her once more.

The next morning Amy arranged to be off work for a week. Then, she hurried to the department store to buy herself a trousseau. She didn't tell anyone about her plans. She and Barry wanted it kept secret. She would call Joan after they were married to tell her why she wasn't at the apartment. She was so busy she didn't have time to be nervous. She went to the grocery store and bought breakfast foods and snacks. She wanted to fix Barry breakfast every morning.

When Barry called Amy on her cell phone she met him at the clinic for the blood test. The nurses cooperated and gave them the papers they would need for their license after their test results. Amy agreed to be ready to meet the Justice of the Peace by three p.m. Barry would pick her up at her apartment.

Amy spent the afternoon packing a suitcase of clothes for herself and washing her hair and getting dressed for the ceremony. She wondered if Barry was as busy as she was, at his house.

Sharply, at three, Barry was at Amy's door. He was dressed in a navy blue suit that complimented her beige suit that she was wearing. He presented her with a sparkling diamond necklace, which he fastened around her neck. He carried her things to his car, and then they were on their way to the courthouse. Amy was excited and nervous, now that the time had come. She couldn't believe that this was her wedding day. Before they realized it, they had purchased the license and the Justice of the Peace finished performing the ceremony. Suddenly, she was Mrs. Barry Reeser and he was escorting her back to his car.

Once they were inside, he kissed her tenderly and said, "Hello, Mrs. Reeser." His blue eyes were shining as he looked into her eyes.

"Hello, husband," she giggled, nervously.

"Where would you like to go first?" he asked. "Would you like to eat an early dinner at a restaurant?"

"I couldn't eat a bite, at the moment," she said truthfully.

"Me neither," he grinned. He started the car and drove in the direction of their house.

"I bought steaks to grill later, if you'd like to do that, Sweetheart," he said. "We could do that down by the pool."

"That sounds wonderful!" she agreed.

He turned down Chandalar Court and was soon in the driveway.

"I'll come back and get your things in a moment," he said, escorting her to the door. "First of all, I want to do this right," he grinned. He unlocked the door and picking her up in his arms, he carried her over the threshold. He set her down and said, "Welcome to our home, Mrs. Reeser."

Amy hugged him tightly and their lips met in an ardent kiss. Finally, she asked, "You want me to help bring my things in?"

"No, you make yourself at home. I'll be right back. Don't go away," he grinned.

"I won't," she answered. She held the door for him when he came in, and then he helped her put up the groceries she had bought.

"I didn't know you brought food. Were you afraid I wouldn't feed you, Sweetheart?" he teased.

"For your information, I plan to fix you breakfast every morning," she answered, playfully.

"Wow! What a wife I have!" He hugged her tightly

and their eyes met. She caught her breath sharply as his warm lips covered hers and he kissed her passionately.

Finally, he said, huskily, "I can't think about food right now, Sweetheart." He picked her up and carried her to their bedroom and laid her on their bed, gently.

After more ardent kisses, Amy whispered, "Do you realize we still have our suits on?"

"Yes, I know. Would you like to change into some of those 'unmentionables' you bought today?" he teased.

Amy blushed. "I think so."

He helped her up and went to his closet and removed a robe and slippers.

"I'll use the bathroom down the hall to dress in. You can use this one. I'll be back shortly." He kissed her once more, softly and then disappeared down the hallway.

Amy unpacked her suitcase and chose a white satin gown and negligee to match. As she was tying the bows, her hands were trembling with anticipation. She brushed her dark hair, which cascaded down her back. She noticed that Barry had turned back the covers on the bed and there were scented candles burning on the nightstand. She smiled, thinking that he was so considerate and thoughtful. She knew that she was fortunate to have him as her husband.

There was a knock at the door and Barry stuck his head inside the room. "May I come in?"

She stood before him, looking radiant, her gaze never leaving his. She heard him draw in his breath, sharply.

"You look lovely," he said huskily, as he moved to take her into his arms.

She closed her arms around him. He was clad in a burgundy and black robe and slippers. "You look very dashing, yourself," she whispered, her heartbeat racing.

He kissed her softly. Picking her up, he lay her on the bed, lying down beside her. He caressed her cheek gently with his fingertips. "Just think, Sweetheart; you don't have to leave me tonight," he whispered.

"I know," Amy answered, trembling slightly.

"Don't be afraid," he whispered, kissing her on her neck.

"I'm not afraid. I just love you so much....and want you so much."

When he began kissing her again, she forgot everything else.

Later, Amy woke and knew it was dark outside. Only the candles were burning on the nightstand, casting a romantic glow on everything in the room. She looked lovingly at Barry lying beside her, his eyes closed, his arms around her, holding her close. She moved, slightly, and he opened his eyes. "I thought you were asleep," she said, shyly.

He pulled her closer. "I was, for a while," he answered "but not now." He trailed his lips along her cheek and her throat, sending shivers throughout her body.

"I want you to know, Darling, I never imagined that being married could be so wonderful. You've made me very happy!" Amy said.

"Do you realize, Sweetheart, that you have given me the most precious gift a woman can give a man? To know that you have only given yourself to me, your husband, is a feeling that I can't even begin to describe."

"I am happy if I have pleased you, Darling," she said, innocently.

"Couldn't you tell?" he teased.

"I just know that I don't want to leave this room," she teased.

It was even later when Amy and Barry realized how hungry they were. Barry suggested that they don their robes and grill steaks beside the pool.

"Won't the neighbors see us?" Amy asked.

"Not at all. Don't you remember? The yard is completely enclosed with a privacy fence."

"Then, let's go. I'm starving!" she exclaimed.

"All that 'work' has increased your appetite, Mrs. Reeser," he teased.

She wrinkled her nose at him, teasing him.

Amy baked potatoes in the microwave and fixed a salad while Barry cooked the steaks. When she brought the food and drinks from the kitchen he had the steaks ready. They ate at a table beside the pool, the lights reflecting on the water.

"That water sure looks inviting," Amy said, between bites as she watched the tiny ripples made by the warm breeze.

"We can go for a midnight swim," Barry suggested.

"Let's do!" Amy agreed.

"We have to wait a few minutes after we eat, you know," he said.

"I don't even own a bathing suit!" she realized. "I forgot all about buying one."

"You don't need one," Barry said, seriously.

"What?" She looked at his serious face and when it dawned on her what he was suggesting, she laughed merrily. "You're wicked! You know that?" she teased.

"Why? You're my wife, aren't you?" His blue eyes were twinkling.

Amy clasped her arms around his neck and looked up into his handsome face.

"Yes, I am, thank goodness!" she said. "Why did I wait so long?"

Later, when Amy and Barry went back inside, they had a message to call Captain Adams.

"Darling, it's three in the morning! Why would he call you at this hour?" Amy asked.

"He wouldn't, unless it was important. I guess I need to call him back. Do you mind?"

"Of course not. Call him, Darling."

"Barry," Captain Adams began, "I hate to bother you at this hour, but I thought you would want to know that

Joan Caulfield called me a while ago. She is worried about Amy Fontell. She has disappeared. Joan said some of her clothes and a suitcase are missing. Her car is still at the apartment. Also, she doesn't answer her cell phone. It's not like her to leave without telling Joan."

"Captain, Amy is here with me," Barry said, trying not to laugh.

"I beg your pardon?" Captain Adams asked.

"I said, Amy is here with me. We were married yesterday, Captain. She forgot to call Joan, and her cell phone was turned off. I can't imagine why she forgot," he chuckled.

"I am so sorry to disturb you, Barry. But, I am very happy to hear the good news! I will certainly call Miss. Caulfield and tell her not to worry anymore," he chuckled.

"Give her our apologies, Captain. Thank you for calling," Barry said.

When Barry hung up the phone, he turned to Amy and said, "We forgot to call Joan."

"Oh dear! She called Captain Adams?"

"Yes, she did."

"She's going to kill me! Should I call her now?" Amy asked.

"No, Captain Adams will. You probably need to call her tomorrow. Well, it's tomorrow already, isn't it?" he grinned. "Call her sometime this afternoon."

"I can't imagine why I forgot to call her," Amy teased.

"You must have had your mind on something really important," he grinned.

"I can't imagine what!"

Amy and Barry stayed secluded in their private world for four days. On the fifth day, they ventured out to have dinner at a restaurant. Afterwards, they returned to their house to resume their 'honeymoon'. Barry promised Amy a real honeymoon when they could take a long, extended trip. Amy was happier than she had ever dreamed possible.

***

Amy and Barry planned how to decorate their new house. She noticed that there were no pictures of his first wife, Audrey on any of the walls. She didn't ask him about this, but she felt more comfortable not seeing them. She tried not to think about Audrey, and Barry's relationship with her. In her quiet moments she wondered if he thought of Audrey. She even wondered if he thought of her when they made love. As hard as she tried, she could not erase that thought from her mind.

Amy and Barry went to see Joan at her apartment to pick up Amy's car and to pack her belongings.

Joan hugged Amy tightly. "You're a fast worker, girl!" she laughed. "You scared me to death by not telling me where you were."

"I'm really sorry about that, Joan," Amy said, truthfully. "But, we forgot to call."

"I don't understand why," Joan teased. She looked at Barry's handsome smile and added, "Now, I have an excuse to hug you, too," she said, as she hugged him tight. "I am so happy for both of you!"

When it was time to go back to work, the days were long for both Amy and Barry. They looked forward to the quiet evenings they spent together and to sharing events of the day.

Barry came home one evening with good news for

Amy. "You'll be happy to know that the surveillance team that was watching Sara Benson's house apprehended Tommy Pinkerton. They've already run the DNA test and it proved, without a doubt, that it was his blood on the cabin door. He was the person who kicked the door in. He's being charged with that, plus, the murder of Rodney Benson."

"Do you have enough evidence to prove that he was the murderer?" Amy asked, amazed.

"We've got the plaster casts of footprints and tire treads found near the crime scene. It certainly puts him at the scene." He looked at her, thoughtfully. "You can rest easy, now, Sweetheart. He's behind bars."

"But, will he stay there? Can he get out on bail?" she asked.

"Unfortunately, it's possible," Barry answered, reluctantly.

"He'll be gone again, Barry! I just know he will!"

"I hope you're wrong. Arthur Morgan's trial is coming up soon. You realize that we'll have to be there to testify, don't you?"

"Yes, I figured we would. What about Tammy Morgan? I'll have to be there for hers, too."

"Her court date isn't set yet," he answered.

"What about Sara Benson? Was she arrested too?" Amy asked.

"They couldn't even get her for 'harboring a fugitive'. Pinkerton was apprehended in the woods near her place. It would be impossible to prove that she was hiding him. He is not likely to turn her in, either."

"So, she gets away with it?" Amy asked.

"That's what it looks like, Sweetheart. After all, she did lose a husband and now, a lover, perhaps. Maybe she will be going through a lot, on her own. Maybe she cares, maybe she doesn't. Who knows?"

"Will Uncle Curtis' pictures be used as evidence?"

"In Morgan's trial, I am sure; maybe in Pinkerton's, too. That's what he was after when he trashed the cabin. He'll find out about the pictures being held as evidence. He shouldn't be looking for them anymore, even if he had the chance. He'll know that Morgan identified him in one of those pictures."

"Have you seen Pinkerton, yourself?" Amy asked.

"No, Captain Adams told me most of this."

"Would you like to go to the cabin for a weekend sometime, since we don't have to worry about Pinkerton any more?" Amy asked.

"That sounds like fun, Sweetheart. We haven't been there since we were married."

"I didn't tell you that I cleaned up the floor for you, did I? I'm afraid there's still a dark stain on the wood. I scrubbed it with everything I could find, but you know how blood stains everything."

"Oh, Darling! I forgot all about that! I'm so sorry you had to clean that up yourself! You're such a sweet, thoughtful person. You did all that, even after I threw my engagement ring at you."

He grinned, enchantingly. "Being there made me feel closer to you."

"Barry, what a sweet thing to say! If only I had known how much you loved me and how much I love you, I wouldn't have wasted all that time. I am so sorry!" She sat in his lap and closed her arms around his neck. "Will you forgive me?"

"For what?" he teased, as he kissed her tenderly. She seemed to melt into his arms as she returned his kisses.

17

***

Amy and Barry went to the cabin for a weekend. Amy found cane poles that her uncle had stored under the porch and she and Barry fished in a small pond on her property. They caught small bream but threw them back. Late in the afternoon they walked through the woods. Barry showed her Mr. Rafferty's cabin from a distance.

"I hope Mr. Rafferty isn't involved in the drug dealing," Amy said. "He seems like such a nice old gentleman."

"I hope he isn't. It may all come out in Morgan's trial. One thing about shady characters, they like to squeal on one another."

"It sounds so complicated. Will the DEA have to investigate the drug dealing?" Amy asked.

"That's their specialty, like forensic science is mine, now."

"Have you had any interesting cases lately?" she asked.

He grinned. "I thought you didn't want to hear any 'gory details'."

"Well, no gory details, but I am interested in your work, Darling."

"I've learned a lot about collecting evidence at a

crime scene. It's amazing what you can find and preserve. It's not always that easy. We had to identify a body last week by the dental records and DNA. It was a missing person from another state."

"How sad," Amy said.

"It was a young woman in her twenties. She had a bullet hole in her skull."

"Oh, no! Some crimes are never solved, I know. But, I hope they catch her killer," Amy said, sympathetically.

"Can you imagine having a daughter that disappeared?" Barry stated.

"No, I can't imagine it," she answered. After a moment, she added, "You know, that's one thing that we have never discussed, Darling; having children."

"You're right. I'm not getting any younger, either," he teased.

"Be serious, Darling. Do you want children?" she asked.

"Of course I do. Don't you?"

"I'd love to have a little 'Barry,' with that charming smile of yours."

"Or, a little girl with your dimples," he said.

Barry stopped on the trail leading back to the cabin and pulled Amy close. "Why don't we 'order' one of those little ones now?" he whispered.

"Now, right here?" she teased.

"How about the cabin? I've always wanted to share that bedroom with you, Sweetheart. Finally, I can."

"You mean, you didn't like our sharing the couch?" she teased.

"The couch was very nice. The bed will be even better."

18

***

Amy was preparing dinner on Friday evening for Barry's family, who had come for a visit. This was their first time to visit since she and Barry had married. Amy wanted everything to be just right. She was taking a roast from the oven when Barry came home from work. He greeted his family and then Amy. Amy knew, instantly, that something was bothering him. She didn't want to ask in front of his parents, so she waited until they had retired for the night.

"Darling, what's wrong? I can tell that something is bothering you."

He sat down on the bed and drew her down beside him. "You know me rather well, don't you, Sweetheart?"

"I should, don't you think?"

"I didn't want to worry you, but you have a right to know. A few weeks ago, Tommy Pinkerton's bail was set at $250,000.00. Sara Benson posted his bail by mortgaging her land."

"Oh, no!"

"It gets worse. His trial date came up and he didn't show. He jumped bail."

"Barry, I knew this would happen!" Amy exclaimed.

"There's always that chance. Try not to worry about it, Sweetheart. He knows that you don't have the pictures now.

There's no reason he would bother you again. There's a state-wide search for him. Hopefully, we'll find him soon."

"What about Sara Benson?" Amy asked.

"She is gone, too. The bondsman will take her land for payment. I figure she is with Pinkerton."

"He may never be found," Amy said.

"Unfortunately, it happens, Sweetheart. Now, enough talk of murder suspects," he said, pulling her down beside him. He kissed her softly. "Let's concentrate on more pleasant things."

Amy felt the fire ignite in her body at his touch. She soon forgot about Tommy Pinkerton.

19

***

Summer was over and fall came. There were no more midnight swims for Amy and Barry. Instead, they sat before the fireplace or lay on the sheepskin rug before the fire. Life had never been better for either of them.

Barry surprised Amy one evening when he presented her with tickets for a cruise to the Bahamas. She stared at them, blankly.

"A cruise? Barry, you're not serious?" She was overwhelmed.

His blue eyes were shining. "This is the honeymoon trip I promised you."

"What about work? What if I can't get off?" she asked.

"Sweetheart, you could give your notice at work. Wouldn't you like to stay home and do as you please? You don't have to work, you know."

"I have never thought of not working. It might be nice to stay home and pursue my hobbies, like writing and cooking."

"It's your decision, Sweetheart. I like the idea of your being at home during the day." He grinned mischievously and added, "I could come home to eat lunch with you and we could find other pleasant things to do."

"You're wicked," she teased, "but it's tempting."

She hugged him tightly. "Thank you Darling. You are so good to me."

Then, she kissed him tenderly and added, "If we have a baby I could be at home to take care of it, too."

He looked at her, lovingly. "It will happen one day, when we least expect it," he said. They had been trying for several weeks now, but he knew it could take more time.

Amy turned in her notice at work. She was surprised at how good it felt to stay home. She stayed busy until it was time for their cruise. She was so excited, that, Barry laughed at her childish excitement at the airport. They flew to their port of departure and were soon on the ship. The steward showed them to their cabin. Amy looked around her, enchanted at what she saw. The cabin was decorated as a bridal suite. There was a lace canopy over the bed and the bathtub was red and heart-shaped.

"Darling, it is absolutely beautiful!" Amy exclaimed. "It's like being in paradise!"

"Welcome to our bridal suite," Barry said, huskily, as he took her into his arms. He kissed her warmly and she returned his passion.

As soon as they left the port, Amy and Barry strolled along the deck exploring the ship. There were mountains of food in the dining areas. There was dancing and various games to choose from. They sampled tropical fruits and exotic dishes. Anything their heart desired was provided.

Later, Amy and Barry swam in the pool. Then, in the privacy of their suite they danced to romantic music. Then, lying together in the huge canopied bed they whispered endearments and dreamed of their future together.

When the ship docked, they took a tour, buying souvenirs to remind them of their wonderful time together.

On their last night of the cruise, Amy snuggled closer to Barry. She kissed his cheek and ran her finger along his strong jaw.

"Let's stay here forever," she said. "It has been so

wonderful! I don't want it to end."

"It doesn't have to end, Sweetheart. We'll be together, always," he answered.

"I want you to know, Darling, that you have made me so happy! You are the most considerate husband. I never dreamed life could be so wonderful!"

"Can't you see how happy you have made me, Sweetheart? It brings me joy to see you this happy. I always want to please you."

"You please me so well, Darling!" she confessed, lavishing him with kisses.

He chuckled. "For a shy, conservative girl, you certainly have come a long way."

"It's your fault," she grinned, "you have corrupted me."

"Have I?"

"I was an innocent babe, until you came into my life," she teased.

"Is that a fact?"

"Uh-huh. I never knew what loving a husband was like."

"You're certainly learning that well," he teased.

"You think so? Do you like it when I kiss you here.... and here?" She kissed the dark, curly hair on his chest and his navel. She felt his body tense and knew that he was under her spell once again.

20

***

Spring came again. Arthur Morgan's trial date was set. Amy and Barry were subpoenaed to appear as witnesses for the prosecution. Both of them testified to what had happened at the cabin when Arthur Morgan shot Barry. Amy testified to all the times he had harassed her. They did not bring up the incident of her being kidnapped. That would come up later in Tammy Morgan's trial. Mr. Rafferty hadn't been called to testify, after all. The ordeal brought it all back to Amy; the horror of that morning that Barry was shot. The pictures that Amy's uncle had taken were admitted as evidence. Arthur Morgan explained that he thought the pictures would incriminate him and he wanted to destroy them. He confessed that he had been doing business with Curtis Fontell and that they had bought and sold crystal methamphetamine drugs and transported the drugs in a small plane that Curtis had chartered when needed. Morgan said he did not know who supplied the drugs, that Curtis handled that. In exchange for a lighter sentence for attempted murder of Lieutenant Reeser, Morgan gave them three names of buyers that they had supplied with the 'meth'. Morgan still swore under oath that he had not intended to shoot Barry and wasn't even aware that he was at the cabin with Amy until he broke in on them.

The jury deliberated for only an hour and found Arthur Morgan guilty of second-degree, attempted murder. The judge was to sentence him at a later date.

Amy left with Barry, relieved that this much was behind her. She still had Tammy Morgan's kidnapping trial to go through. Tammy's trial date was set for the following week.

Barry accompanied Amy to Tammy Morgan's trial. Tammy was hostile in her attitude and denied everything. Amy gave her testimony as to what happened the day Tammy forced her to drive to meet Arthur Morgan. Amy's coat was used as evidence, showing the cut made with the switchblade. Amy was afraid that the jury would not convict Tammy Morgan because it was her word against Amy's. Then, Arthur Morgan was brought in to testify for the prosecution. He told the jury that it was true that Tammy had forced Amy to drive the car to meet him and he told the jury why. The jury deliberated only thirty minutes to reach a verdict. They found Tammy Morgan guilty of first degree kidnapping. The judge would sentence her at a later date.

This time when Amy and Barry left the courtroom, Amy felt that they had finally received justice for the crimes committed against them by the Morgan's.

On the way home, Barry said, "The only thing that is still unresolved is Rodney Benson's murder. That's where all of this mess really started."

"You haven't had any luck finding Pinkerton?" Amy asked.

"Not a clue. Captain Adams said an unidentified man called and reported that he had seen Pinkerton, or someone fitting his description. Nothing ever came of it. That was a couple of months ago."

"What about Sara Benson?" Amy asked.

"She's still gone, too. Her land was auctioned off to pay the bondsman. I don't think he got $250,000.00 for it."

"Will there be an investigation concerning the drug dealing?" Amy asked.

"The DEA is handling that already."

"We won't be involved in that, will we, Barry? I don't want to have to testify in court again."

Barry laughed, his blue eyes twinkling. "Not unless you have a meth lab set up somewhere that I don't know about."

"Be serious," Amy said.

"They will use your uncle's pictures for evidence, but that won't involve you, Sweetheart."

"You know, that was something, the way Arthur Morgan testified against his own wife," Amy said. "He must not have loved her very much. I did see him slap her that time."

"Most folks aren't as blessed as we are, Sweetheart," Barry said. "Some never experience what we have together."

Amy wanted to ask him how their relationship compared to his relationship with his first wife, but she didn't think this would be a good time to ask.

21

***

When Amy began to feel nauseated in the morning, she didn't think much about it. At first, she thought it was something she had eaten. When it occurred regularly, she began to wonder if she could be pregnant. She was careful to keep it from Barry, not wanting to get his hopes up until she knew for certain.

Amy made an appointment with her doctor and he confirmed her suspicion. She was six weeks pregnant. When she left his office, she was thrilled. She started planning how to tell Barry the good news. She decided to prepare him a romantic, candlelight dinner and tell him then.

When Barry came home from work that night, he found the table set for two with candles burning. The aroma of a roast cooking filled the kitchen. He found Amy taking the roast from the oven.

"Wow," Barry said, grinning. "This is what a man likes to come home to, a beautiful wife with a delicious dinner on the stove! Is this a special occasion?" he asked, viewing the romantic setting.

"Every day is a special occasion with my husband," she said, shyly.

He kissed her; a long, lingering kiss that left her breathless.

Finally, she managed to say, "Our dinner is getting cold."

"I don't mind, do you?" he asked, huskily.

"What do you think?" she answered, breathlessly.

He picked her up in one swift motion and carried her to their bed. It was a long time later, before they thought of their dinner that was waiting.

Later, Amy remembered that she hadn't told Barry about the baby. She waited until he was reading in bed and snuggled close to him, interrupting his reading.

"Are you ready for 'dessert' now, Sweetheart?" Barry teased. "Didn't you get enough of 'the main course'?"

"I can never get enough of being with you, Darling," she whispered.

He chuckled and pulled her closer, kissing her again and again.

"You are such a joy to me, Audrey, Sweetheart," he sighed.

Amy's body grew rigid as he continued to kiss her throat and neck. When she didn't respond, he drew away and looking into her eyes, asked, "What is it, Sweetheart?"

Tears filled Amy's eyes and rolled down both cheeks.

"What's wrong?" he asked, concerned.

"Let me up!" she sobbed, as she pulled away from him, trembling. She snatched her robe off the chair and pulling it on, she ran from the room.

Barry caught her in the hallway. Grabbing her by the shoulders, he forced her to look at him.

"Amy! What happened? What is wrong with you?" he asked.

"Nothing is wrong with me!" she cried. "What is wrong with you?"

"I don't know what you're talking about!" he said, confused.

She twisted from his grip and stood trembling, tears streaming down her face. She tried to calm herself but couldn't.

"Sweetheart," Barry pleaded, watching her closely, "please tell me what's wrong. What have I done to upset you?"

She met his gaze with her own. "What have you done? You dare ask me that?"

He shook his head, at a loss for words. He had never seen Amy react in such a way.

"You don't know, do you?" she cried.

When he didn't answer, she continued, her voice barely above a whisper.

"You called me Audrey! Audrey!" she exclaimed.

His face looked stricken, as though she had slapped him. "Amy, I'm so sorry! I didn't realize…."

"You don't realize who I am, when I am in your arms? When we are making love, do you pretend that I am Audrey? Do you, Barry?"

"Amy, don't be absurd!"

"Now, I'm being absurd!" She turned from him and rushed back to the bedroom. Barry followed and watched as she got dressed and began packing a suitcase.

"What do you think you're doing?" he asked, angrily.

"I'm leaving!"

He grabbed her, roughly. "Stop this! You're being ridiculous! Amy, you're not leaving!"

She jerked away from him. "Don't touch me!" she cried. "I don't ever want you to touch me again!"

He dropped his hands to his side and his expression changed. He looked at her coldly.

"If you walk out of this house, don't come back," he said, softly.

She stopped, surprised at what he had said. She hesitated only a moment and then resumed her packing.

Suddenly, he turned and left her in the bedroom, alone.

Amy burst into tears, barely able to see what she was

doing. When her suitcase was full, she got her backpack and walked to the front door. She didn't see Barry anywhere. Subconsciously, she wanted him to stop her, to take her in his arms and make everything better. But, he didn't. He let her go. As she got into her car she saw him standing in the doorway watching her. He didn't make a move to stop her.

Amy could hardly see how to drive to Joan's apartment for the tears. She was almost hysterical when she banged on Joan's door and waited for her to answer it.

When Joan saw how distraught she was, she exclaimed, "Amy, what has happened? Has something happened to Barry?"

Amy managed to shake her head as Joan led her inside. Joan took her suitcase from her, and led her to the couch.

"I have left him!" Amy said sobbing.

"You have left him? I don't believe it! Amy, tell me what happened."

Amy refused to tell Joan.

"Is this the first fight you two have had, Honey?" Joan asked.

Amy sniffed and nodded, fresh tears filling her eyes.

"Look, all couples have fights just so they can have the fun of making up. This will pass, you'll see," Joan assured her.

"You don't understand," Amy said, finally. "He....he called me Audrey!"

Joan's face was blank. "Who's Audrey?" she asked, confused.

"His first wife, the one who died!" Amy explained.

"Oh." Joan was silent for a moment. Then, she said,

"Amy, you're over-reacting. I'm sure it was just a slip of the tongue."

"Sure it was! Because, he's still in love with her! Why else would he call me by her name?"

Joan couldn't answer that. Instead, she asked softly, "Amy, were you two making love when he called you Audrey?"

"Yes!" she stammered. Then, she said truthfully, "Well, not exactly. We had been, earlier, and would have been again....., until he called me that."

"That's a lot different, Amy, than his saying it in a moment of heated passion. You must know that."

"I don't know anything of the sort! I don't want to discuss it any more! Please, Joan!"

"Okay, we won't discuss it. Not now, anyway. But, I will tell you this up front; I think you're making a grave mistake. The guy is crazy about you! I don't care what name he called you. Look at what he has done for you, Amy."

"You said we wouldn't discuss it!" Amy retorted.

"Okay, have it your way," Joan said.

"Thank you. May I stay here for a while?"

"Are you serious?"

"I'm here, aren't I?" Amy said, sniffing.

"You know you're welcome, Amy."

Amy stopped her before she could continue. "I'll take a shower and then go to bed in my old room. Thanks, Joan." She left Joan staring after her.

Amy cried herself to sleep that night. When she awoke during the night she imagined Barry's arms around her and remembered the times he had held her close. When morning finally came she was tired and irritable. She tried to be cheerful with Joan but failed. Joan fixed her scrambled eggs and toast and Amy tried to eat. The first bite sent her scurrying to the bathroom. Joan heard her gagging. When Amy came back to the kitchen her face was pale.

"Are you all right?" Joan asked, concerned.

"I don't feel very well, but I'll be fine. I just need some coffee." She poured herself a cup and sat down.

Joan saw that Amy's hands were trembling. "Amy,

you're pregnant, aren't you?" Joan asked, bluntly.

Amy saw no use in denying the obvious. "Yes, I'm pregnant," she admitted, tears filling her eyes again.

Joan smiled. "That explains why you're over-reacting, Honey. Women are always temperamental when they're pregnant. Are you happy about it?"

"Of course I'm happy about it. Or, I was," she confessed.

Joan came around the table and hugged her tightly.

"You goose! Why don't you go home to that hand-some husband of yours this morning?"

"I can't," Amy admitted, her face stricken.

"What do you mean, 'you can't'?"

"He told me if I walked out of the house, not to come back."

"Wow! You must have made him really mad. You know he didn't mean it."

"He meant every word of it."

"Did you say hateful things that you didn't really mean, Amy?"

Amy remembered telling him that she never wanted him to touch her again. "Yes," she admitted, shamefully.

"See there? I'm sure he didn't mean what he said, either. Both of you were hurting and lashing out. Would you like for me to call him for you?"

"No, I don't!" she answered, trembling.

"Amy, don't you remember what you did once before that caused so much misery? You broke off your engage-ment and wasted all that precious time together! You two need to be together right now. You need to be sharing eve-rything about this baby that's on the way."

"It's over, Joan. It isn't me that he wants, it's 'Audrey'."

"Don't be ridiculous! You have a great husband who adores you and you're throwing it all away because of a ghost that haunts you. So what if he called you by his dead wife's name? People do that, Amy! They don't erase all memories from their mind. Don't you realize that?"

"What are you, Joan, a marriage counselor? Have you ever been married?"

"You know I haven't."

"I rest my case," Amy said, haughtily.

"Okay, you're making your bed. You'll have to lie in it."

"What is that supposed to mean?"

"It means, you better give this some serious thought, Girl. You may be throwing away your only chance for happiness."

Amy ignored her statement. "I'm tired of discussing it, Joan. Can we drop the subject, please?"

"Sure, I've got to go to work, anyway. You can do whatever you please."

"Do you want me to leave?" Amy asked, a tear sliding down her cheek.

"No, I don't want you to leave, you goose! I just want what's best for you." Joan hugged her, tears shining in her own eyes. "Why don't you go back to bed? I doubt if you slept a wink last night. You need to keep up your strength. You have a baby to consider now."

"I think I will," Amy agreed, feeling exhausted.

As soon as Joan got to work her secretary greeted her and said, "You had a call earlier from a 'Barry Reeser'. He said he would call back." "He's on the line now."

"Thanks," Joan replied, shutting the door to her office behind her. She picked up the phone "Hello," she said.

"Hello, Joan," Barry said.

Joan couldn't help the tingly feeling he evoked in her at the sound of his voice. Lord, Amy was a fool, she thought. "Hi, Barry. How are you?"

"I'm okay. I know Amy is at your apartment, Joan. I drove by there last night and saw her car. I guess she told you she walked out?"

"Yes, Barry, she told me. I'm sorry to hear it. I hope you two can patch things up."

"That's entirely up to her. I just wanted to make sure she was safe, that's all. I was afraid she would take off to the cabin alone."

"She may do that, yet," Joan said.

"I know." He seemed at a loss for words.

"Barry, what can I do to help?"

"I don't know, Joan. Nothing, I guess." After a moment he asked, "Did she tell you what she got so angry about?"

"Yes, she told me that you called her 'Audrey'."

"It was a stupid mistake," he admitted.

"I understand, completely, Barry. I tried to reason with her, but she wouldn't listen."

"I appreciate it, Joan. Thanks for trying."

Joan sensed that he needed someone to talk to. "Maybe the two of you could talk to a marriage counselor. I hear they have helped a lot of couples."

"I don't know. I guess I'd try it, if she were willing. Maybe I am to blame."

"Don't blame yourself, Barry. I think she is over-reacting."

"Do you?"

"I certainly do. I told her so, too. She didn't like it much, though."

"I bet she didn't," he chuckled.

"Barry, I think she's a darn lucky girl," Joan confessed.

That caught him off-guard and he chose not to answer. Finally, he said, "I won't keep you, Joan. I appreciate what you're doing for her. If she needs anything let me know. She would probably do without before she'd ask me for anything right now."

"Amy has her inheritance from her parents, Barry. She doesn't have to be dependent on you. You know that, don't you?"

"I forgot. She never talks about things like that. Money has never been important to her," he said.

"Lord, what a mixed-up girl!" Joan laughed. "If I could only trade places with her!"

"I need to get to work," Barry said, reluctantly. "Will you keep in touch? I want to know how she's doing."

"You know I will," Joan said, hurting because of the misery she knew he was feeling right now. What a fool Amy was, she thought once again.

***

Amy had been at Joan's apartment for a week. She had not heard a word from Barry. He was keeping his distance. She ached with the need to see him and talk to him, but she was too proud to call him. She still cried herself to sleep at night, snuggling up with her cool pillow for comfort. She was sick in the mornings. She decided not to tell Joan that Barry didn't know about the baby. She hoped Joan wouldn't let it slip if she talked to him anytime. If Barry wanted her back, she wanted it to be for herself and not because of the baby. She wondered if he would ever call her. So far, he hadn't. She remembered how she had stormed out of the house and what she had said to him. She didn't believe he would make the first step toward reconciliation. She was at a loss as to what she should do. She loved him dearly. She was sure that he loved her. Yet, she couldn't get the thought out of her mind, that he still missed Audrey and still grieved for her. Why else would he call her 'Audrey'?

When Joan suggested to Amy that she and Barry see a marriage counselor, Amy refused.

"We shouldn't have to see a marriage counselor when we haven't been married very long," Amy said.

Joan looked at her, incredulously. "The fact that you

are separated is reason enough, Amy. I can't believe you haven't gone back to him before now."

"He hasn't even called me!" Amy retorted.

"You walked out on him, Girl! He didn't walk out on you! You need to make the first move."

"That's your opinion. If he loves me, he should have come after me."

Joan shook her head in disbelief. "You need to see a counselor or shrink, Amy. You are married to a wonderful man! You are driving him away! If you keep acting like this, you may not get him back. Don't you understand?"

"What are you saying?" Amy asked, her face ashen.

"I'm saying, you need to stop and think about what you are doing. Any woman would jump at the chance to trade places with you!"

"Including you, Joan?" Amy asked quietly, her heart almost stopping inside her chest.

"Including me, Amy," she admitted honestly. "The guy is hurting and you're too naïve to realize it."

"How do you know so much? Have you seen him?" Amy asked, defensively.

"No, but I have talked to him."

"When?"

"He called me at work, Amy, the day after you came here. He was worried about you. He drove by to see if your car was here. He keeps track of you even if you aren't aware of it. I'm telling you, the guy is crazy about you! He wanted to make sure you didn't want for anything!"

Tears filled Amy's eyes at this revelation. He hadn't stayed away entirely. He had still thought of her.

After several days had gone by Amy was bored and depressed. She wished she could see Barry's mother and talk to her about her problem. She had a good relationship with her and felt that Mrs. Reeser could help her. She decided to drive to her house for a visit although she had never been there before. She didn't want to call until she got to town. That way, she felt that Mrs. Reeser wouldn't have time to talk to Barry before she got there.

Amy packed an overnight bag and left a note for Joan, saying that she was going out of town for a few days. She didn't want to argue with her about what she had decided to do.

The drive took Amy two hours since she wasn't familiar with the roads. When she arrived, she called Mrs. Reeser from her cell phone.

"Amy, what a pleasant surprise," she said over the phone.

"Mrs. Reeser, would you like some company for a while? I am in town," Amy asked, hesitantly.

"Of course, Dear! It would be a pleasure. Is Barry with you?"

"No, he isn't," she admitted.

"Well, that's all right! We girls will have a nice visit," she said, pleasantly.

She told Amy how to find their street and she was waiting at the door with Mr. Reeser when she arrived. Seeing Mr. Reeser made Amy's heart flutter. He reminded her so much of Barry. They hugged her warmly and kissed her on the cheek.

"It's so good to see you, Amy," Mr. Reeser said cordially. "Come in, come in."

Amy entered their modest home, which was decorated simply but was cheerful and inviting. The aroma of spiced potpourri flowed throughout the rooms.

"Your home is lovely," Amy said, feeling at home already.

"Thank you, Dear. Here, let me take your bag," Mr. Reeser said. "You'll have Barry's old room, of course." He disappeared to that area of the house.

"Come on into the kitchen, Dear," Mrs. Reeser said. "May I get you something to drink? We will be eating dinner shortly."

"I hope I am not imposing, Mrs. Reeser, but I could use a glass of tea if you have it."

"I have plenty of tea." She fixed Amy a frosty glass of tea and set it on the table in front of her.

"What brings you here, alone, Amy?" Mr. Reeser asked, coming back from the bedroom. "Couldn't Barry get time off from work?"

Amy was at a loss for words. She didn't want to start right out by telling them her troubles. But, she couldn't lie, either.

Mrs. Reeser came to her rescue. "David, let's not start bombarding Amy with questions all at once. Let her relax and have her tea. I'm going to put dinner on the table and we will eat."

Mr. Reeser looked at his wife, puzzled but refrained from asking any more questions.

"May I help you?" Amy asked, relieved.

"No thank you, Dear. You visit with David. It will just take me a moment."

As they were eating, Amy asked about Joey.

"He has gone to a bowling party with a group of his friends and will spend the night at a friend's house," Mr. Reeser explained.

"This is delicious stew, Mrs. Reeser," Amy said, thoroughly enjoying it. She hadn't been able to eat much lately because of her condition.

"Thank you, Amy. It was always Barry's favorite, too. It is too bad he isn't here to enjoy it with us," she said, watching Amy closely.

"Yes, it is," Amy agreed quietly, aware of their eyes upon her.

"How is Barry's work going? Is he still enjoying working in the forensic lab?" Mr. Reeser asked, cautiously.

"He loves his work," she managed to say in spite of the lump forming in her throat. She must not cry, she told herself sternly.

"More cornbread, Dear?" Mrs. Reeser asked, passing her the dish.

"No, thank you. I have had more than enough. Will you please excuse me?" Getting up, she hurried to the room that had been Barry's. She managed to close the door before she burst into tears.

Barry's parents looked at one another across the table, concern on their faces.

"What do you suppose is wrong?" Mrs. Reeser asked, softly.

"I have no idea, Becky. Why don't you go in there and talk to her? Something is definitely not right."

Mrs. Reeser knocked softly on the bedroom door. "Amy, may I come in?"

"Yes, please do," Amy answered. She was lying across the bed but sat up quickly. "I am sorry I upset your dinner," she said, sniffing.

Mrs. Reeser sat down beside her. "You didn't upset our dinner, Dear. Would you like to talk about what is bothering you? It is obvious that something definitely is."

Amy burst into tears again and buried her face in Mrs. Reeser's bosom. Mrs. Reeser put her arms around her and drew her closer. She stroked Amy's hair and let her cry until her tears were spent.

"There, there. Now, you'll feel better. Tell me, Amy, have you and my son had a quarrel of some kind?"

Amy looked into her sweet, loving face and knew why Barry had always been so loving and considerate. She had taught him that. Amy nodded, sniffing back her tears. Mrs. Reeser handed her a small, lacy handkerchief from her apron pocket and Amy blew her nose noisily. Twisting it in her fingers, Amy kept her eyes downcast as she began to tell her mother-in-law what she had said and done to her son. When she finally raised her gaze to meet Mrs. Reeser's, she saw only love and compassion there, not the hatred that she had feared would be there.

"I don't deserve Barry, Mrs. Reeser. All I seem to do is hurt him. He is everything I ever dreamed a husband could be. I can't seem to take 'her' place."

"Has he ever said anything to make you feel that he is comparing you with his first wife?" she asked, softly.

"No, never. But, I can't help but wonder. Why can't I accept our relationship as man and wife without having her come between us?"

"I can't answer that, Dear. Have you ever discussed Audrey with him, openly?"

"Not intimately."

"Perhaps you should. Maybe getting your feelings out in the open would help."

"I'm afraid. What if it upsets him?"

"Haven't you upset him, already?" she asked, wisely.

Amy nodded, tears filling her eyes again.

"I wish I had all the answers," Mrs. Reeser said. "But, I don't. I do know that my son loves you very much. I believe you love him just as much. I believe the two of you can work this out, if you try. Would you like for me to call him and ask him to come up here?"

"I don't think I can talk to him just yet. I'm just not ready."

"Don't put it off too long, Amy," Mrs. Reeser advised.

"My roommate, Joan, suggested that I see a counselor. What do you think of that idea?"

"It sounds like a good idea. Would you want Barry to go with you?"

"I don't think so, not at first, anyway. Maybe I need to talk to the counselor alone."

"Do you know a counselor?" Mrs. Reeser asked.

"No, but I can find one. I am sure that Joan will help me."

"That's good. That's a good 'first step'. Now, why don't you call Barry and talk to him? Let him know that you are thinking of him, Amy."

"How can I?" she asked, afraid that he would reject her advances.

"It's easy," Mrs. Reeser said, smiling. "Just pick up the phone and dial his number."

23

***

When Joan came home from work, she found Amy's note telling her that she had gone out of town for a few days. The first thing that she thought of was that Amy had gone to the cabin alone. She knew that Tommy Pinkerton was still at large. She decided to call Barry and give him this bit of news. She didn't mind talking to him again.
She was disappointed when she got his answering machine, but he called her back an hour later.

"Joan, I have a message here to call you," Barry said.

"Yes, Barry. Thanks for returning my call. How have you been?"

"I'm okay, thanks."

"I have some news about Amy," she said.

"What?" he asked, alert.

Joan told him about the note and her assumption that she had gone to the cabin.

"Did she mention the cabin to you at all?" Barry asked.

"No, she didn't. But, you know how she loves that place. I guess I have been giving her a hard time lately."

"Why?" he asked, bluntly.

"Hell's bells, Barry! You know why! She's acting like a spoiled brat. You need to show her who is boss.

Maybe she just needs a good spanking."

He chuckled. "Joan, I wish it were that simple, I really do."

"Are you two going to call it quits? Is that it?" she asked.

"I don't want that," he admitted. "But, that's her decision to make."

"Well, if 'you' won't make the first move, and 'she' won't make the first move, what else do you think is going to happen?"

"I don't know. I wish I did," he said, wearily. "I need to go now, Joan. Thanks for telling me this. I'll drive up to the cabin to make sure she is okay."

"Good luck, Barry. Remember, I'm here if you need me," Joan said, earnestly.

"Thanks, Joan."

"Sure, any time." She heard him hang up the phone. Once more, she wished that she could trade places with Amy.

24

***

Amy found enough courage to dial Barry's number while Mrs. Reeser sat on the bed beside her, encouraging her. To their disappointment she got the answering machine. Even listening to his voice on the machine made her heart beat faster. She didn't leave a message.

"He's not at home," she said to her mother-in-law.

"That's too bad. You could have left him a message, Amy."

"I'd rather not. I will try again, later."

"You look tired, Dear. Would you like to retire for the night?"

"Would you mind? I am rather tired, especially after the drive here."

"You go ahead and get ready for bed. I'll say good-night to David for you." She kissed her on the cheek. "If you need anything, just ask."

"Thank you, Mrs. Reeser. You are so kind."

"You are my daughter now, Amy."

"Thank you." Amy hugged her tightly. Before she could leave the room, Amy added, "I do love your son. I love him more than you'll ever know."

She smiled at Amy. "I do know. When I see the two of you together, I do know. A person would have to be blind not to see the love you both share. Don't throw it away, Amy." She slipped quietly from the room.

Amy lay across the bed, exhausted. This was Barry's bed, she thought; Barry's room; the room he had grown up in. For the first time she looked around her. She saw the pictures on the walls. There were pictures of Barry at various ages, growing up. A dark-headed, blue-eyed little boy of approximately five looked down at her. Amy smiled. That is what Barry's son would look like, she thought, like the little boy smiling back at her with a twinkle in his blue eyes. Instead of tears in Amy's eyes, there was a smile on her lips as she fell asleep. The blue eyed boy looked down at her in the quiet room that belonged to him, and now, to her. For the first time in days, she slept peacefully.

25

***

Barry drove to the cabin but did not find Amy there. He hung around for an hour in case she showed up, but she didn't. He even drove over to Mr. Rafferty's house and asked if he had seen her. He hadn't. Barry asked him to keep an eye on the cabin in case she returned. Mr. Rafferty didn't ask any questions. If he found the request odd, he didn't comment. Barry returned to the city.

As Barry unlocked the front door to his house the phone was ringing. He hurried to answer it before the answering machine picked up.

"Hello."

There was a pause before he heard Amy speak.

"Hello, Barry," she said, softly.

"Amy, it's good to hear from you. Where are you?" he asked, relieved to hear from her.

"I am at your parents' home."

"You didn't tell Joan where you were going. We've been worried, Amy."

"I'm sorry. So, you have talked to Joan?" Amy asked.

"She called me. She was afraid that you had gone to the cabin alone. I just got back from there, looking for you."

"I'm sorry to have caused so much trouble, Barry."

"Never mind. I'm glad you are at Mom and Dad's. How are you, Amy?"

"I don't know how to answer that, Barry," she said, hesitantly.

"What's wrong?" he asked, concerned.

"I miss you so very much," she admitted, softly.

He was quiet for a moment, and then said, "You are the one who left, Amy."

"I know. I am thinking of going to see a counselor. I think he could help me with these mixed-up emotions."

"Would you like for me to go with you?" he asked.

"I don't think so. I think it's my problem, not yours."

"This is 'our' problem, Amy. You are my wife."

"Yes, I know," she said, tears streaming down her cheeks.

"Let me help," he said, softly. "You find someone you want to counsel you and I'll take you."

"Let me think about it. When I get back to Joan's, I will make an appointment, and I'll call you."

"You don't have to go to Joan's, Amy. You have a home with me. Why don't you come home?"

When Amy didn't answer, he continued, "If you prefer to stay in the guest room, I won't pressure you."

Amy was so choked up she could hardly answer. She wanted to go home. She wanted to share their home and be his wife in every way.

"Amy?" he asked, when she still hadn't answered, "will you come home?"

"Do you really want me to, Barry? After what I have done to you?"

"I love you, Amy. I always will. Do you still love me?" he asked, bluntly.

"You know I do!" she exclaimed.

"No, I don't know that, Amy. I don't know you, when you get angry and leave me. I know I upset you. I know I called you 'Audrey' by mistake. I can't promise that I won't ever do it again. Will you leave again, if I do, Amy?"

"I don't ever want to leave you again! I want to understand and forgive and forget. I need help doing that, Barry. That's why I want to see a counselor, to help me understand and get through this. I want to be able to talk to you about Audrey, openly, without it upsetting either of us," Amy explained.

"Let's take it one step at a time," Barry said. "Come home first. Then, we'll find a counselor. You talk to him, and then we'll talk to him together. Will you do that, Amy?" he pleaded.

"Yes, Darling. I will come home," Amy answered, crying.

"Will you come today?" he asked, softly.

"Yes, I will. I love you, Barry," she said, trying to stop crying.

"I love you, Amy."

When Amy hung up the phone, she went to tell Mrs. Reeser that she was going home. Mrs. Reeser hugged her warmly.

"See, Dear, I told you everything was going to work out."

"Thank you for being here when I needed you. You are a 'second mother' to me."

"Thank you, Amy, for coming to talk to me. I will always be here for you. I want you to know that."

Amy was tempted to tell her about the baby. But, she decided not to. She felt that she should tell Barry first.

26

***

Amy felt better than she had in weeks as she drove from her in-laws' home to her home with Barry. She was nervous as she pulled into the driveway. It was four p.m. She knew that Barry would be waiting for her. He met her at the door. Her breath caught sharply when she saw him standing there. He smiled, but she thought there was sadness in his smile. He took her in his arms without saying a word and hugged her tightly. She looked up into his eyes and she saw dampness there. She pulled him toward her, her face uplifted, waiting for his kiss. He kissed her softly, but she returned his kiss passionately. Finally, he released her.

"I have steaks ready for the grill. I thought you might be hungry," he said.

"I'm starved!" she said, honestly.

They grilled the steaks together and had a pleasant dinner. Afterwards, they did the dishes, and then sat together in the den. Amy watched him closely, her heart yearning for him to hold her again.

"How was Mom and Dad?" he asked.

"They are fine. I never did see Joey. He had gone bowling with friends." After a moment, she said, "Barry, could we talk? Will you tell me about your relationship with Audrey?"

He was surprised at her question. "I don't think that would be such a good idea, right now," he answered.

"I really want to know. Maybe it will help me if we discuss her."

"Sweetheart, there was nothing about our relationship that is threatening to you. That part of my life is over. I have a new life with you."

"Your mom told me a long time ago, that you were devastated when Audrey died," she ventured.

"Of course I was. I did love her, Amy."

"I know you did. She was fortunate to have you love her, Barry."

"Where are you headed with this, Amy?"

"I want to know, that you don't think of her.....when we are making love....," she said, breathlessly.

Barry looked at her, incredulously. "I can't believe you would ask that!"

"Won't you tell me?" Amy asked, cautiously. She sensed that he was irritated with her, but he remained calm.

"No, Amy. I have never thought of anyone but you when we are making love, or any time that I have held you in my arms. Don't you understand that? I love you. I love being with you."

"Do I make you as happy as she did?" Amy asked, blushing at her own question. She saw him draw in his breath sharply. She did not realize how she was trying his patience.

"Amy," he explained, "what we share together is special. It couldn't be better. Don't you know that, Sweetheart? Do I have to tell you that? I could ask you the same question; do I satisfy you?" he added, bluntly.

"I don't think you have to ask that, Barry," Amy answered, blushing crimson. I believe you know the answer to that."

"You shouldn't have to ask me these questions either,

Amy. Didn't you believe a word I told you, when we were together?"

"Yes, I do believe you," she confessed, tears coming again to her eyes.

"Then, don't question our relationship together. I don't feel comfortable discussing my intimate relationship with Audrey, even with you, Amy. Would you want me discussing 'our' relationship with someone else?"

"No," she answered, truthfully. She was embarrassed that she had asked him such an intimate thing.

"There is one thing I will tell you. I probably should-n't, but I will. There is one thing that you have given me that Audrey never could. You came to me as a virgin on our wedding day. You know what that meant to me, I have told you. Audrey wasn't able to do that. She regretted it, but she had a fling with someone in college before we met. She was honest with me and told me this before we were married. I respected her for telling me."

"Darling, you make me so proud. Thank you for tell-ing me that." Amy said.

"Now, can we drop the subject?" Barry asked.

She nodded. "I am sorry if I have upset you. I am sorry I left you, Darling. Please forgive me."

"I will, Amy, but I can't keep doing it over and over. Either you choose to accept me and our marriage, or you don't," he said, watching her closely.

Tears filled her eyes and spilled over. "I do want you, Barry. I want our marriage to work. I love you more than life itself," she whispered as she pulled him toward her until their lips met.

Finally, he released her and asked, softly, "Do you plan to sleep in the guest room tonight?"

"Do you want me to?" she answered.

"What do you want to do?" he asked, avoiding her question.

"I want to sleep beside you in our bed," she answered

breathlessly, her heartbeat racing.

For the first time that evening, he showed her the charming smile that she loved so well. His blue eyes looked into her dark ones.

"What are we waiting for?" he asked softly.

He led her to their bedroom and pulled her down beside him on their bed. She sighed deeply as he began kissing her and caressing her. This was where she belonged, she told herself. This was the man she loved with all her heart and soul. She returned his passionate kisses. She didn't think of his first wife a single time. All she could think of was how wonderful it was to be in his arms and how much she wanted to please him as well.

Later, as she lay quietly in Barry's arms, Amy thought of their baby; the baby that he still knew nothing about. A smile spread across her lips and he noticed.

"What are you thinking about right now?" he asked, softly.

She turned slightly, so she could look into his beautiful blue eyes.

"You wouldn't believe me, if I told you," she teased.

"Try me," he said, waiting.

"There's something that I haven't told you," she began.

A shadow crossed his face, for a fleeing moment.

"It's something pleasant," she grinned.

He smiled. "That's a relief. I don't have the energy for anything unpleasant."

She chuckled. "Have I worn you out, Darling?" she teased.

"You certainly have. It's the age difference, you know," he teased.

"That's odd, that you'd bring the subject up. Do you remember telling me once that you weren't getting any younger?" she asked, baiting him.

He looked at her, puzzled. "Yes. What are you leading up to? Have I gotten too old for you now?" he teased.

"I hardly think so! I am wondering how you'll be as a father."

"What?"

"I'm wondering, how you'll be as a father," she repeated.

"What brought that up?" he asked, still puzzled.

"I was lying here thinking about that picture of you that hangs in your bedroom at your Mom's. That little blue-eyed boy watched over me all night long," she said, dreamily.

"You're talking about the picture of me? I'm totally confused," he said, watching her closely.

"I think we'll have a little boy that looks just like you."

"Oh, you do?"

"Yes, I do."

"When do you think this will take place?" he asked, his hold on her tightening. She could feel his heartbeat quickening and wondered if what she was saying was finally sinking in.

"Oh, in less than seven months, probably," she said. She watched as his blue eyes grew wider and the handsomest smile she had ever seen spread across his face. He squeezed her so tightly she could hardly breathe.

"Are you serious?" he asked. "Sweetheart, are you going to have a baby?"

She nodded, tears brimming her eyes. "Yes, Darling. 'We' are going to have a baby. I hope it is a little boy just like his daddy."

"Have I hurt you? I didn't know! You should have told me! Why haven't you told me, Amy?"

She laughed. "I have just told you. No, you have not hurt me. Yes, I should have told you earlier. Any more questions, Darling?" she teased.

He pulled her over on top of him and locked her in a

bear hug. "A baby!" he repeated. "We're going to have a baby!"

"Unless you squeeze me to death first," she squeaked.

He laid her down on the bed beside him, gently. He examined her flat tummy.

"You don't look pregnant. Are you sure? Have you been to the doctor?" he asked.

"More questions?" she teased. "Yes, Darling. I am sure. I have been to the doctor. You are going to be a Papa."

He kissed her softly, a long, lingering kiss.

"Do you know how happy this makes me?" he whispered.

"Probably as happy as it makes me, Darling," she answered.

"I love you so much, Amy. I wouldn't mind if you had a dozen little babies, just like you."

"Hold on now!" she exclaimed. "Not a dozen, please," she said, laughing. "I've already said, I hope it is a little boy that looks like you."

"Are we going to let the doctor tell us what it is, if he knows?" he asked.

"I think I would like for it to be a surprise. What do you think?" she asked.

"Me too. I'd rather not know until it's born. Maybe we'll have a boy and a girl," he grinned.

Amy looked alarmed. "You don't have twins in your family, do you?" she asked, seriously.

He laughed aloud. "No, Sweetheart. I'm just teasing. There aren't any twins that I know of. But, would twins be so bad?"

"That's frightening to think of. I'll settle for one at a time," she said, truthfully.

"Okay, whatever you say," he agreed, humoring her. He hugged her to him again and kept her close as they both slept.

Amy awoke during the night. Her cheek was on Barry's chest. He was sleeping, his heart beating steadily, his arms still encircling her. She was overwhelmed with her love for him. She was thankful that she could give him the gift of love and the gift of a baby. She had seen the happiness in his eyes. She wanted to make him happy, to try to make amends for the heartache she had caused him. She snuggled even closer in his warm embrace. Soon, she was asleep again.

27

***

Amy was happy to be at home again with Barry. She knew that he was happy having her home. Sometime she found him watching her closely and she knew that he still worried about her state of mind. She decided to have Joan help her find a counselor. Joan asked her co-workers and came up with a name. Amy called to make an appointment the following week.

The day of Amy's appointment arrived. She decided to tell Barry about it before he left for work. He had finished his breakfast and was having coffee when Amy told him that she had an appointment at two p.m.

"I'm glad to hear it," Barry said. "Do you want me to go with you, Sweetheart?"

"Not this time, but thank you for offering. I will be fine."

"Okay. I'm willing to go any time the doctor thinks I need to, or when you want me to."

"Don't you worry about me, Darling. I'll be here when you get home this evening." She kissed him goodbye before he left for work.

Amy was nervous as she entered the counselor's office. She almost changed her mind before the receptionist escorted her inside. The doctor was an elderly man in his sixties. He shook her hand cordially.

"Mrs. Reeser, I am Dr. Simpson. I am happy to meet you. Please have a seat."

Amy sat in a comfortable, over-stuffed chair directly across from the doctor. She thought the room was charming, decorated in blues and grays and mauve. The doctor began by asking Amy to tell him about herself. At first she was shy talking about herself, but he encouraged her by asking specific questions. Soon, she felt at ease with him and began to enjoy talking to him. Before she realized it her time was gone and it was time for her to leave. She made her next weekly appointment and was already looking forward to it.

Amy's next appointment with Dr. Simpson was even more comfortable for her. She answered his personal questions and then he asked her about the problem that had brought her there. She tried to explain her feelings concerning the memory of Audrey and related to him the problems those feelings caused. He asked her questions about her intimate relationship with Barry. Although she found herself blushing, she told him how fulfilling her relationship was with Barry. Dr. Simpson told her that he wanted to talk to Barry later and asked her if Barry would be willing to come. She assured him that he would.

When Barry met with Dr. Simpson, the doctor asked him some of the same questions that he had asked Amy. Barry answered them willingly until he began to probe into his intimate relationship with Amy and Audrey. Barry hesitated to answer some of the questions.
Finally, he addressed the doctor. "Doctor, I appreciate your concern and I respect your integrity. However, I will not discuss with you, my sexual relationship with Audrey or with Amy. I will say that the relationship I had with Audrey pales in comparison to my relationship with Amy."

"I understand, Mr. Reeser. You have told me what I need to know."

"I love Amy more than I can describe," Barry continued. "Her happiness means everything to me. I would never hurt her, intentionally. I am sure that she told you about the problem that started all this, my calling her 'Audrey'."

"Yes, she did," the doctor answered.

"I regret that, but it can't be undone. Surely, I am not the first person to make that mistake."

"No, Sir. You are not the first, I assure you," Dr. Simpson said. "Now that I have talked to both of you, I feel that the problem can be resolved without much difficulty. I believe as time goes on Amy will stop focusing on the past and will focus on your future together and focus on the coming baby. She seems happy about the baby, doesn't she?"

"Yes, definitely. She seems very content now and looking forward to the birth of the baby."

"That's good," the doctor said. "I want to continue Amy's sessions. I don't believe it will be necessary to see you again, Mr. Reeser. I believe that you have your wife's welfare as your top priority and I believe that you sincerely love her. If you will give her some time, I believe that she will soon forget about your previous wife."

"I hope you are right, doctor," Barry said, getting up to go. "Feel free to call me if you need to."

"I will, I assure you." He shook hands with Barry and added, "Best wishes to both of you."

"Thank you, Sir," Barry said.

28

***

Amy continued her sessions with Dr. Simpson for five months. By that time she seemed perfectly happy with Barry. She never mentioned Audrey's name again. She told Barry that Dr. Simpson suggested that she discontinue the sessions for a while. He felt that Amy was doing fine and that she could concentrate on the coming baby.

Barry was pleased with the results that Dr. Simpson had achieved with Amy. He could see the difference in her after a few weeks.

As the months passed, Amy blossomed as the baby grew. At seven months she began to restrict her activities, considerably. She began to see the gynecologist more often as he required.

29

***

Barry decided to take Amy out to dinner one evening instead of her having to cook. He was even more considerate of her now, as she grew large with the baby and seemed to be more uncomfortable. They had come home from the restaurant and Amy was lying down, resting. She was trying to find a comfortable position but couldn't. Barry grinned, watching her tossing about.

"Sweetheart, I am sorry you are so miserable," he said, kindly. "If I could carry that 'boy' for a while, I would."

Amy glared at him, but her eyes were twinkling."

"That 'boy' of ours may be a girl, you know," she said.

Barry chuckled. "We'll know in a few weeks, won't we?" he teased. He lay down beside her and gently stroked the round mound of her stomach that was their baby. He kissed her on the nose and she hugged him tightly.

"I miss being closer to you, Barry," she said, wearily. "You know I love you, don't you, Darling?"

"I know I am loved," he teased. "Don't worry, after this baby gets here, we'll make up for lost time, I promise."

She snuggled closer to him and stroked his dark hair

and strong jaw. She looked into his blue eyes and saw the love there.

"I am so lucky to have you, Barry," she said, softly. "You are so kind and gentle. I know all men can't be this gentle. I remember seeing Arthur Morgan slap his wife."

Barry frowned. "Don't think of Arthur Morgan, Amy," he said, seriously.

"I can't help it. He just popped into my head."

"Let him 'pop right back out'!" Barry instructed. He kissed her softly. Looking into her dark eyes he saw her smiling at him. "What are you thinking of now?" he asked.

"You don't have to wait until after the baby comes," she teased. She raised his shirt and planted a warm kiss on the curly hair of his chest and trailed her ruby lips down his stomach. He ran his fingers through her dark, flowing hair that cascaded over his body. He forgot about whatever it was that they had been discussing.

30

***

Two months later, Amy awoke during the night. She knew that something unusual had awakened her. She lay very still. Barry was sleeping soundly beside her. She felt an aching sensation begin low in her back. It seemed to build in intensity until a searing pain crossed her abdomen. She winced with the sharpness of the pain. She looked at the clock in the darkness. The illuminated digits showed that it was twelve-thirty. Her due date was in three more days. She knew that this could be her labor beginning. She didn't want to wake Barry until she was sure that this was the real thing. She watched the clock. Fifteen minutes later she again, felt the ache begin in her lower back and pierce through to her abdomen. The pain was sharper this time. She had chosen to have the baby 'naturally', never realizing what it would be like. Barry had trained to be her 'coach'. They had attended natural birth classes together. At fifteen minute intervals, she watched the clock for an hour, and then she woke Barry. He was awake, instantly when he heard her voice.

"Sweetheart, what's wrong?" he asked, concerned.

"I think I'm in labor," she answered. "I have timed the contractions for an hour. They are coming every fifteen minutes."

Barry got out of bed quickly and dressed. Amy was sitting on the side of the bed but had to lie down when another contraction began. She groaned aloud with this one.

Barry's blue eyes revealed his concern for her. "I need to call your doctor," he said, flipping through the index of names. His hands were trembling as he dialed the number.

The doctor's answering service answered. The lady instructed him to take Amy to the hospital immediately when Barry explained the circumstances.

Amy was having another contraction. "Barry, it hurts really bad!" she exclaimed, when she could catch her breath again. "I didn't know it would hurt so much!"

"I'm sorry, Sweetheart," he said, soothingly. "Let me help you get dressed. We've got to get you to the hospital." He reached for her robe and helped her put it on. He put her shoes on her feet, and grabbed up her suitcase that had been packed for two months. Before they could get to the door, Amy was having another contraction. She stopped walking and held tightly to Barry.

"Ohhhhh....." she groaned, holding her stomach.

When her pain subsided, she continued on to the car. It was a ten- minute drive to the hospital. By the time they arrived, Barry was perspiring in the November night. When they arrived at the emergency room a nurse met them with a wheel chair.

"We'll take her to the 'birthing room'. You'll need to move your car, Sir."

"Move my car?" Barry asked, blankly.

"Yes, Sir. You can't leave it in the emergency entrance."

"Oh, okay. I'll be right back, Sweetheart," he addressed Amy. When he returned, Amy was in a room with monitors already hooked up.

"I understand that you're having your baby natural,"

the nurse said to Amy.

"Yes," she managed to say.

"Are you her coach, Mr. Reeser?" she asked.

"Yes, I am. Is there something that I need to do now?"

"Encourage her to do her rhythmic breathing and you can begin to massage her back as she has her contractions."

"How long will it be before the baby is born?" Barry asked.

The nurse chuckled. "It will be quite a while, yet, Mr. Reeser. She has only dilated four centimeters. She has to dilate ten centimeters."

Barry brushed Amy's damp hair from her brow and kissed her lightly. "Let me rub your back, Sweetheart," he said, tenderly. He massaged Amy's lower back as her contractions began. He watched the monitor that showed her contractions peaking and subsiding. He tried to encourage her by telling her when they were beginning to peak and then recede.

"Sweetheart, you need to breathe the way they taught you, when you have a contraction," Barry said, encouraging her.

Amy was perspiring and her dark hair stuck to her face. "I'm hot, Barry. I want a drink of water."

"I'll have to ask the nurse," Barry replied.

The nurse heard and replied, "Amy, you can only have a sip." She handed Barry a cool, wet cloth and said, "You can use this to bathe her face." She gave Amy a sip of water.

Amy saw the concern on Barry's face as her contractions began again. She tried to do her rhythmic breathing, but it was hard to concentrate. Time dragged on for her. Her body was racked with pain as the contractions came closer and harder until they were five minutes apart. The nurse checked her progress often.

"How much longer, nurse?" Barry asked, his eyes

mirroring the pain he bore for Amy's agony.

"She's coming along fine, Mr. Reeser. You've dilated eight centimeters, Amy. Just keep doing your breathing exercise."

"I need something for pain. I don't think I can stand this much longer," Amy said, weakly.

"I'm sorry, Honey," the nurse answered. "You're too far along now. If I give you something, it might stop your contractions. You sure don't want that, do you?"

"I'm sorry, Sweetheart," Barry said, concerned. He stroked her lower back gently, trying to relieve her pain.

Amy groaned as another contraction began to peak. She squirmed on the bed, in agony. When she began to cry as her contractions became harder, she knew that Barry could hardly bear it. Tears streamed down his own cheeks and he had to turn away to wipe his eyes. He could no longer massage her back but tried to hold her hand or wipe her face.

"Why can't they give me something for pain?" she asked angrily, between contractions.

"Sweetheart, she told you why. Please try to endure it. Surely it can't be much longer. I wish I could bear the pain for you," he said, truthfully.

She looked at him, angrily. She wasn't angry with him, she was angry with the nurses. "I want to see my doctor!" she said to the nurse.

"He will be here shortly, Amy. You have dilated nine centimeters. Just one more to go," the nurse answered.

Soon, the doctor appeared. He spoke to Barry and went directly to Amy to examine her. "You're coming along fine, young lady," he said, patting Amy tenderly. "You'll soon have that big boy."

Barry looked at him, surprised. Amy saw his expression and smiled.

"He says it will be a boy, like you, Darling," she said to Barry.

"I've got 'the inside scoop'," the doctor said, grinning.

Amy gasped as another contraction was upon her. She squeezed Barry's hand until it hurt. She groaned as she tried to bear the pain, writhing in agony. The doctor was examining her.

"I can see the baby's head, Amy. I want you to push with your next contraction. Now!" the doctor instructed.

Barry watched helplessly as Amy strained to help push the baby out.

Amy cried out and the doctor said, "The head's out, Amy. One more push, for the shoulders to come out. You're doing fine." Then, he announced "It's a boy!" He held up a wiggling, crying baby for Amy and Barry to see.

Amy burst into tears of joy and reached for the baby. Tears were streaming down Barry's cheeks. The nurse wrapped the baby in a blue blanket and laid him on Amy's chest. Amy held the baby, gently, taking in all of his features. Barry watched in awe, unable to see clearly because of the tears in his eyes. He touched the baby's hand and the baby curled his hand around Barry's finger. Barry's face broke into a broad smile. Amy was aware, for the first time, of what he had just gone through, with her. His face was strained and she realized he was crying. She reached for him with one hand and pulled him closer.

"You were right, Darling. We have our baby 'boy'."

"Thank you for our baby boy," he said, kissing her softly. "I love you so much, Amy."

"Meet your father, little one," Amy said, cuddling the baby close.

The doctor interrupted them to take the baby. He handed the baby to the nurse. "Time to get him cleaned up and finish with you, young lady," he said. "We'll have him back with you, shortly."

"Sweetheart, I need to call Mom and Dad to tell them about the baby. I'll be back in a few minutes," Barry said, leaning over and kissing her once again.

"Be sure to tell your dad that we are naming him 'David' for him," Amy said.

"I will. See you soon."

When Barry came back from calling his parents, Amy was in her own room. She was sitting up in bed with a fresh gown on and her hair had been combed and fluffed. When she saw him, she smiled and reached for him. He seemed relieved to see her looking better. Barry leaned over and took her in his arms. He buried his face in her damp hair. She made him raise his head and look into her eyes. She saw tears in his eyes.

"Are you all right, Darling?" she asked.

"I am now, since I know that you are. I am so sorry that you suffered so."

"It was worth it. We have a beautiful little boy, but I am very, very tired and sleepy. I wonder if they will bring him to me soon?" she asked.

"Why don't you rest now and go to sleep? I'll be right here," he said.

She closed her eyes even before he finished talking. Soon, she was sleeping soundly.

Barry tried to relax in the chair beside Amy's bed. He realized that he was exhausted, himself. He closed his eyes and kept seeing the baby in his mind. When the nurse brought the baby, he was fretting. Barry was instantly alert. The nurse saw that Amy was asleep.

"I hate to wake her," she said, "but this little fellow is ready to eat." She shook Amy gently. Amy opened her eyes slowly. When she saw the baby she was awake instantly. She reached for him and the nurse placed him in her arms.

"You are breast feeding him, aren't you?" she asked.

"Yes," Amy answered.

"That's good. That's better for the baby," the nurse said.

The baby began to nuzzle his tiny, pink mouth about, looking for nourishment. Barry watched, intrigued, as Amy placed the baby to her breast and he began to suckle. Barry thought it was the most beautiful sight he had ever seen. The baby's dark, curly hair was a contrast to Amy's pale, silky skin.

"You won't actually have your milk for three days," the nurse said, "but this nourishment he gets now is very important for him. I wish more mothers would breast feed their babies. Call me, if you need anything," she said as she left the room.

When the baby was nursing contentedly, making soft, gulping noises, Amy looked across to find Barry watching them, his blue eyes shining. "Come closer," Amy said, smiling.

He pulled his chair as close as he could and leaning over, played with the baby's soft, curly locks of hair. "He's beautiful!" he exclaimed, grinning proudly.

"He looks like you, Darling," Amy said.

"You think so?" he asked.

"Of course, see the dark hair and blue eyes?" she teased.

"I guess he does," Barry said, grinning broadly. "By the way, Mom and Dad said they were coming right away. They were excited and said to give you their love."

"That's good. This is their first grandchild, you know."

When the baby stopped nursing and was asleep, Amy touched his soft, tiny chin to wake him. He began to nurse again. She was overcome with love for him and cuddled his warm, little body closer.

"Just think, Darling, we made this precious little baby together, with our love. He is part of each of us," she said, softly.

"Yes, it is amazing, isn't it?" Barry said, his face beaming.

After a while the nurse came to get the baby to take him to the nursery. Barry dozed in his chair while Amy slept soundly.

Barry awoke and couldn't go back to sleep. He paced the floor, wondering when the nurse would bring the baby back to the room. He decided to walk to the nursery to see him. When he got there, the curtains were closed. Then, he walked to the nurse's station down the hall.

"Excuse me," he said, addressing a nurse, "I am Amy Reeser's husband. She is in room 303. It has been over two hours since our baby was brought to my wife. Can you tell me when she can have the baby again?"

The nurse looked at the chart. She glanced at another nurse before she answered. "Mr. Reeser, your baby has started running a low-grade temperature. It's nothing to be alarmed about, I'm sure. We feel that it would be best to keep him in the nursery until his next feeding."

"Why would the baby be having a temperature?" Barry asked, alarmed.

"We're not sure, Mr. Reeser. We have called the doctor and he has told us to keep him posted if there is any change."

"What should I tell my wife? This is going to upset her, considerably," Barry said.

"I will bring the baby shortly, Sir, for his feeding. He has been fretting and is probably hungry again. I will explain to her about the temperature," the nurse said.

"Thank you," Barry said, his brow creased with 'worry lines'. When he entered Amy's room, he found her awake.

"Barry, where have you been?" she asked. "Did you go see the baby?"

"I went to the nursery, but the curtains are closed. They only open them at six in the evening, according to the sign," he answered.

"They can bring David to me anytime. He should be

getting hungry."

"The nurse said they would be bringing him shortly," Barry said.

Amy noticed the worried look on Barry's face that he couldn't conceal.

"What's wrong, Darling?" Amy asked.

"What?" he said, evading her question.

"Something is wrong, I can tell. Is it the baby?" she asked, alarmed.

Barry hurried to her side. "Sweetheart, the baby is running a temperature."

"How much of a temperature?" she interrupted.

At that moment the nurse brought the baby in for his feeding. Amy was relieved to see him although he was fretting. She took him from the nurse and began to talk to him, soothingly, caressing his warm cheek. He nuzzled her breast, wanting to nurse and began to cry.

"There, there, Sweetie Pie," Amy crooned, "don't cry, Mommy is right here." She placed him at her breast and he began to suckle. "Why does he have a temperature?" She asked the nurse.

"We don't know, Mrs. Reeser. Sometime babies do that. Sometime the trauma of the birth canal and their swallowing too much mucus causes it. We are watching him closely. It is only ninety- nine degrees now, but we don't want him having any temperature, do we?" she said, smiling.

"He seems okay," Barry said, tracing the baby's chubby cheek with his finger.

"He will be fine, I am sure," the nurse assured them. "He is nursing well."

"He seems to be," Barry grinned as he heard tiny, gulping sounds coming from David.

Amy continued to talk soothingly to David as he nursed. Barry took his tiny hand and it closed around his large finger, again.

Barry smiled at Amy. "He seems okay, don't you think?" he asked, softly.

"Our Sweetie Pie is going to be fine, Daddy," she said, smiling sweetly at Barry.

When David finished nursing, he was fretful again.

"He probably needs to burp," the nurse said. "Put him on your shoulder and pat him gently."

Amy did as she was instructed. Soon, a soft, 'burp' erupted from the baby's pink mouth.

"He liked that," Barry said, chuckling.

Amy laid the baby across her lap and he was content. He closed his eyes and was asleep again.

"I will leave the baby with you for a while, if you'd like for me to," the nurse said. "I will have to come to get him before long to check his temperature again."

"Yes, I want to keep him," Amy said, reluctant to part with him even though she was tired. When the nurse was gone, she asked Barry, "Would you like to hold your son?"

"You know I would," he said, grinning, "but he seems so tiny!"

"He weighs seven pounds, four ounces," Amy said, "and he is 21 inches long."

"That still seems tiny," Barry chuckled, "but let me hold him." He took David from Amy and watched as he wiggled and stretched in his arms. Then, he was sound asleep again. Barry sat down gently, holding David in his arms. Amy watched the expression on Barry's face as he looked at their son. He was beaming.

"I'm glad that we didn't wait any longer to have a baby," Barry said, softly. "Look what we have been missing!"

"I know," Amy said. "He is so precious."

"Look at his tiny little hands and feet, so perfect, like a miniature adult," Barry continued.

"He's amazing, isn't he?" Amy agreed.

Soon, the nurse came to get David to take him back to

the nursery.

"You rest, Sweetheart," Barry encouraged her. "You've been through a lot. I will keep an eye on our boy." He kissed her warmly and tucked the sheet around her.

Amy closed her eyes and was soon sleeping soundly. Barry got up and walked to the nursery. The curtain was still closed, but he paced back and forth, listening. He could hear the faint cry of more than one baby. He wondered if one of them was David.

Finally, the same nurse that had been with Amy came out of the nursery. She seemed surprised to find him in the hallway.

"Mr. Reeser, the visiting hours for the nursery aren't until six," she said.

"I know. I am just killing time, letting my wife sleep right now."

"I see," she said, skeptically.

"Nurse, did you take David's temperature again?" Barry asked before she could leave.

She hesitated a moment. "Yes, Mr. Reeser. I am sorry to say it is one hundred degrees now."

"What? What are you going to do? It's getting higher!"

"I realize that. I have a call in to the doctor. He has already gone for the day."

"Isn't there another doctor you can call until you locate my wife's doctor?"

"Yes, Sir, there is. He has already ordered Tylenol for the fever. I just gave it to the baby."

"Is that him I hear crying?" Barry asked, concerned.

The nurse looked annoyed. "Mr. Reeser, we are doing everything we can for the baby, I assure you. If you will excuse me, I have other patients to attend to." She left him standing in the hallway.

Barry could still hear babies crying in the nursery. He wanted to jerk the door open and find David. Instead, he walked to the nurses' station.

"Excuse me, nurse," he said. "I want to see my baby in the nursery."

A different nurse looked up from her work, a look of disbelief on her face. "Pardon me?" she said.

"I'm Barry Reeser. My wife is Amy. She gave birth to a baby boy earlier today. He is in the nursery. I want to see him."

The nurse searched for David's chart, read something on it and looked up at Barry. "Your baby is confined to the nursery right now. You cannot go in there."

"Bring him outside the nursery for a moment so I can see him," Barry insisted.

"Sir, that is not possible right now! He is fine."

"He is 'not' fine! He has a temperature of one hundred! I want to see him, myself!"

"Who told you that?" she snapped.

"Does he, or doesn't he, have a temperature?" Barry asked, about to lose control.

"Well…, yes. You are out of line, Mr. Reeser! I suggest that you calm down and go back to your wife's room. You do not need to upset yourself or her. A lot of babies have a temperature at one time or another."

Barry stared at her coldly. His hands were trembling from the mounting anger inside him.

"Maam," he said, calmly and coldly, "I am not going anywhere until you let me see David. Do you understand?"

The nurse stared back at him, coldly. "Sir, you are causing a scene!"

"No, Maam, I am not causing a scene. But, I definitely could!" he said, his blue eyes a cold gray.

She snorted under her breath. Grabbing a keypad, she snapped, "Very well! Follow me! I will let you see your baby for just a moment." She stomped down the hallway and Barry followed her to the nursery. Her attitude angered Barry even more.

At the nursery door the nurse stopped. "You wait here. I will bring the baby out for a moment." She disappeared inside. After a few moments she appeared at the door holding David. He was crying.

"Let me hold him," Barry said evenly, as he took him from the nurse.

"There, there, big boy," he soothed, rocking the baby gently in his arms. For a few seconds David quit crying but began again. Barry touched the baby's brow with his lips.

"He's hot," he said to the nurse.

"Yes, I know," she answered. "I should take him back now. He will cool down when the Tylenol has time to take effect."

"I suggest that you locate my wife's doctor or a pediatrician," Barry said, levelly.

"Mr. Reeser, we are doing our best for this child!"

"Your 'best' is not good enough," Barry retorted.

The nurse reached for David and Barry gave him back to her, reluctantly.

"Mr. Reeser, please calm down and return to your wife. I hope you do not alarm her, also."

Barry said nothing. He simply stared at her until she disappeared through the doorway, closing the door behind her. He felt miserable. He wanted to vent his anger somehow but knew that he couldn't. He had never felt so helpless. He needed someone to talk to. He thought of his father, but he knew that he and his mother were already on their way to the hospital. He dropped change into the pay phone and dialed Captain Adams' number, without thinking. When the captain answered, Barry related to him everything that was going on and unloaded his frustrations on him.

When Barry paused long enough for the captain to speak, Captain Adams said, "Barry, I'll be there in ten minutes." He hung up the phone.

Barry hung up the receiver and then remembered that

they hadn't even told Joan about the baby's birth. He glanced at his watch. It was already five p.m. He picked up the phone again, dropped more change in and dialed Joan's number. When she answered he told her about the baby's birth and that Amy was fine.

"You sound tired," Joan teased after she congratulated him. "Were you two up all night?"

"No, just half the night." Then, before he realized it, he was telling her about the baby's problem.

"Oh, no, Barry!" she exclaimed. "He's going to be okay, isn't he? What does the doctor say?"

"I haven't even seen a damn doctor!" he exclaimed. "I'm sorry, Joan. I'm angry right now. I don't mean to vent my frustration on you."

"Barry, you and Amy need someone with you right now to help you through this. I'm coming up there. I'll be there in a few minutes."

"Thanks, Joan. Maybe you can cheer Amy when she wakes. She is going to be worse than I am if they don't let her see the baby." Somehow, Barry felt better after having vented his frustrations on Captain Adams and Joan. As he hung up the phone he saw the captain walking toward him in the hallway. He met him, half way. They shook hands warmly and the captain patted Barry on his shoulder, affectionately.

"How about having a cup of coffee with me, Barry? It might help you unwind," Captain Adams said.

"Okay, first let me look in on Amy to see if she is still sleeping."

The captain followed Barry to Amy's room. When they peered in they saw that she was sleeping soundly.

"Good, she was exhausted," Barry whispered as he closed the door to Amy's room.

They went to the cafeteria for coffee and were sitting there talking, when they saw Joan waiting for the elevator. They intercepted her.

"Hello, Joan," Barry said. "I wanted to warn you that Amy is sleeping. Also, she doesn't know the latest about David's temperature still rising. Nor, does she know about my encounter with the nurses," he continued.

"I won't say a word," Joan said, hugging him suddenly. Her eyes were moist. "I am sorry that you two are having to go through this. Hello, Captain Adams," she said, belatedly.

"Hello, Joan. Good to see you again," the captain said.

"I'm going to her room now. I won't wake her if she is still asleep," Joan announced, as she stepped into the elevator.

Barry tried to relax as he talked to Captain Adams, but he was too worried about the baby. He decided to wait until the nursery window was open at six before going back to Amy's room. He wanted to see the baby again. They finished their coffee and took the elevator up. Then, they walked to the nursery window. Promptly at six a nurse opened the curtain. Other families gathered around peering inside to see their babies. Barry scanned the interior of the nursery looking for David. There were five babies in the nursery, three with blue, 'boy' tags on the beds. He spotted David's dark, curly hair and pink cherub face. He was crying, kicking his tiny feet and flailing his arms in the air. Barry pointed him out to the captain.

"He has an IV in his little hand," Barry said, concerned. "He didn't have that before."

"He's a fine looking boy, Barry," Captain Adams said, smiling. "They're probably giving him medication through the IV."

As they stood watching, a nurse walked up to David's bed. She had a large syringe in her hand.

"My God!" Captain Adams exclaimed, "Look at the size of that syringe!"

They watched as the nurse pushed the needle into

David's IV. Instantly, the baby's body jerked, his arms stiffening in the air. The nurse looked shocked. Staring at the baby, and then at the syringe, she suddenly yanked the IV loose from the baby's hand and grabbed him up in her arms. She held him above her head, shaking him gently. The baby's mouth bubbled with foam. Barry's knees almost buckled beneath him. He grabbed the window- sill for support.

"Oh, my God!" a lady behind them exclaimed aloud. "Did you see that? Something happened to that baby over there!"

Barry and Captain Adams were speechless, in a state of shock as the nurse disappeared into the back of the nursery carrying David. Suddenly, the nurses' loud speaker boomed, announcing 'code blue' to the nursery.

"I'm going in there!" Barry exclaimed, recovering enough to speak. He lunged for the door and found it locked. He pounded on it, loudly.

"Wait, Barry! There's another entrance to the nursery. I saw another door," Captain Adams said. Taking Barry's arm, he forced him away from the locked door.

Terror that Barry felt inside was mirrored on his face. He stared at the captain blankly as he led him down the hallway to the next door.

"This should be where the nurse disappeared to," Captain Adams said. He tried the door and it was, also locked. He knocked soundly and waited.

Barry knocked loudly. "This is not working!" he said weakly.

At that moment, a young doctor came running down the hall and stopped at the door beside Barry and Captain Adams.

"Excuse me, please! Please stand back!" he instructed as he used his touch pad code to unlock the door. As he entered the nursery Barry and Captain Adams pushed their way inside before the door closed behind him. No one noticed as they inched their way into the nursery. They saw a cluster of nurses gathered around a table where the tiny baby lay. The baby wasn't even crying and hardly moved. Barry started to call out to them, but Captain Adams stopped him.

"Wait, Barry! Don't distract them," he whispered. "Let them do whatever they can for the baby!"

Barry stared at the captain, his breath coming in raspy gulps. He felt as though his heart was going to explode, but he listened to the captain and was silent.

"What have you done?" they heard the doctor exclaim. "What dosage did you give him?"

The nurse's face was chalky. "Six hundred thousand. That's what the pharmacy sent up," she answered, weakly.

"That's a hundred times too much! Didn't you question the order?" the doctor snapped.

"No, Sir. Well, yes, Sir, I did. I called down to the pharmacy and they said it was correct. So, I administered it."

"Idiot!" the doctor snapped. "You knew it was wrong!"

The nurse's face grew even paler.

Barry could hold his fury no longer. He lunged for the baby, pushing the startled doctor and nurse aside. "Get out of my way! Let me see my baby!" he exclaimed. "What have you done to him?"

The doctor's face turned red as he said, "What are you doing in here? Get out of here! Nurse, get this man out of here!"

Cold fury surged through Barry. He grabbed the doctor by the collar. Looking him straight in the eye, his voice was calm and cold as he said, "How dare you order me out. That's my son you've probably killed! I saw it all! If he dies, so help me God, someone will wish he were dead!"

For a moment the doctor was speechless and his face paled. Finally, he said, weakly,

"Turn me loose, if you expect me to save your boy."

Captain Adams was at Barry's side. He put a hand on Barry's shoulder. Barry dropped his hands to his side. He stared at his lifeless son and felt of his tiny, warm body. He realized that David was still breathing, but it was shallow.

The doctor snapped orders to the nurses and they began to scurry around following his instructions. The doctor turned to Barry.

"Sir, please let us attend to your child. If you will please wait outside, I promise that you can see him as soon as possible. It is imperative that we try to reverse the damage that has been done. I will come to talk to you even before you see the boy."

Barry hesitated and Captain Adams tugged at his arm. "Barry, he's right. Let's leave them alone and let them help David."

Reluctantly, Barry backed away and allowed Captain Adams to escort him into the hallway. Once there, Barry leaned against the wall, his head buried in his arms. He lost control of his taut nerves and began to sob, uncontrollably.

Captain Adams put his arm around him trying to console him. "Barry, don't give up. The boy is going to make it! I just know he is!"

"What damage will have been done? What did they give him and why? I have to know!" Barry said, trying to get control.

"We'll find out soon, when the doctor comes out," Captain Adams said.

"I'm not budging from this spot," Barry said, watching the closed door.

Barry and Captain Adams paced the floor, waiting. Moments seemed like hours before the doctor emerged. Barry was at his side instantly.

The doctor looked tired, his face drawn. "Mr. Reeser, your son is stable. I believe he is going to be all right."

"What did the nurse give him that did this?" Barry

questioned.

"I ordered penicillin and potassium. The dosage got messed up. The pharmacist or the nurse added too many zeros. The boy got a hundred times the amount prescribed."

"For Christ's sake!" Barry swore. "How could anyone be so careless? What damage has been done?" he demanded to know.

"We won't know for some time. It could take as long as five years," the doctor said, reluctantly.

"Five years! What kind of damage are you talking about? You'd better level with me, doctor! Somebody is going to pay for this mistake! What have you done to reverse the damage?" Barry demanded.

"We're giving him enemas to draw out the potassium," the doctor said.

"For the love of God!" Captain Adams said, disbelieving.

"You're putting that child through hell!" Barry exclaimed, hurting inside at the thought of it. "You still haven't answered my question. What type of damage are you talking about?"

The doctor was evading the question. Under Barry's direct gaze he had to answer, truthfully. "The boy has a small blood clot on the left side of his brain. That side controls the right side of his body. There may have been minor damage that controls his motor skills on that side. We have no way of knowing the extent of the damage until he fails to do what he should normally do at any given age."

"How do you know about the blood clot?" Barry asked coldly, furious inside.

"We did a CT scan on the boy," the doctor answered.

"When? You didn't leave that room!"

"There is another hallway, Mr. Reeser, from the nursery. It leads to various treatment rooms."

"I want to see my son, now!"

"Of course," the doctor agreed, quickly. "Follow me."

Barry and Captain Adams followed the doctor inside, where they found David sleeping in the tiny bed. A nurse was sitting by his side with David's chart in her hand. She looked up and smiled as they entered.

"His temperature has gone down, Dr. Jones. He is sleeping comfortably now," the nurse said.

"That's good news," the doctor said.

"Would he be better off at Children's Hospital?" Barry asked.

"I don't believe that they could give him any better care than he is receiving now," the doctor answered. "However, if you'd like a second opinion, feel free to do whatever you feel is necessary, Mr. Reeser."

"I want a pediatrician to check him, to be sure. Can you arrange for one to come from Children's?" Barry asked.

"Of course."

Barry caressed David's tiny body, feeling his plump cheek with his finger. The baby stirred slightly and stretched. Then, he settled down and was still, breathing evenly. He had an IV in his tiny hand once again. Tears filled Barry's eyes. He ached to hold his son.

"What are you doing about feeding him? He should be starving now." Barry said.

"He has been given supplementary feedings. It won't interfere with his mother's breast- feeding. He should be able to nurse when he awakes to eat again," the doctor answered.

"What am I going to tell his mother? She is not aware of what has happened to him," Barry asked the doctor.

"That is up to you, Sir. I leave that to your discretion. It is certainly not in her best interest to upset her, especially with her nursing the baby. It could possibly interfere with her ability to produce milk for the baby."

"Are you serious?" Barry asked, surprised.

"I am, Sir. New mothers are very emotional and sensitive. It is important that they stay calm and eat the correct foods. Everything about their body affects the production of their milk. Therefore, everything affects the baby."

"Are you saying not to tell her, Doctor?" Barry asked.

"I am suggesting that you wait a while, Mr. Reeser," he answered.

"He's right, Barry," Captain Adams said.

Barry watched the baby for a few more minutes. Finally he said, "I won't tell my wife right away…. as long as David continues to improve. I don't want any more complications. I'm sure she is distraught by now, wondering how the baby is and why he hasn't been brought to her."

"Barry, she is probably wondering where you are," Captain Adams reminded.

"I am sure she is," Barry answered. "Doctor, as soon as the baby is able, I want him brought to his mother."

"He will be I assure you. In fact, if your wife feels well enough, she can come in here now and sit with the baby and hold him."

"I will tell her," Barry said, relieved at the thought.

As Barry and Captain Adams entered Amy's room they found Barry's parents and Joan with her. As they greeted them, Amy interrupted.

"Barry, where have you been? Have you seen the nurse? Why hasn't she brought David to me? He must be starved!"

Barry went to her side and planted a kiss on her brow.

"Calm down, Sweetheart. Everything is under control," he said, forcing a smile. "The baby's fever has gone down, but they want to keep him under close observation in the nursery. You are allowed to go in and hold him if you want to."

"Of course I want to! He probably needs to nurse.

He's probably starved!"

"I believe they fed him something," Barry said, reluctantly.

"I don't want them to do that! I don't want him to get used to a bottle," Amy said.

"They said that you can nurse him when he wakes up to eat next time."

"Okay," Amy said, relieved.

Barry felt Amy watching him. He knew that he looked strained and tired. He had slept very little since they came to the hospital.

Barry's mother spoke, interrupting his thoughts.

"Amy, if you want to go to the nursery to be with your baby, go right ahead. We need to go to the lobby anyway, before they run us out of here."

"Thank you, Mrs. Reeser. I would like to be with David."

Barry's parents, Joan and Captain Adams went to the lobby as Barry and Amy walked to the nursery. The curtain was closed for the night. Barry knocked on the door that they had used before. A nurse came to the door. Recognizing Barry, she stepped aside for him to escort Amy inside. Looking around for David, Amy saw him and hurried to his side.

"Oh, my baby! They have an IV in your little hand! My poor baby," she said, touching his tiny arm. "It looks so uncomfortable."

Barry was at her side. "It's necessary, Sweetheart. It's probably not as uncomfortable as it looks, is it, nurse?"

"No, Sir. It's just for precautionary measures. We'll be able to take it out soon, hopefully," the nurse said.

The nurse placed a rocking chair beside the baby bed for Amy. "You may sit here, Mrs. Reeser. I will get the baby for you."

Amy sat down and waited as the nurse picked up David, careful to keep his IV lines intact. She placed the baby in Amy's arms. David stretched and yawned and opened his eyes.

"Hello, Sweetie Pie," Amy crooned. "Have you missed Mommy? Mommy is right here."

Barry wiped tears from his eyes as he watched Amy and David. He knew that the baby was too young to focus his eyes yet, but David seemed to know her voice and stared at her.

"You're such a handsome little boy," Amy said softly, toying with his dark curls. "You're going to be as handsome as your daddy, little one." She looked up at Barry and saw the tears in his eyes. "Come here, Daddy," she said and drew him close as he squatted beside the rocking chair. "Let your little boy see his daddy, Darling."

Overcome with emotion and strain, Barry got up quickly, turning his back to her. When he regained his composure he turned back to her.

Amy was watching him, a confused expression on her face.

"I'm so happy to see both of you together and you're all right," he managed to say.

"Of course we're all right, aren't we, little David? See, Darling, he doesn't have a temperature any more. He's just warm, like he is supposed to be. Our baby is going to be fine," she smiled.

Barry squatted beside her again and planted a kiss on top of the baby's head. Then, he kissed Amy on the cheek. "Sweetheart, you stay here with the baby as long as you want. I'll go to the lobby and see the folks. I'll come back in a little while."

"Okay, Darling," she said, gently rocking the baby.

Barry walked to the lobby where he found his parents and Captain Adams and Joan. He knew that Captain Adams had not told the others about the baby. He explained to them what had happened. He related to them that David seemed okay at the moment and that he was in his mother's arms. Mrs. Reeser began to cry and Barry's father had to comfort her. After a while, his parents decided to go out to Barry and Amy's home for the night. Then, Captain Adams left and only Joan remained.

"Barry," Joan asked, concerned, "Have you eaten at all, today?"

"I guess not," he admitted, "how could I?"

"You need to eat something. Is the cafeteria still open?" she asked.

"Probably," he answered, not feeling hungry at all.

"Will you come with me and eat something?" Joan asked. "I will eat with you."

"If you insist," he smiled, reluctantly.

"I insist," she said, returning his smile.

Together, they went to the cafeteria. When Barry saw and smelled the appetizing food he realized that he was hungry after all. He ate a hearty meal and Joan ate a salad. Afterwards, he felt better. He was finally able to relax as he drank a cup of coffee with her.

"When are you going home, Barry?" Joan asked.

He looked surprised at her question. "I'm staying here tonight. I wouldn't sleep a wink if I went home."

"I figured you'd say that," Joan said, smiling at him. "You're already worn out, I can tell."

"I'm just thankful that the baby seems okay or we would all be feeling a lot worse right now."

"Yes," Joan agreed, "you're right about that. When will you tell Amy about what happened?"

"I don't know. I'll probably wait a few days, at least."

"She's going to be furious, Barry. You know that, don't you? Not only at what happened to the baby but for your not telling her right away."

"You're probably right, Joan, but that is a chance I have to take. I told all of you what the doctor said about not upsetting her," he explained.

"I know. You are only trying to do what is best for her."

"I really need to get back to the nursery, Joan," Barry said, finishing his coffee.

"Sure. I need to be going. Give Amy my love." Reaching across the table, Joan took Barry's hand in both of hers. "Try not to worry so much, Barry. We're all pulling for that little fellow. He's going to be all right, he has to be."

Barry looked into Joan's eyes and read more than he wanted to. Slowly, he pulled his hand away. Getting up from the table, he said, "Thanks for sitting with Amy for so long, Joan."

"Barry, I didn't only do it for Amy," she said, huskily.

He stared at her, his eyes narrowing. He hoped that he wasn't reading her correctly.

"Good bye, Joan," he said, levelly.

"Good bye, Barry. I'll keep in touch. Call me if there is any change, okay?"

"Okay," he agreed, not wanting to have to call her again.

31

***

Barry went back to the nursery and found Amy nursing the baby. The nurse brought him a chair and he sat across from Amy, enjoying the scene before him. David was making smacking and gulping sounds as he nursed. Barry chuckled, watching him.

"He's a greedy little fellow, isn't he?" Amy said, smiling.

"He sounds wonderful!" Barry answered.

"I know. Darling, while you were gone the nurse gave him some Phenobarbital. Why do you think they did that?"

For a fleeting moment Barry was alarmed. Calmly, he asked, "Did you ask her about it?"

"Of course, she said it was to prevent seizures. That's all she told me."

"It probably has something to do with his having a high temperature earlier. By the way, I requested that a pediatrician from Children's Hospital look David over just to be safe."

"That's a good idea, Barry." David was wiggling and seemed uncomfortable. Amy put him on her shoulder and patted him gently on the back until a burp erupted.

Barry chuckled. "He's learning how to do that rather well."

"Just like his daddy," Amy teased. David was awake, his blue eyes wide.

"I'd like to hold him," Barry said.

"Of course, Darling." Amy handed David to him.

Barry cuddled David in his arms. Except for the IV the baby looked perfectly healthy. He was kicking his tiny feet and tossing his arms about, staring at Barry.

"This is your daddy, little fellow." He lifted David up and gently placed his cheek against the baby's soft cheek, feeling the warmth of him. The baby fidgeted and Barry laid him back in his lap. "I forgot about this stubble," he chuckled, feeling of his growing whiskers. I need a shave, don't I?"

"You look beautiful, Darling," Amy said, gazing at him warmly. "Are you going home tonight? There's no reason for you to stay here, you know."

"I'm staying."

"Is that final?" she teased.

"That's final." His blue eyes met hers, making her body tingle.

"You do look tired, Darling. Aren't your mom and dad at our house? You know that I will be fine. The baby is fine now, don't you think?"

"I certainly hope so." He noticed that David was asleep again. "Is he supposed to sleep this much?" He was wondering if the Phenobarbital was making him sleep.

Amy laughed, softly. "Yes, Darling, babies sleep all the time when they are tiny. You'll be wishing that he slept more, one of these days."

Barry felt more at ease concerning the baby. David looked fine and was sleeping soundly. Barry handed him back to Amy.

The nurse appeared and asked, "Would you like to put him back in his bed? You need your rest too, Mrs.

Reeser."

"Okay, if you will come for me when he gets hungry."

"I promise," she agreed as she put him in his bed once again.

Amy and Barry looked at him once more before leaving the nursery.

Barry sat with Amy in her room while she ate her dinner. He was dozing in the chair so he got up and paced the floor.

Throughout the night Barry checked on David and sat beside Amy's bed. The pediatrician came to see David and talked to Barry. He assured Barry that the medical treatment that David was receiving was all that he needed. He predicted that the damage done to David would be minimal, if noticeable. Barry was relieved after talking to him. However, he was determined to see a lawyer, soon. Such negligence couldn't go unpunished.

By five in the morning, Barry was exhausted. He had only slept a few minutes in the chair. Mr. Reeser surprised him by appearing and encouraged him to go home to shower and sleep. Barry was too tired to argue and did as his father urged him.

Barry's mother was preparing breakfast for him when he got home. He showered and then ate heartily, barely able to keep his eyes open. When he finished eating he went to bed. He slept six hours without waking. When he did awaken he was irritated with himself for having been away from the hospital for so long. Mrs. Reeser assured him that Amy and David were fine. Mr. Reeser had called during the day to update her on their condition. Barry shaved and dressed and then took his mother to the hospital with him. They found Mr. Reeser in Amy's room. Amy had David with her.

"I've been holding my grandson today," Mr. Reeser said, beaming.

Barry went to Amy's side. Leaning over the bed he kissed her softly and examined his son. David was sleeping again.

"Has he slept all day?"

"Not all day, Darling. He has been awake several times and even cried a few times.

"Cried?"

"Barry, babies are supposed to cry. It is the normal thing that they do," Amy said, laughing.

"Barry, you worry too much," Mrs. Reeser said, teasing. She gave him a knowing look.

"I guess you're right, Mom."

"Darling, you look like you feel a lot better. You've even shaved," Amy said, smiling.

"Mom let me sleep too long."

"You needed it, Dear," Mrs. Reeser said.

"We can go back to the house now and leave these young folks alone," Mr. Reeser suggested. "We'll come back tonight."

"Is there anything that we can bring you, Amy?" Mrs. Reeser asked.

"No, thank you, Mrs. Reeser. I am fine. I hope we get to go home tomorrow."

"Have you seen your doctor today?" Barry asked when they were alone.

"Yes and the baby's doctor. We're doing fine. Both doctors said that we should get to go home tomorrow."

"Really? That's good news. Will you let me hold David again?" he grinned.

"Of course, Darling." She handed the baby to him.

Barry talked to David softly until he opened his eyes. Then, he sat down with him and propped him up on his knee. Barry moved his hand in front of David's face and David followed the movement with his eyes. Barry smiled.

"What are you doing?" Amy asked, watching him.

"Just checking," he said.

"You're a goose," she laughed. "You're checking him out, aren't you? Our baby is fine. He has no fever and he has ten fingers and ten toes."

Barry laughed. "You're right. I'm checking him over."

Mr. and Mrs. Reeser visited with Amy again that evening. Captain Adams came back to make sure that David was all right. He brought a gift for the baby. Then, Joan made her appearance, carrying a huge fruit basket with a teddy bear inside.

The following day, Amy's breast milk was plentiful. Barry watched in awe as she nursed David.

"You're a milk fountain this morning," he teased. "Don't drown our boy."

"I hope he eats a bunch! I believe I could feed twins," she said.

David was smacking between gulps as he nursed, contentedly.

"Isn't that uncomfortable, Sweetheart? Does it hurt at all?"

"Just a little. The nurse gave me some ointment to use. She also said that the more David nurses the easier it will be."

When the pediatrician made his rounds he examined David thoroughly.

"This young man looks fine. All I want you to do is to continue to give him the Phenobarbital for a couple of months. Then, you can discontinue it."

"Why does he need to take that?" Amy asked, puzzled.

Barry looked, uneasily, at the doctor.

The doctor hesitated only a second and then answered, "It's just for precautionary measures, Mrs. Reeser. If you have any problems after you're home, call my office. Otherwise, I'll see this little fellow for his six-weeks checkup."

After he had gone, Amy said, "I don't understand why David has to have medication."

"Sweetheart, don't question the doctor. I'm sure he knows what he is doing," Barry said.

"Okay, if you say so," she said, reluctantly.

When Amy's doctor made his rounds, he dismissed Amy. She and Barry were happy to be going home.

When Amy and Barry arrived at their home Mrs. Reeser had lunch cooked. Mr. Reeser had set up the baby's cradle in Amy's bedroom.

"I knew you would want the baby close," he said, grinning, "not in the nursery just yet."

"You read my mind," Amy said to her father-in-law.

Mr. Reeser left for home later that afternoon to go back to work. Mrs. Reeser stayed to help Amy for a few days.

Everything progressed smoothly with David and Amy. Amy was regaining her strength and David was growing daily. Barry observed David obsessively. He couldn't see any problems at all.

32

***

Barry made an appointment with a lawyer and explained everything that had happened to David at the hospital. The lawyer could hardly believe what had happened. He assured Barry that he had grounds for a lawsuit against the hospital and the individuals that were responsible. The lawyer took a deposition from Barry and told him that he would begin proceedings immediately.

When Barry left the lawyer's office he knew that the time had come to tell Amy what had happened. He dreaded telling her.

Amy had a light dinner cooked when Barry got home. He kissed her warmly and held David for a few minutes before they ate. Afterwards, Barry helped Amy clean the kitchen before they retired to the bedroom where David lay in his cradle. He wasn't asleep but lay in his cradle kicking his feet. Barry chuckled, watching him.

"I believe he has grown an inch since I left this morning."

"He's growing like a weed!" Amy agreed.

When David began to fret Amy took him out of the cradle and reclining on the bed, she began to nurse him. He suckled greedily.

"That's why he is growing so fast," Barry chuckled, "he eats like a little pig."

"That's what he is supposed to do," Amy teased, "he's my little piglet."

Barry sat beside her on the bed and waited until the baby finished nursing before he brought up the subject of the hospital. When Amy put the sleeping baby back in his cradle she sat beside Barry and snuggled close.

"I have missed our sweet times together, Darling. Have you missed me?" she asked.

"What do you think?" he answered softly. He kissed her tenderly, taking her breath away.

She sighed, wanting him. "We still have three weeks until my six-week checkup. Do you think we really have to wait that long?"

Barry grinned. "I don't know the answer to that, Sweetheart, I have never had a baby, you know." Amy pinched him, lovingly.

"Surely we don't have to wait that long," she said, dreamily.

"Sweetheart, there is something that I need to discuss with you," he said, reluctantly.

"What?" she asked absently, as she began unbuttoning his shirt.

"I'm afraid I have been keeping something from you, Sweetheart. I hope you understand that I did it for your own welfare."

She looked at him puzzled. He was much too serious. "What are you talking about?"

Barry took a deep breath and proceeded to tell her all that had happened to David at the hospital and about the talks he had with the doctors. He watched as Amy's face grew pale and then flushed with anger.

Barely above a whisper, she said, "I can't believe that you kept this from me! How could you, Barry? What if David had died? It was so horrible to put this child through that! How could anyone be so ignorant, to do that to a tiny infant? How do we know that he is all right, even now?" She bombarded him with questions and then burst into tears. Barry pulled her into his arms and let her cry to get it out of her system. Finally, her tears spent, she raised her gaze to his. His blue eyes were also filled with tears. He kissed her again and wiped her tears with his lips.

"Don't cry, Sweetheart," he said, gently. "David seems fine. We only have to observe him for the next five years to see if his motor skills develop normally."

"Five years? Barry, No! You can't be serious!"

"I know it's outrageous!" he exclaimed. "That's why I've been to see a lawyer this afternoon. We are filing a lawsuit against the hospital and whoever else is responsible for hurting our child. I don't know how long it will take, but they're not going to get away with what they did. Hopefully, it will keep this from happening to another child."

When Amy was finally calm, she lay in Barry's arms, her head on his chest. She looked up into his eyes and said, "I'm not angry with you, Darling. I know that you did what you thought was best for me. I'm angry about what they did to little David."

"I know, Sweetheart," he said, gently. "We have to be optimistic. We have to believe that David will be all right." Amy followed his gaze and they watched their baby sleeping soundly in his cradle.

33

***

Amy and Barry adjusted to having a baby in the house. David was a good baby. He slept during the night and only woke to nurse. He was healthy and hardly ever cried except when he was hungry. The doting parents began to relax when they could find no fault in David's growth.

Amy had a routine to her days and was perfectly happy until Barry came home one evening and told her that he had to go to Huntsville, Al. for four weeks to train in a forensic lab. She was dismayed.

"Barry! Not a whole month! What will David and I do without you for that long?"

Barry grinned. "Sweetheart, I will come home on weekends. I can't stay away from you and David that long."

"I miss you already," she pouted.

"Me too," he said, pulling her close.

"When do you have to leave?"

"I have to fly out early Monday morning."

"I need to help you pack your things," she said.

On Monday morning Amy took Barry to the airport and waved forlornly as his plane disappeared into the sky.

"There goes Daddy," she said to David . "We miss him already, don't we, Sweetie Pie?"

The house seemed empty that night until Barry called to give Amy the name of his hotel and the phone number.

"I miss both of you," he said softly, "but I had an interesting day today. This lab up here is awesome! I'm going to have plenty to do."

"I wish you were home already," Amy said.

"I know. It's lonesome in this room without you, Sweetheart. I did get to eat dinner with my colleagues and didn't have to eat alone tonight."

"David is eating now. Can you hear him smacking?"

"I thought it sounded like him," he chuckled. "I can see both of you in my mind right now. It's a wonderful picture to go to bed with."

The next day Amy decided to call Joan and invite her to eat dinner with her that night. Joan accepted. They had a nice visit. Joan played with David until Amy put him to bed. Joan visited with them twice that week.

On Friday night Amy met Barry at the airport. He didn't want to leave her side. He spent every moment with her and David until he had to leave again on Monday.

The second week that he was gone passed slowly for Barry. Then, it was Tuesday of the third week. Barry left the forensic lab at five and was having dinner at the hotel. When he finished his coffee he went to his room. He kicked off his shoes and was getting comfortable, ready to call Amy, when there was a knock at the door. Puzzled as to who it could be, he opened the door. Standing before him was Joan Caulfield. She was dressed in a revealing black sheath with white pearls. She smiled, seductively.

"Hello, Barry."

"Joan! What are you doing here?" Barry asked, shocked to see her.

"May I come in?"

He hesitated, feeling uncomfortable with her. "I

don't think that's a good idea, Joan. Why are you here?"

Ignoring his question, Joan walked into the room and closed the door behind her. Barry stared at her, disbelieving, as she sat down on the couch and looked up at him, coyly.

"Joan, what are you doing here?" he asked, again.

"I had an opportunity to come to Huntsville and I grabbed it. I thought I'd drop in on you while I am here. You don't mind, do you?" Her eyes were sparkling. She patted the couch beside her. "Come, sit beside me."

Barry shook his head, annoyed at her brashness. He sat on the edge of a chair across from her.

"How did you know where to find me?"

"Amy told me, of course," she said, smiling sweetly.

"Does Amy know you are here?" Barry asked, bluntly. "Did you tell her that you were coming to my hotel?"

"Of course not! I'm not stupid!" she teased.

"I think you are, Joan," he retorted.

Joan laughed merrily. "Maybe I am, at that, Barry. I can't help how I feel." She looked at him lovingly. "Surely you have guessed my feelings for you by this time, Darling."

"Joan, you are out of line," Barry said, angrily. "You are supposed to be Amy's best friend! Are you out of your mind?"

"I've been out of my mind thinking of you for a long time, Barry," she admitted. "Yes, Amy is my best friend. I love her dearly, but I love her husband, too. I'm crazy about you, Barry. I can't sleep at night, for thinking of you...... and wanting you."

"Joan, if I have ever given you the impression that I was even remotely interested in you in that way, I am sorry. I had no idea! I love my wife, don't you understand? I have no intention of having an affair with you or anyone else. I will not be unfaithful to my wife!"

"God! That's what I love about you! You're so different from other men! Any one of them would be ready to jump in the sack with me. Not you, Barry. You're different. That makes me want you even more."

"Joan, you need to leave," Barry said, watching her warily.

"You can't blame a girl for trying. I figured, what Amy doesn't know, won't hurt her. You know what I mean? I should have told you all this before, when she left you alone. I guess that was stupid of me."

"It wouldn't have made any difference, Joan. I've always loved Amy and I always will. I wouldn't hurt her like that. I couldn't live with myself, if I did."

Joan looked at him longingly, her gaze taking in all of his handsome features. "Like I have said before; I wish I could trade places with her. You and I could be wonderful together. I hope she really appreciates you, Darling."

"I'm sorry, Joan. I'm sorry you haven't found someone to love who can love you in return."

"Oh, I have found someone to love," she teased, her eyes shining. "As for the latter, only time will tell."

"How can you face Amy, or even me, after this? This alters our friendship in every way. You have betrayed that friendship."

"There's no need to tell Amy anything about this, Barry," she said, smugly.

"You can't be serious!" he exclaimed.

"Why tell her and hurt her? I won't betray my feelings for you in front of her. We can go on as before. I can admire you from a distance," she said, daringly.

"It won't work, Joan. Amy and I don't keep secrets from one another."

"For Christ's sake! You can't be serious! Everyone has secrets," Joan exclaimed. "She won't learn it from me. If she finds out, you'll be the one to tell her."

Barry got up and walked to the door. "You should

go, Joan," he said seriously. He was annoyed and disappointed in her.

She did as he asked and followed him to the door. As he opened it, she suddenly grabbed him and planted a warm kiss on his mouth. When he didn't respond, she drew back, laughing.

"Darling, I know you can kiss better than that," she teased.

He took her by the shoulders and pushed her away from him, gently. "Go, Joan. Don't come back," he said, angrily. He pushed her gently through the doorway into the hallway. Before he could close the door she blew him a kiss, her eyes twinkling. He closed the door, leaving her standing in the hallway. He locked the door. He expected her to pound on the door but was relieved when she didn't. He heard the sound of her footsteps receding down the hallway. He sat down heavily, feeling as though he had just done battle. He was disgusted with Joan. He thought back to different encounters with her, trying to figure out if he had done or said something to give her the wrong impression. He could think of nothing. He remembered things she had said to him in the past. It dawned on him that Joan had been interested in him for some time. The phone rang, shattering his thoughts. Reluctantly, he picked up the phone, expecting it to be Joan.

"Hello," he said.

"Hello, Darling," Amy's voice said, cheerfully, "I've been waiting for you to call."

"Hello, Sweetheart," he said, relieved that it was Amy. "How is my girl and our little one?"

"We're fine. But, it's so lonesome here. Hurry and come home, Darling."

"Just three more days, Sweetheart and I can come home for the weekend. After that, just one more week away and I can come home for good. The days seem to be getting longer and longer without you."

"I know. They are long for us, too. David has been sleeping in your place at night."

"What?" Barry laughed. "You know he is going to be spoiled to that, don't you? He'll want to sleep with us from now on."

"Do you think so?" Amy asked, innocently.

"Yes, I think so. He'll want to sleep between us, you'll see," he teased.

"Oh, Dear. What will we do?" she asked, alarmed.

Barry laughed, picturing Amy at that moment. "I guess we'll have to make room for him, won't we?"

"Barry, you're teasing me," Amy said, giggling.

Barry heard David cry in the background. "What's wrong with my boy?" he asked.

"I think he wants me to hold him. He can't be hungry," Amy said.

"Uh-oh. Sounds like you've spoiled him, Sweetheart," Barry teased. "That's okay, though. He's only a baby for a little while."

"You're so right! I think he has grown an inch this week, though. You'd better hurry and come home, Darling."

"I wish I were there right now, Amy. You don't know how much I wish I could hold you right at this moment."

"Yes, Darling. I do know. I ache for your arms around me, too. I love you so much."

"I love you with all my heart, Amy," Barry said, wiping the moisture from his eyes.

When Barry flew home on the weekend he was afraid that Joan would come over, but she didn't. He was relieved. He hadn't decided what to tell Amy yet. He hoped he could forget what had happened if Joan would do the same. Everything depended on how Joan conducted herself when they were together. Barry dreaded seeing her again and didn't know if he could be civil to her. He felt guilty for keeping it from Amy. Amy had been betrayed by her best friend, yet he hated to be the one to break up Amy's friendship with Joan.

34

***

It had been two weeks since Barry had gotten home from Huntsville. He had worked overtime a couple of nights. There was so much going on that the forensic investigators could hardly keep up. The latest crime scene that Barry investigated was a shooting. It seemed to be drug related. Barry wasn't planning to work late tonight until Amy called him and informed him that she had invited Joan over for dinner.

Hearing the news, Barry hesitated and then said, "Sweetheart, I really need to finish some work here tonight. I'm sorry. You can still enjoy your dinner with Joan, can't you?"

"Oh, Barry, must you?" Amy asked, disappointed.

"You'll enjoy the evening without me, I'm sure," he answered, evasively.

"Well, if you have to, but we'll miss you. David won't get to see his daddy before he goes to bed."

"I'll try to spend time with him in the morning before I come back to work," he said.

When Barry hung up the phone he felt guilty, but he was determined not to spend the evening with Joan. He still did not trust her.

35

***

When Joan got to Amy's house she looked around for Barry. Not seeing him, she asked, "Where's that handsome husband of yours?"

"Oh, he had to work late tonight."

Joan couldn't hide her disappointment. "Rats! I know you hate that. Does he often work late?"

"He has been working late recently," Amy answered.

"How's little David doing?" Joan asked, playing with the baby.

"He's wonderful!" Amy exclaimed. "Isn't he growing? He can roll over now."

"Wow! How about that? He's such a handsome little fellow, too. He looks just like his dad, doesn't he?"

"Of course!" Amy agreed, smiling.

"You haven't seen any signs of a problem have you, Amy? You know, with his motor skills or anything."

A shadow crossed Amy's face for an instant. Then, she answered, "It's too soon to tell. So far he seems perfect. It's awful, though, having that worry in the back of our mind."

Joan left soon after dinner. Amy fed David and put him to bed for the night. She read for a while but had fallen asleep before Barry got home. He woke her as he got into bed beside her and kissed her softly. She clasped her arms around him and pulled him closer.

"We missed you tonight," she whispered sleepily.

"I missed you and my boy, too," he answered softly. "But, I'm here, now."

"Hmmm," she muttered, as she snuggled closer.

***

It was Friday night. Barry planned to take Amy and David out to eat, but he had to wait in his office to meet with a forensic investigator from Huntsville. He asked Amy to meet him at his office and as soon as he was finished with his meeting they would leave from there. Amy bundled David in a warm, winter outfit and drove to Barry's office. He wasn't in his office, so she sat down in the waiting room outside his office. She was juggling David on her lap when he began to bounce excitedly as he looked past her and down the hall. Amy heard Barry talking and turned to see him and another gentleman walking toward them. Amy laughed at David, who recognized his dad at a distance.

"Hey, big fellow!" Barry said, taking him from Amy and turning to the man beside him. "Mr. Honeycutt, this is my son, David, and my wife, Amy," he grinned proudly.

"Glad to meet you, Mrs. Reeser. That's a fine boy you have there, Barry."

Barry handed him back to Amy after planting a kiss on his soft cheek. "Sweetheart, I'll just be a few more minutes," Barry said as he and Mr. Honeycutt entered his office.

"Nice to meet you, Mrs. Reeser," Mr. Honeycutt said

as they disappeared into Barry's office, leaving the door ajar.

After a pause, Amy heard Mr. Honeycutt continue: "You're a sly fellow, Barry," he chuckled. "That charming wife of yours isn't the same woman I saw in your hotel room in Huntsville."

Amy's face flushed crimson and her heart felt as though it had stopped beating. She sat in shock, listening.

Barry hesitated and then replied, "What are you talking about? Were you in the hallway?"

Amy heard Honeycutt laugh. "The door was partly open. I wasn't eavesdropping. I had come to ask you to eat dinner with me in the lobby. When I saw a woman in your arms, I figured you had better things to do."

"You've got it all wrong, Mr. Honeycutt," Barry explained. "That wasn't the way it was at all. The lady didn't stay. I asked her to leave."

Amy heard the irritation in Barry's voice, but she realized that he didn't deny that there was a woman in his room. She had heard enough. She snatched up the baby's diaper bag and hurried outside. Her breath caught in her chest. She took deep breaths trying to get control of her emotions. She tried to tell herself that there was an explanation. There had to be. She trusted Barry! He would never be unfaithful to her! Yet, why was a woman in his hotel room?

David began to fret, so Amy got into Barry's car to get out of the cold wind. She knew that the baby was hungry. Absently, she began to let him nurse, careful to keep him covered and warm. She was trembling, but it was not from the cold. When David finished eating, she burped him and continued to wait for Barry to return. When he finally appeared, he wore a puzzled expression as he got into the car beside her.

"Amy, I've been looking everywhere for you! What are you doing out here in the cold? I asked you to wait inside."

"I had to feed David," she said, weakly.

"Oh." He leaned over for a kiss. He didn't notice her hesitation before she let his lips touch her own.

"Are we still going to the Steak House?" he asked, starting the car.

"That's fine."

Somehow, Amy got through the meal, although she spent more time with David than she did eating. She could barely force herself to swallow.

Barry noticed. "Sweetheart, what's wrong? You've hardly touched your food."

Amy's eyes were brimming with tears. "I overheard what Mr. Honeycutt said.....about a 'woman' being in your room," she said, hardly above a whisper.

A startled expression crossed Barry's face and he actually blushed. It was the first time that Amy had ever seen him blush.

"You overheard Honeycutt?" he stammered. It was more of a statement than a question. After a long pause he sighed, wearily. He leaned back in his chair, watching her face closely.

"I knew I should have told you. I apologize for not telling you, Amy."

"Apologize for what, Barry? For having a woman in your room?" Amy was trembling.

"How could you?"

"Sweetheart! Let me explain!"

"How can you 'explain' a thing like that?" she asked, visibly shaken.

He leaned forward and grasped her hand in his.

"Amy, let me explain! Don't do this!" he pleaded. "I wanted to spare you."

"Of course you did!"

"Amy, listen to me!"

"Barry, I want to go home. This is not the place to

discuss this!" She got up with David, suddenly, leaving Barry to pay the bill and follow her. When he got into the car, he was silent. Amy wondered if she had made him angry but didn't care if she had. They were both silent as he drove to his office to pick up her car.

"Leave David in the car seat. I'll be right behind you."

Amy was reluctant to leave David even for a moment. When she hesitated Barry said,

"Amy, he's asleep. He will be all right."

She closed the door and went to her car. They were at home within ten minutes. Before Amy could get David, Barry had carried him inside and put him in his bed.

"Let's talk in the den so we don't wake the boy," he said.

Amy followed him into the den and sat on the end of the couch a short distance from him.

He looked discouraged. "I won't bite, Amy."

"Tell me what you have to tell me." She steeled herself to hear the worse.

"I explained it to Honeycutt. Didn't you believe me?"

"I don't know what you're talking about! I heard you admit that there was a woman in your room. Were you having an affair with someone?"

"I was not having an affair and have never had an affair with anyone! That's what I am trying to tell you, Amy!"

"I am trying really hard, Barry. If you only knew how hard! Who was the woman? Why was she in your room?"

"That is what I had hoped to spare you from finding out. The woman was 'Joan'."

Amy was speechless for a moment. Then, she said, barely above a whisper, "You can't be serious!"

"I'm dead serious, Amy. As God is my witness, I am

telling you the truth. Joan came to see me at the hotel. I had nothing to do with her being there. Please believe me."

"My 'best friend'? Why would she be in Huntsville?"

"She had some fabricated story about being in town. I'm sure it was a lie. She came on to me, Sweetheart, but I wanted no part of her. I told her so and I told her that I love you and always will."

Amy stared at Barry, trying to comprehend all that he was saying. Her best friend had betrayed her? "He said that she was in your arms...."

"Sweetheart, she grabbed me, I swear. I did not initiate it! I want no other woman but you! I love only you!"

Amy stared at the only man she had ever loved, the man who held her heart in his hands at this moment. She knew that he was telling her the truth.

"Did she kiss you?" she asked, barely above a whisper, her heart aching. Amy saw his expression of shame as he answered.

"Yes, Amy, she did. But, I pushed her away. I never wanted it to happen. I'm sorry. I had no idea that she was interested in me. Did she ever give you that impression?"

Amy tried to remember. "I should have guessed from things she said in the past. She's a snake, isn't she?"

"She was your best friend, Amy. I hated to be the cause of your losing that friendship."

"I don't need that kind of friend, Barry; not one who stabs me in the back, trying to seduce my husband."

"Then, you do believe me, Sweetheart?" Barry asked.

"I believe you, Barry, but it hurts. It hurts to know that she was there in your room and you held her....and kissed her." Tears slid down Amy's cheeks.

"Sweetheart," he said, moving closer to her side, "I did not 'hold her' and I did not respond to her advances. I am not interested in anything that she has to offer."

"I believe you, Barry, but why didn't you tell me?

You kept something from me once again! Something that I needed to know! Let me deal with my problems. Don't try to protect me anymore! I am a big girl. I can handle it!"

Barry pulled her into his arms and buried his face in her dark, flowing hair. After a moment he raised his gaze to meet hers. There were tears in his blue eyes.

"I'm so sorry, Sweetheart. Please forgive me for not telling you. I know now, that it would have been the right thing to do. I hoped that her infatuation would pass and you could still be friends. I doubt that is possible now."

"Of course it isn't possible, Barry! I know how Joan is toward men. I lived with her for years. She won't give up on you. The fact that you spurned her advances will only make her more interested in you. She has dated married men before, I am sure of it." Amy thought for a moment and then added, "That is why you stayed at the office the last time I invited her over for dinner, isn't it?"

He nodded. "I didn't want to be around her, Amy."

"Thank you for doing that, Darling. A lot of men would enjoy that situation and boast about it."

"I'm not like most men, Sweetheart," he grinned. "Haven't we talked about this before?" After a moment he asked, "What do you plan to say to Joan when you see her?"

"I plan to give her a piece of my mind!" she answered.

"Do you want me to go with you to talk to her?" he asked.

"No, Barry. I'll handle Joan, trust me," she said.

37

***

Amy decided to talk to Joan as soon as possible. She called Joan one afternoon and told her that she was coming over. When she arrived she lay David on the couch and propped pillows around him so he wouldn't roll off. He was kicking his feet and cooing.

"My goodness! That little fellow is growing!" Joan laughed. "Can he walk yet?"

"Joan, this is not a social visit," Amy said, meeting her gaze bravely.

Joan looked at her sharply but didn't comment.

"Do you have any idea why I am here?" Amy asked.

Joan's ruby lips curled in a smile. "Not really. You look so serious."

"I had a long talk with Barry about one of his weeks in Huntsville," Amy began.

A slow smile spread across Joan's lips. "I see. What did he have to tell you, Amy?"

"He told me everything, Joan. He told me about your visit to his hotel room. You have a lot of nerve!"

"You can't blame a girl for trying," she grinned.

"Yes, I can blame you! Barry is my husband, not some guy you picked up in a bar! I thought you were my friend!"

"I always wondered what it would be like to kiss Barry," she teased, her eyes sparkling.

Before she realized what she was about to do, Amy reached out and slapped Joan hard on the face.

Joan glared at her, her face crimson. Then, enjoying herself, she continued wickedly, "I wasn't disappointed. He knows how to kiss."

"You're a liar! He pushed you away! You'll never know what a wonderful husband he is, Joan. You wouldn't understand! He didn't fall for your trap."

Joan stared at her, a twinkle in her eyes. "I could tell you a good story about the two of us, Amy, but I won't. You're right. Like I have told you before, he's crazy about you. He is the first man who ever turned me down, flat. You better appreciate what you've got."

"Joan, you have no shame! You could have any man you want, yet, you want mine."

"Do you blame me? Compare him to anybody else we know. Just looking at him makes me tingly," Joan teased.

Amy picked up David, ready to leave. "Look elsewhere for a man, Joan. I don't want you around mine."

Joan walked her to the door. "I hope we can still be friends, Amy."

Amy stopped and stared at her. "You think I'm stupid, don't you, Joan? I know you!"

"I'll see you around," Joan said.

"Not if I can help it," Amy answered as she left.

Joan never called Amy and Amy never called her. Amy was sorry that she had lost her best friend, but she was relieved that Joan would not be a threat to her marriage.

***

Barry asked Amy if she would like to go to the cabin for a weekend.

"We can buy a crib to keep out there and buy electric heaters to keep the baby warm," he said.

The idea appealed to Amy. "I would like that very much." She would be happy to get away and get her mind off the episode with Joan.

When they arrived at the cabin, Barry built a fire and then set up the baby's crib. With the electric heaters the cabin warmed up comfortably.

After eating soup and sandwiches for supper, they sat on the couch before the fire and played with David. Barry looked lovingly at Amy, bouncing David on her knee.

"You're beautiful, Sweetheart. Do you know how happy you have made me? My life is complete with you and our son." He leaned over and kissed her softly.

Amy sat David in Barry's lap and snuggled closer. She caressed Barry's cheek with her fingertips.

"Thank you, Darling. My life is complete with you and David. I hope you know that I do appreciate you and I know how fortunate I am to have you love me."

He looked at her for a long moment. "I'm the lucky one," he said softly, reading her mind. "No one will ever come between us, I promise."

Amy was surprised at his statement, surprised that he knew why she had said that, although neither of them had mentioned Joan for weeks.

Later, lying in Barry's arms, Amy marveled at how their love grew from day to day.

In the morning Amy dressed David in one of his winter outfits and she and Barry dressed warmly. They went for a walk through the woods checking to see if there were any poachers baiting deer. They found that the troughs were empty and there was no sign of poachers.

"Why don't we walk across to Mr. Rafferty's house, Barry? He has never seen the baby."

"Okay, it's not far." Barry carried David as they walked through the woods. David was alert, watching the trees as they passed. Before they reached the clearing where Mr. Rafferty's cabin was, Barry stopped suddenly. Amy bumped into him from behind.

"What is it?" she asked, startled.

Barry was sniffing the air and his eyes narrowed. "Do you smell something? Smells like paint or paint thinner," he said softly.

"Maybe Mr. Rafferty is painting his cabin," Amy suggested.

"It wouldn't be this potent, Amy." He handed David to Amy. "You stay right here. I'm going to walk close enough to see the cabin. Then, I'll be right back. Don't follow me, Amy," he said emphatically. Before she could question him, he had disappeared through the trees.

Barry stopped at the edge of the woods where he could see Mr. Rafferty's cabin. He saw no sign of life, although there was smoke coming from the chimney. He sniffed the air again and realized that the chemical smell was less noticeable here. He back-tracked until he found Amy where he had left her.

"What are you doing?" she asked, alarmed.

"Sweetheart, I don't think this smell around here is paint. This is what crystal methamphetamine smells like. It's more noticeable in this area than closer to the cabin. There may be another cabin secluded in these woods. I want you and David to go back to the cabin. You don't even need to be breathing the fumes, if that is what it is. Let me take you back to the cabin," he said, as he took David from Amy and started hurrying back through the woods the way they had come.

"What are you going to do?" Amy asked breathlessly as she tried to keep up with Barry.

"First, I am getting you and David back safely. Then, I am going back to find where the smell is coming from."

"No!" Amy said, grabbing his shirt from behind and forcing him to stop. "I don't want you going back alone!"

"Sweetheart, I have to investigate this. I have to be certain before I call anyone else out here. I'll be okay. I'll be careful, I promise."

"Barry, I'm scared! You're not even armed!" she cried, trying to keep up with him again.

"Sweetheart, I'll get my weapon at the cabin."

Amy saw that there was no changing his mind. He saw them safely to the cabin and she watched as he buckled on his shoulder holster and secured the gun beneath his coat.

"Lock this door, Amy. Don't open it for anyone but me. If I'm not back within the hour, call Captain Adams. You have his number and your cell phone?"
She nodded, biting her lower lip. Visions of his getting shot flashed through her mind. Her eyes filled with tears.

Barry raised her chin with his fingers and planted a quick kiss on her lips. "I'll be back soon," he said softly. He kissed David on top of his head, his curly locks tickling his lips. He turned quickly and said, "Lock the door behind me!" Then, he was gone.

Amy locked the door behind him, her hands trembling. She sat down and hugged David tightly. He kicked and whined and she automatically placed him at her breast to nurse. He suckled greedily as she tried to still her racing heart.

***

Barry slipped quietly through the woods, his weapon drawn. He smelled the chemicals again as he neared the area where they stood before. Instead of heading toward Mr. Rafferty's cabin he cut through the woods in another direction. After a moment he saw a rundown, weathered cabin through the leafless trees. He hid behind a hickory tree and observed the cabin for any sign of movement. Smoke was coming from the chimney and two trucks were parked near the front door. A well-used trail led off into the woods in the opposite direction. As he watched, his heart-beat quickened at the sight of a car coming along the trail. He watched as a woman got out and carried a large paper bag full of something into the cabin. He knew it had to be heavy by the way she struggled with it. Five minutes passed and then the back door opened and a man emerged. He was carrying two heavy boxes which he put over into the back of one of the trucks. He made another trip inside and emerged again with two more boxes. Barry wondered how many people were inside and was trying to decide what he should do, when a noisy old truck drew his attention to the trail coming through the woods. Barry recognized Mr. Rafferty's truck and watched as he drew to a stop and getting out, sauntered through the front doorway of the cabin.

A feeling of disappointment swept over Barry. He had hoped that Mr. Rafferty wasn't involved in the drug trafficking. He knew from the smell, that there was a meth lab inside. Now, he knew there were three people inside, probably four. He knew that he needed to get back to his cabin and call for backup. He knew that Amy would be getting worried about him. He slipped back through the woods the way he had come. When he reached the cabin, Amy was watching for him through the window and opened the door before he could knock. He proceeded to tell her what he had seen, ending with Mr. Rafferty's appearance. He knew that she was as disappointed as he.

Barry called Captain Adams and then hung up the cell phone.

"They're on the way," he said, quietly. "I don't like your being here with David. You can leave now and I will ride back with the Captain."

"No, Barry! I don't want to leave you! Please, don't make me." Her gaze met his and held.

He pulled her into his arms and held her tight. He stroked her soft hair and watched David as he slept.

"Sweetheart, I don't want anything to happen to you and David," he said huskily.

"I'll lock the door when the police get here, after you leave," she pleaded.

"You don't have your pistol do you?" he asked.

"No. I never dreamed I might need it."

He was quiet, weighing her options. Finally, he said, "Okay. Promise me you won't open the door for anyone but me."

"I promise!"

***

When Captain Adams arrived with four other officers, heavily armed, Amy watched through the window as Barry joined them and then they disappeared into the woods.

Barry led the officers to the spot where they could observe and still remain hidden. He saw that Mr. Rafferty's truck was gone as well as one of the other trucks.

"We have to let the DEA boys lead the way," Captain Adams whispered.

Barry nodded and watched as they circled the cabin and then rushed it.

"Okay! Let's go!" Captain Adams exclaimed, following.

One of the inhabitants burst through the back door, only to be yanked back by a DEA officer who quickly handcuffed him. Once inside, Barry recognized the woman whom he had seen earlier. She was handcuffed. Looking around he saw bowls of diet pills containing pseudoephedrine, the ingredient that provides the 'high' that users get from the meth. He found lithium strips, needed for the hydrous ammonia they contained. The shelves in the kitchen were lined with denatured alcohol and lighter fluid, iodine and iodine crystals. Camp fuel and propane tanks sat around on the dirty floor. Other ingredients for the lethal drug were strewn all over the counters. The stench was almost overwhelming.

"Barry, do you know who that woman is in there?" Captain Adams asked as he joined him in the dirty kitchen."

"No, who is she?"

"That's Sara Benson."

"You're kidding me!" Barry exclaimed. "Is the guy Pinkerton?"

"No, but my guess is that he was here earlier. You said there were two other trucks here, didn't you?"

"That's right. One of the trucks belonged to Homer Rafferty."

"I reckon we need to pay Mr. Rafferty a visit. I'm sure he can tell us the identity of the other fellow, even if these two aren't talking."

The officers secured the scene before they left, so it would be ready for the forensic investigators to come in with Barry later. Then, they led the suspects back through the woods to transport them to jail.

When Amy heard voices she looked through the window and saw Sara Benson as the men were putting her into a police car. She opened the door wide, after Barry's knock.

"Barry! That's Sara Benson!" she exclaimed.

"That's what I just found out. Captain Adams and I are going to see Mr. Rafferty now."

"Be careful!" she implored.

"I doubt that Homer Rafferty is dangerous, Sweetheart. He just doesn't seem the type."

41

***

As Barry and Captain Adams approached Homer Rafferty's cabin in the police car, he came to the door.

"Howdy, neighbor!" he said, grinning slightly.

"Hello, Mr. Rafferty. This is Captain Adams. We'd like to talk to you."

"Sure, come on in," he said, opening the door wider. "You'll have to 'scuse the mess. My wife passed away six weeks ago and I ain't much on housekeepin'."

"I'm sorry to hear about your wife," Barry said, truthfully.

"Yall' take a seat," he said, moving wrinkled clothes out of the way so they could sit on the couch.

"Mr. Rafferty," Captain Adams began, "this isn't a social call. We're here to take you in for questioning." He read him his rights and continued, " I'm arresting you for participating in the illegal production and trafficking of Methamphetamine drugs." He was about to handcuff him when Barry stopped him.

"Captain, do you have to handcuff him?" he asked.

The captain looked at Barry, a surprised expression on his face.

"I ain't goin' to run no where, young feller'," Mr. Rafferty said.

"Do you give me your word?" the captain asked, reluctantly.

"Yessir!" Turning to Barry, he continued, "How'd ye' find out about me, son?"

"I saw you at the cabin, Sir. Why did you lie to me before?"

"I ain't lied to ye'. I just ain't told ye all I knowed, affore'."

"You've been working in the lab all along, haven't you, Mr. Rafferty?" Barry continued.

"I just leased the cabin. They did the cookin' and sellin'."

"Who was the other guy that left earlier with the boxes? Was it Pinkerton?" Barry asked.

Homer Rafferty nodded. "I guess there ain't no use to hide nothin' now."

"Do you have a lawyer, Sir?" Barry continued.

"Ain't never had no need fer' no lawyer. They's a bunch of crooks."

Captain Adams laughed in spite of trying to keep a straight face.

"You don't have to talk to us without a lawyer present," Barry informed him. "If you can't afford a lawyer, the court will appoint one for you."

"Suit yerself'. Don't rightly know iffn' I need one or not."

Barry escorted Homer Rafferty to the police car. The captain dropped Barry off at his cabin and then, left for the city.

Everyone had gone by the time Amy met him at the door.

Amy handed Barry a glass of tea and he sat down wearily.

"I hated to see Mr. Rafferty arrested," Barry said. "He said his wife died a few weeks ago."

"Oh, no. I still like the old gentleman, Barry. I can't

help it. He has been a good neighbor to us."

"He admitted that Pinkerton was there. He's the one who loaded up the truck with the drugs and left. Hopefully, the police will be able to find out more at the station."

There was a knock on the door and Amy jumped, startled. Instantly, her face was a picture of alarm.

Barry looked out the window before he opened the door. "It's the guys from the lab. They just now got here to help me with the investigation. This may take a while, Sweetheart. I want you and David to go back to the city. The guys will drop me off later. We have a lot to do at that cabin and at the lab. I'd feel better if you were safe at home."

The police weren't able to locate Pinkerton. It was as though he had disappeared since he was last seen at the cabin in the woods. His fingerprints were everywhere and with all the evidence gathered, it would be easy to send him to prison for years, if he was ever caught. Barry was relentless in his work and was confident that he would be caught, eventually. He wanted closure to the nightmare that had plagued them for months.

42

***

Amy and Barry watched their son grow, wary of finding anything wrong, physically. They were amazed when he took his first step at eight months, taking his first steps from one piece of furniture to another. He would look up at his parents, his eyes shining. He knew he had accomplished a great feat. When he giggled, Amy's heart melted.

She squeezed him tightly. "You precious little Darling!"

Barry watched them quietly, the love showing in his own eyes. He handed David a toy car and observed as he reached for it with his left hand.

"Do you suppose he is going to be left handed?" he asked, absently.

"We're both right handed, Darling. Is that likely?" Amy answered.

David immediately placed the car in his mouth.

"You don't eat it, Sweetie, you roll it." She showed him how to roll it on the table.

"He tries to eat everything." Barry chuckled as he watched him use his left hand to roll the car. Barry reached over and placed the car in David's right hand.

"Are you supposed to do that, Barry? If a child has a tendency to be left handed, I don't think you're supposed to try to change that."

"I'm not doing that, Amy. I am just checking."

David changed the car to his left hand and then stuck it into his mouth again.

"Well, if he is left handed, that will be perfectly fine!" Amy announced.

Barry sat down on the floor beside David and opened his canister of blocks. David immediately dropped the car and grabbed for the colored blocks. Barry started building a tower with the blocks and watched as David knocked them down with his left hand. He noticed that David held his right arm close to his side. David squealed with delight as he knocked down another tower with his left hand.

A frown crossed Barry's brow and he said, "I think we need to encourage him to use his right hand more." He placed a yellow block in David's right hand and guided his arm to stack the block.

Realization dawned on Amy's face and she grew pale. "Barry! What's wrong with his right arm?"

"Don't panic, Amy," Barry said softly.

"But, I see it now! You've known all along! He's not left handed! Something is wrong!"

"Maybe we need to have him checked by the doctor," Barry suggested.

Amy grabbed the phone nearby and dialed the doctor's number. She made an appointment for the following day.

"Sweetheart, I didn't mean that you had to do it immediately," Barry said.

"I know, but we don't need to waste time. Will you go with me tomorrow?"

"Of course."

At the doctor's office the next day Barry watched as the doctor played with David, testing his responses and reflexes. The doctor laid a red, circular disk on the floor near David's right side and watched as he tried to pick it up with the fingers of his right hand. Failing to do so, he quickly used his left hand to pick it up.

Tears ran down Amy's cheeks as her gaze met Barry's. He put his arm around her and drew her closer as they sat quietly, observing.

The doctor took a purple ball the size of a basketball and told David to catch it. He gently pitched it into David's arms and watched as David tried, unsuccessfully, to catch it.

Turning to Amy and Barry, he said, "That's encouraging. He tried to use both arms to catch the ball." He pulled his stool around so that he faced Amy and Barry. "Mr. and Mrs. Reeser, I do believe that David has more mobility in his left arm than his right. It's hardly noticeable if you aren't looking for it. Don't try to make him use his right hand all the time, but do encourage him to use his right arm more. You might even want to take him to a therapist to make sure he has every advantage possible."

Amy asked, "Is it going to be a handicap for him, Doctor?"

"In my opinion, no. If he continues to develop in every way that he has up until now, it's possible that he will only be left handed, like millions of folks, Mrs. Reeser," the doctor said, smiling. "We'll continue to monitor his growth as usual, unless you discover something else that you think is important. Otherwise, I will see you for his next checkup."

Barry shook the doctor's hand. "Thank you, Sir," he said, more relieved than he wanted to admit.

"Try not to worry about the boy," the doctor continued, addressing both of them. "David is doing so well, I cannot believe he will have a serious problem later on."

After Amy and Barry got home they put David down for a nap and stood beside his bed watching him. Barry slipped his arm around Amy and pulled her close.

"He's going to be okay, Sweetheart. I really believe

that," he said.

"I know," she said, wiping a tear from her cheek. "I just love him so much!" Meeting Barry's gaze, she added, "I can't describe how much I love both of you ."

"You don't need to try. I know already," he whispered. He kissed her warmly, making her catch her breath. "Do you know how much I love you, Sweetheart?" he whispered.

"I'm not sure," she teased, "would you show me?"

He scooped her up into his arms and carried her to their bedroom.

David saw a therapist once a week for the next year. She did exercises with him, to strengthen his right arm. David grew rapidly with no further indications of any developmental problem.

Barry talked to their lawyer about the case of negligence at the hospital. The lawyer suggested that they wait another two years before going to court to be sure that no other problems would arise.

Barry agreed.

43

***

One afternoon as Amy was outside letting David play on his swing set Barry came home from work and found them there. David ran to meet his father. Barry picked him up and sat down on the grass with him. Barry began to wrestle with him and lay down flat while David bounced all over him, squealing with delight.

Amy laughed at them, enjoying the sight. She thought that David was a miniature 'Barry' in looks and mannerisms.

Finally, when David tired of this, he ambled off to his sandbox and began to play with his dump truck.

Amy and Barry sat on the glider and watched as David filled the truck with sand. After a quiet moment Amy looked at Barry inquisitively.

"You're awfully quiet, Darling. What's on your mind?" she asked.

His gaze met hers and he smiled, weakly. "You know me well, don't you, Sweetheart?"

Amy became alarmed at the far away look in his eyes. "What's wrong?"

"A body was found in a creek just off a logging road near Sara Benson's old house. It was so decomposed that we won't know who it is until we finish all the tests in the lab."

A chill ran through Amy's body. "Was it a homicide?"

"It was definitely that; a bullet in back of the skull."

Amy gasped, envisioning the skull.

"Here I am discussing 'gory details' with you again," he said, as though to apologize.

"That's okay. Do you think it could be related to the meth lab and all that?" Amy asked.

"We suspect it is related. As a matter of fact, we suspect it is Pinkerton. We'll know for sure when the DNA test is finished."

"Wow! Pinkerton at last…, maybe."

"Maybe."

"I guess that's good. Well, not good that he is dead but good that he will be accounted for and out of the picture, finally."

"Except, another murderer is running loose somewhere out there."

"Yes, unfortunately." Amy shivered at the thought. "Whatever happened to Mr. Rafferty?"

"He was given fifteen years for his crimes. He may not live to be a free man again."

"That's so sad."

"Yes, it's sad, but that doesn't excuse what he did, Amy, or the heartache associated with the meth. There is no telling how many people were hooked on the stuff, kids included, or who may have died because of him."

"Keep me posted when you find out more, will you?" Amy asked.

"I'll let you know."

44

***

In a few days all the evidence was collected and the body found in the creek was identified as Tommy Pinkerton. True to his word, Barry filled Amy in on all the details.

"We'll never know now, if he really murdered Rodney Benson," Barry said.

"You may never know who killed Pinkerton, or why," Amy stated.

"You're right. But, we can go on with our lives now, Sweetheart. With the meth lab closed down and all the culprits in jail or dead, I think it is safe for us to go to the cabin without ever having to worry. Probably Pinkerton's killer was one of the drug dealers."

"I hope you're right, Barry. I hope all this is behind us and we can start fresh."

At that moment, David walked steadily into the room holding a red caboose in his right hand. "Daddy," he said in his sweet baby voice, "let's play 'choo-choo'!"

Tears filled Amy's eyes as her gaze met Barry's.

"Sure, Pal! You can be the conductor and I'll be the porter. How's that?" Barry asked, his blue eyes shining as much as his son's. "Who can Mom be?" Barry continued.

"Mom can be the 'train rider'," David answered.

"That's perfect, Sport, just perfect!" Barry exclaimed as he took his son and his wife by their hand and led them to the colorful, metal train cars.

Everything was falling into place. Everything was going to be fine. Barry knew it.

45

***

Barry's parents came for a visit one weekend. When Barry was outside with his dad watching little David play in the pool, Becky Reeser confided in Amy.

"Amy, I am so worried about Joey. You know he moved out and we never hear from him. I am ashamed to say it, but I believe he is living with an older woman."

"Oh, no. Are you sure?" Amy asked.

"Some of his friends from work told us. It seems that he has missed work because of her. David is really worried but tries not to let me know how much," Becky confided.

"What can Barry and I do to help?" Amy asked, concerned.

"David will probably talk to Barry about it. Hopefully, Barry will have a suggestion. Do you have Joey's address and phone number? At least, he did give us those," Becky said.

"Barry may have it, but give it to me, just in case he doesn't."

Becky copied the information down for Amy and handed it to her.

"We'll get in touch with him and try to find out what is going on. I hate to see him get mixed up with the wrong person," Amy said.

"Thank you, Amy. I wish Joey would meet someone like you."

Amy blushed, pleased. "Thank you, Becky. That's such a sweet thing to say."

After Barry's parents had gone home, Amy and Barry were discussing Joey one evening . Barry decided to take a day off from work and drive to Joey's place and find out, first hand, what was going on.

Barry knew where Joey worked and was waiting for him when he got off work on Tuesday.

Joey saw Barry standing beside his car as he walked toward him.

"Barry! This is a surprise. What are you doing here?" Joey exclaimed.

"Waiting for you, Joey."

"When did you get in town?" Joey asked.

"Just now. I came to see you."

Joey had a puzzled look on his face and seemed uncomfortable. Barry was watching him closely. He noticed his drawn appearance and his clothes practically hanging on him.

"You want to go get a drink, Barry? I mean, a coke?" he asked, blushing.

"A 'drink', Joey?" Barry asked quietly, watching him."

"Aw, well. I know you don't drink, Barry."

"Do you drink, Joey?" Barry asked.

"Just a social drink, now and then; nothing more. Want to get a burger?" he asked, avoiding Barry's piercing blue eyes.

"Sure, I'll drive. You can ride with me. My car is over there," Barry said.

Joey followed Barry to his car and getting in, he immediately flipped open a pack of cigarettes.

"Are you smoking now, Joey?" Barry asked, displeased.

A shocked expression crossed Joey's face and he put the pack inside his pocket.

"Did Dad send you?" Joey asked, defensively.

"Why would Dad send me?" Barry asked, coolly.

"Hell! He has left a dozen messages for me at work. He keeps bugging me!"

"Watch your tongue, Joey! Has it ever occurred to you that he is worried about you? What has happened to you? You've changed and not for the better."

"I'm still the same old 'me'," Joey laughed, nervously.

He directed Barry to a Bar & Grill a few blocks away and once there, they went inside. The place was smoke-filled and dimly lit. Joey found an empty table and sat down.

"You don't mind if I order a drink do you, Barry?" Joey asked, hesitantly.

"That's up to you, Joey," Barry answered, annoyed at his brother.

When the waitress came, Joey ordered himself a Scotch and a cheeseburger. Barry ordered a cheeseburger and coffee.

"It's kind of early for a Scotch, isn't it, Joey?" Barry asked, when the waitress left.

"Don't even go there, Barry," Joey said testily, meeting his gaze.

"What has happened to you, Joey? You've gone crazy! Mom and Dad raised you to do better."

"I'm doing fine! I've grown up, that's all! I'm living my own life now," he said, daringly.

"You look like crap!" Barry gritted between his teeth. "You must have lost twenty pounds. Are you on drugs, too?"

"No, I'm not on drugs!" Joey denied.

"Who is the woman?" Barry asked, bluntly.

"What woman?" Joey asked, looking around.

"The woman that you're shacked up with!"

"Who told you that?" Joey snapped.

"Joey, Mom and Dad know. I know. Who is she and how old is she?"

"What damn business is it of yours?" Joey exclaimed. "I've got my own life to live, you've got yours!"

"After looking at you and listening to you, Joey, I'd say that you're not doing a very good job of living it." Barry had to stifle the urge to reach across the table and jerk Joey up by the collar and beat some sense into him.

The waitress interrupted them to bring their dinner and drinks.

Barry didn't feel like eating, but he knew that Joey needed food.

"Let's call a truce," Barry said, "let's eat." He picked up his burger and took a bite. Surprisingly, it was good and he realized that he was hungry. He hadn't stopped to eat on the way. Neither of them spoke as they ate their meal. Joey downed his Scotch and ordered another one. Barry stared at him, silently. Finally, Joey shoved his empty plate away and leaning back in his seat, he took out the pack of cigarettes. This time he lit the cigarette and drew on it hungrily. He tried to blow the smoke away from Barry.

Then, he started talking. "I met this woman that you asked about at a party. She's really something! You should see her," he grinned.

"How old is she, Joey?"

"How should I know? What difference does it make, anyway? She's a beauty, Barry. She knows all the right moves, you know what I mean?"

"No, tell me." Barry said, baiting him.

Joey grinned, blushing. "Aw, you know what I mean. She's real sexy."

Barry felt nauseous, hearing this from his younger brother.

When Barry didn't reply, Joey continued. "She's a dancer."

"A dancer?" Barry stated, blankly.

Joey's eyes narrowed, watching Barry. "Well, you wanted to know, she dances at a nightclub."

"For the love of God, Joey! Have you lost your mind? You have better sense!"

"Don't judge me, Barry! Wait until you see her and get to know her."

"I have no desire to get to know her! No wonder you won't go near Mom and Dad! You know they wouldn't accept her."

"That's crap! I'm not a little boy any more!"

"I'm beginning to understand now, Joey. This Gal is working her spell on you. Did she get you to drinking and smoking? What else? Are you doing drugs?"

"No! I'm not doing drugs!" he said, angrily. He got to his feet. His face flushed, he said, "I'm ready to go. Are you ready?"

Barry knew that the liquor was working on Joey already. "I'll take you home. You're in no shape to drive."

Joey opened his mouth to reply, his eyes blazing. Seeing his brother's stern face, he backed down. "Whatever," he spat, angrily.

Barry drove to the apartment that Joey directed him to. When he stopped the car in front, they both sat staring into space.

"Joey, I can't stand seeing you like this. Let me help you," Barry said, softly.

"I'm okay, Barry. I'm fine, believe me!"

"You're killing yourself! You look awful."

"You said that already. What's wrong with the way I look?"

Barry shook his head, at a loss for words.

"Come inside and meet Linda. She's supposed to be off tonight."

"No."

"Aw, come on, Barry, give her a chance. You don't even know her."

Barry hesitated, wondering if he could influence Joey better if he knew with whom he was dealing. Finally, he made up his mind.

"Okay, I'll come in and meet her," he said, getting out of the car.

Joey led the way to the front door.

"Hey, Linda! We've got company," Joey called, as he opened the door.

They were barely inside the room when the woman appeared in the doorway leading to the kitchen. Barry's gaze met hers, levelly. He saw that Joey was correct in describing her. She was very attractive, but there was a coarseness about her that he recognized readily. She was tall and slim. He guessed her age to be at least thirty-five, not much younger than his own age.

"Well, who do we have here?" she purred, looking Barry over from head to toe. "Don't tell me! I see the resemblance. This has to be your big brother, right, Joey?"

"Yeah, this is Barry. Barry, this is Linda Wells."

"How are you?" Barry said, curtly.

"I'm fine, Darling, how are you? It's so nice of you to drop by. Would you like a drink...Vodka, Scotch?"

"No thank you. I'm fine."

"You're fine, all right," she teased, her gaze sweeping over him again.

Joey spanked her on the rear knowingly and said, "Put your eyeballs back in their sockets, Linda. This is my brother, for Christ's sake!"

She drew closer and was about to take Barry's arm. He avoided her by sitting down warily, in a recliner.

"Well, do have a seat," she said, laughing.

Joey walked to the bar and poured himself another drink.

"Pour one for me too, Sweetie," Linda said.

Barry could stand it no longer. He got up quickly and walked to the door.

"Are you leaving already?" Linda asked, surprised.

Joey turned from the bar, the glass of liquor in his hand. "You just got here, Barry!" he said, uncertainly.

"I've been here long enough, Joey. Think about what I said." Barry closed the door as he went out. He felt as though a rock were buried in the pit of his stomach. All the way home, he kept remembering the scene with Joey and Linda. He felt sick, realizing what Joey had gotten himself into. He remembered how Linda's look had made his skin crawl. He wondered how many men she had been with and how many she had ruined. He vowed to do his best to keep her from ruining Joey. He wondered what he could do to prevent it. He had to figure out a way. For some unknown reason the image of Joan Caulfield popped into his mind. Was he comparing Linda to Joan? Joan seemed like a saint compared to Linda.

At home again, Barry confided in Amy, telling her everything about his visit with Joey. She could tell that he loathed 'Linda'.

"I wonder if he could be an alcoholic," Barry continued. "He kept drinking one drink after another. He looks awful, Amy. I wouldn't be surprised if he is on drugs."

"How can we help him, Barry?"

"I don't know," he answered, his brow furrowed with worry.

Amy went to sit beside him and ran her fingers through his dark hair. She massaged his brow gently with her fingertips. "We'll find a way, Darling. Try not to worry so much."

"He's my brother, Amy," Barry replied, distressed.

"I know. I understand that it hurts you to see him like that. I love Joey, too." She lifted his chin so that his eyes met hers. She leaned over and kissed his lips sweetly. He stared at her a moment and drew her to him roughly and covered her mouth with his in an ardent kiss.

When Barry finally released Amy enough for her to breathe normally, her eyes were shining as she said, "That's more like it."

***

Barry's concern for Joey prompted him to confide in Captain Adams. They discussed the problem over coffee one day.

The captain listened attentively as Barry related to him everything that happened. The captain studied a moment then replied, "Barry, I can think of only one thing that might work to get Joey away from this 'Linda'. If she were to become interested in someone else, that might work."

Barry stared at him, letting that register in his mind. "You may have something there, but who?"

A smug expression crossed the captain's face.

"What?" Barry asked.

"What about 'you'? Amy would probably kill me, if she knew that I suggested this," the captain stated. "From the way you said this 'Linda' came on to you, that just might be a way to prove to Joey that she can't be trusted."

"Are you out of your mind?" Barry retorted.

The captain chuckled, seeing Barry's expression. "I'm serious, Barry. It just might work."

"And probably alienate Joey from me for the rest of my life," Barry stated.

"Would you be willing to give it a try?" the captain asked.

Barry shuddered, imagining being near Linda again.

"Is she that repulsive, Barry?" the captain asked.

Barry's eyes narrowed, remembering. "She's pretty, if all you do is look. But, she is tough looking and coarse. For God's sake, Captain! She dances at a club. What do you expect? She is the type I have despised all my life!"

"Could you ignore your feelings for a short while if it helped to get Joey away from her?"

"Captain, you're asking a lot of me," Barry said, reluctantly. "We're playing with fire here and I could be the one getting burned. There's Amy to consider and you know this could backfire."

The captain nodded. "It's risky, but I think it's worth a try."

"What about you? She would hit on you, too, if given the chance. Why don't you help me out? She can have her choice, you or me."

The captain laughed. "You've turned the tables on me, Barry, but I'll do it. We'll be in this together. First, I think it would be a good idea to have a talk with our wives to clear things with them before we tackle this. We're both happily married and as far as I'm concerned, I want to stay that way," the captain chuckled.

"Now you know how I feel," Barry said.

Barry dreaded bringing up the subject of his discussion with Captain Adams to Amy. He had an idea what her reaction would be and he was right. He had explained what they planned to do and Amy was shocked.

"Barry! I can't believe that both of you planned this! Do you realize what you are getting yourselves into? Isn't there some other way?"

"Can you come up with another idea, Sweetheart? I've wracked my brain trying to come up with something. Then, the captain came up with this idea."

Amy's voice was weak as she asked, "Are you going to the club where she works?"

"No, I'm not going to watch her dance, Sweetheart, I promise."

"Good. This is hard enough to accept, with-out....that....," Amy confessed.

Barry took Amy into his arms. He kissed her softly and meeting her gaze said, "If you don't want me to do this, Sweetheart, I won't. I'll understand and we'll forget the whole thing."

"No, I want you to do whatever you need to do to make Joey realize that he is ruining his life with her. I trust you, Barry. I know that you will be faithful to me."

"Thank you for that trust, Sweetheart. I don't ever want to do anything to betray that trust or to hurt you."

On the weekend Captain Adams and Barry made the trip to see Linda. Barry had called Joey's apartment earlier and Linda answered. He told her that he and a friend were in town on business and would like to take her out for a late lunch. She had jumped at the chance to see Barry again.

As Barry was driving, he addressed the captain. "Before I called Linda, I called Joey earlier and apologized for leaving like I did. He invited me to come back some-time and he'd take me to watch Linda dance."

The captain chuckled. "That part of the discussion with my wife didn't go over very well. How about you?"

"Like a lead balloon," Barry laughed, remembering. After a moment he added, "I just hope I don't forget and call you 'Captain'. We're better off if she doesn't know that you're a policeman. Joey would remember you from the hospital, I'm sure."

When Barry and Captain Adams arrived at the restau-rant where Linda was to meet them the captain said, "Barry, I hope you appreciate what I am doing for you. This is to-tally above and beyond the call of duty."

"Here I was thinking that you were my friend and do-ing me a favor," Barry joked. Both men sobered quickly as they entered the restaurant.

Barry gave his name to the hostess and asked if anyone was waiting for him.

"Yes, Sir. This way, please." She led them to a secluded table in a corner.

Barry recognized Linda at a distance and felt her watching them as they approached. He felt his own heartbeat picking up speed in anticipation of what was coming and what was expected of him and the captain. She sat in a seductive pose, a glass of liquor in her hand. In one glance, Barry's gaze took in her crimson dress that was molded to her perfectly shaped body and her long, platinum hair that hung in wavy strands on her shoulders.

"Gentlemen," she said, seductively, acknowledging them when they stopped before her table, "Please have a seat." Her ruby lips twitched at the corners, suppressing a smile.

"Linda, it's a pleasure to see you again," Barry lied. "I'd like for you to meet my co-worker, Gary Adams. I've been telling him about you."

"Oh? And just what did you tell him about me?" she purred. "Did you have a change of heart, Darling? You left in an awful hurry last time." She reached over and ran her fingers along Barry's hand as it lay on the table. Her gaze met his, daringly.

Barry had the urge to jerk his hand away as though he had touched a hot stove, but he forced himself to keep it still.

She picked up her smoking cigarette and drew on it and laid it back down.

"What brings you two handsome men to town?" she asked, looking the captain over in his turn. "You said 'co-worker'. Do you work in that forensic stuff too?" she asked the captain.

The captain hesitated only momentarily, meeting Barry's gaze and answered, "Yeah, something like that. I work in the lab."

She frowned prettily. "That's a disgusting job to even think about. How can you do it?" Turning her attention back to Barry she added, "Joey has told me a lot about you, Honey."

Barry's heart sank. He hoped she wouldn't figure them out so soon.

"We're not here to discuss our work, Linda," Barry said, forcing himself to give her his charming smile.

"No? Why are you here?" she asked sweetly.

Barry swallowed hard. Glancing at the captain and then at Linda, he said, "We thought you might have something to offer us."

Linda burst into laughter, drawing attention to herself from other tables. She leaned closer to Barry and took his hand in both of hers. She caressed the top of it with her fingers.

"Let me get this straight, Darling. Either that is a proposition or you're interested in something else I can supply. Which is it?"

"Can you supply us with something else?" the captain asked smoothly.

Linda studied both of them for a moment before she answered. Finally, she said, "How do I know you're not setting me up?"

"You can trust us, Linda," the captain said softly.

"Yeah, right!" she laughed. "You sound just like a dozen other guys I know. What did you two have in mind, a three-some?" she teased.

Barry felt sick to his stomach at the thought. Suddenly, Amy's image flashed across his mind. He longed to be at home with her and his son instead of here with this vile woman. He glanced at the captain and saw a smirky grin on his face.

"Is that an option?" the captain asked daringly.

"What do you think, Honey? Don't you think I can handle both of you?"

"What about Joey?" Barry managed to ask, having a problem controlling his urge to break and run. He felt as though they were playing with a rattlesnake.

"What Joey doesn't know, won't hurt him," she said, her hazel eyes narrowing slightly.

"So that's the way it is," Barry said.

"Don't get me wrong, I like Joey a lot. He has been real good to me, but he's too possessive, if you know what I mean. I don't like being tied down."

They were interrupted by the waitress who came to take their order. Then, they resumed their conversation.

"Are you going to tell Joey that we were here today?" Barry asked.

Linda grinned. "You think I should?"

"You can tell him that we came by, but we knew he was working," Barry said.

They got their order and ate their lunch. When they finished eating, Linda lit another cigarette and leaned back in her chair, her eyes sparkling.

"How much are you guys prepared to pay?" she asked.

Both men assumed that she was referring to the lunch. They looked puzzled that she would ask and the captain said, "Of course we will pay for your lunch, Linda."

She laughed aloud, again. "I can tell that you guys aren't used to doing this. I'm telling you, I usually get paid for my services. You understand?"

Barry felt as though he had been socked in the stomach. He was so repulsed by Linda that he could hardly sit there. His gaze met the captain's and he read the same message there. They tried to change their expression before she noticed.

"How much do you usually get?" the captain asked, finally.

Linda smiled seductively. "That depends," she purred. "If it's just one of you, a hundred dollars. Both, three hundred."

"Why don't you take us one at a time for now?" Barry managed to ask.

"Three hundred is pretty steep," the captain said.

"I doubt that you would complain......afterwards," she teased.

Barry was anxious to leave and said to the captain, "You know, Gary, we really need to be going."

"You're right. We hate to eat and run, Honey, but you understand," he grinned.

"Why don't you stick around and watch me dance tonight? I'll dance especially for you."

"Can't tonight, Doll," the captain said. "You pick another time and give me a call. Here's my cell phone number." He handed her a piece of paper with the number on it.

"What about you, Barry?" she asked, meeting his gaze.

Barry wrote his number on a napkin and handed it to her.

"How original!" she teased. "The next night I have off is Tuesday. Morning or afternoon?"

"Whatever," Barry stated as he counted out money to pay for the meal. He left it beside her plate. "That should take care of lunch," he said.

"Thanks. I'll be seeing both of you around. You can count on it," she smiled.

Both men left her sitting at the table. When they were in the car and pulling out of the parking lot they let out a sigh of relief.

"I thought I was going to throw up back there," Barry said, disgusted.

"Man, she's a character, isn't she?" the captain exclaimed. "If this wasn't out of my jurisdiction, I would give her a hundred dollars and then arrest her for solicitation."

"Can you believe that Joey is mixed up with her?"

Barry said.

"A young fellow, yes. I can believe it. How are we going to handle it, Barry? She's going to wonder why we don't go to bed with her. How are we going to keep putting her off and make it believable?"

"Captain, I don't know. I honest, to God, don't know. But, I know one thing for certain. She's not getting 'me' into her bed!"

The captain had to laugh. "Lord, what our wives would say if they had heard that conversation back there!"

"I don't even want to think about it," Barry admitted. After a moment he said, "Linda's going to call, if we don't call her first."

"Yeah, I know. Maybe we need to wear a wire and record everything. Don't you think that would be best?" the captain asked.

"That's a good idea. Then, we can let Joey listen to it and find out the truth about her. Surely that would make him come to his senses!" Barry stated.

"You'd think so, anyway," the captain stated. "Come by my office tomorrow and I'll have a wire ready for you. We'd better not waste any time."

"You think she'll call soon?" Barry asked.

"I figure she'll call soon but not because she needs the money," the captain answered.

"Captain, I know I agreed to this plan, but I'm getting cold feet."

The captain chuckled. "Barry, you can't bail out on me now. We're in this together."

"I know. I'll do my best. When the time comes, I'll come up with some excuse to keep from taking her to bed," Barry said, reluctantly.

"If you figure that one out, be sure to fill me in, will you?" the captain said.

Several days passed before Linda called. Barry was getting worried that their plan had backfired until she called one Monday evening. He was playing with David when Amy answered the phone.

"It's for you, Barry," she said, handing him the phone. He noticed her anxious expression as his gaze met hers. He knew that it was Linda.

"Hello," he said, his heartbeat picking up speed.

"Hello, Darling. Remember me?" she purred.

Barry hesitated a moment and then said, "Can you hold on a moment so I can change phones?"

"Sure, Darling."

He held the phone a moment, long enough for her to think he was alone. Then, he said, "I can talk now, my wife can't hear."

Amy sat down suddenly, her face ashen. Her gaze met Barry's and held. Finally, he looked away and resumed his conversation.

"You didn't call," Linda began, teasingly.

"I was waiting on you," Barry answered.

She laughed, huskily. "Okay. I'm calling now. Tomorrow is Tuesday. I'm not working at the club."

"So, you want me to meet you somewhere?" he asked, avoiding Amy's stricken look.

"I'll be at the Highlight Inn on highway 36, room 215. Do you know where that is?"

"Yes, I know where it is."

"What time can you be there?" she asked.

"You name it," he answered.

"The earlier the better," she said.

"How about eleven?" he asked.

"That's perfect. I'll be waiting, Darling," she said.

Amy was trembling. "You're meeting her," she stated.

Barry felt guilty, as though he had betrayed Amy. He sat down beside her and pulled her into his arms, gently. Amy laid her head on his chest and could hear his heartbeat slowing down to normal. She wondered about the affect

Linda could have on him. She raised her face and looked into his blue eyes. His sadness was reflected there.

"I'm scared," she whispered.

"Don't be scared, Sweetheart."

"I'm afraid of what she might do. I'm afraid of her."

He didn't know how to reassure her. He kissed her softly and passionately. When he released her he said, "I belong only to you, Amy. I won't ever forget that."

Later that night, lying in Barry's arms as he slept, Amy lay awake for hours, worrying. Finally, she slept, fitfully.

Barry woke early and found Amy still sleeping. He got up, showered and dressed. He was making coffee when she joined him in the kitchen.

"Are you getting ready to leave?" she asked, reluctantly.

He was startled and spilled his coffee. She noticed that he was as nervous as a cat. She forced a smile and began to clean up the mess.

"Listen, Amy," Barry began, handing her a phone number, "I want you to call this number at the motel at exactly one. I will try to be the one to answer. I'll pretend that you are Captain Adams and that something has come up and I have to leave. I'll make it sound believable. That should give me enough time to record plenty of stuff for Joey. Can you do that, Sweetheart?" he pleaded.

"I think so," she said, looking up into his cool, blue eyes.

At that moment David came padding barefoot into the kitchen, rubbing sleep from his eyes.

"Good morning, Sport!" Barry said, grabbing him and squeezing him tight.

"Daddy goin' work?" David asked.

"Yeah, Daddy has to go, but I'll be back later, I promise." He hugged his son again and took Amy into his arms and kissed her softly. "I love you," he said, as he looked at her pale face.

"I love you too, Barry," she whispered.

He released her and walked to the door.

Amy watched as the door closed behind him and he was gone. She slumped onto a chair, laid her head on her arms and cried.

"Mommy cry? Why mommy cry?" David asked.

Amy straightened herself and wiped her eyes. She forced a smile for David.

"Mommy's not crying, Darling. Mommy is just fine. Would you like for Mommy to fix you a waffle for breakfast?"

"Yeah! Waffle!" he sang, "I want waffle!"

47

***

Barry almost wished that he smoked if it would help relieve some of the tension that he felt on his way to the Highlight Inn. He checked the tiny tape recorder that was hidden under his shirt near his waistband. He hoped that Linda couldn't feel any wires if she had her hands on him. He knew that he would have to do some 'tall talking' to pull this off. He thought of Joey and hoped that he would understand why he was doing this when it was over. Lord! He wished it were over already! He dreaded tackling that rattlesnake again.

When Barry arrived at the Inn, he went to room 215 and knocked. His heartbeat was racing with dread.

Linda opened the door and stepped aside, letting him enter. She closed the door behind him as he turned to face her. She was wearing a pale pink gown and negligee. Her platinum hair hung in waves on her shoulders.

"Hello," Linda said, huskily, her ruby lips curled in a seductive smile. "I thought you'd never get here!"

"I'm not late." He could think of nothing else to say.

She laughed. Then, she slipped her arms around him as he stood there, at a loss for words. Slowly, she pulled his dark head down until her lips touched his. She kissed him slowly and expertly, causing him to draw in his breath sharply. His arms circled her body automatically and she pressed closer to him. Finally, he pulled away.

"Come, sit down," she said. She had a decanter of wine and two glasses prepared on the table before the couch. "Have a glass of wine with me," she said.

"I don't drink, Linda. I could use a Coke, if you have one."

"She laughed at that. "Sure do, Darling, anything you want. Are you hungry? I have fruit and finger sandwiches; you name it."

"Sounds good," he agreed, stalling for time. "Can I help?"

"It's already done. All I have to do is bring it to you." She disappeared into an adjoining room where there was a tiny refrigerator and microwave.

Barry waited nervously, until she came back with a tray of strawberries, grapes and tiny ham and cheese sandwiches.

She poured his coke into a glass of ice. Picking up a tiny sandwich from the tray, she put it up to his lips. He opened his mouth for it and she made a point of tracing his lips with her fingertips. He chewed the sandwich and tried to swallow. It stuck in his throat, and he coughed.

She looked at him, teasingly. "Need a drink, Darling?" she asked and lifted the Coke to his lips for a swallow.

His cool blue eyes stared into hers. "I can feed myself," he said, forcing a smile. He remembered that he hadn't eaten breakfast and he was actually hungry.

She held the tray closer and he helped himself to another sandwich. She ate one and then poured herself a glass of wine. After sipping on it for a moment she took a grape and ate it. Then, she reached for a ripe strawberry and held it to Barry's lips. He stared at her and opened his mouth. He chewed and swallowed it. She offered him a grape, touching his lips again. He pushed her hand away.

"Are you finished eating already?" she teased.

"I've had plenty, thanks," he managed to say.

"Good! Now, we can get down to business," she said, seductively.

Barry reached for his wallet to pay her. She stayed his hand with her own.

"No, silly, not that! This one's on the house. You're too fine to have to pay, believe me!" she said.

"But, you said your fee is a hundred dollars," he said, baiting her.

"When I'm working. This is play. There's a difference."

"Really?" he managed to ask.

"Yes, really. I'd almost pay you, Honey," she laughed. She put her glass down and curled up close to him. "You've never cheated on your wife before, have you, Darling?"

Shocked by her question, he finally answered, "How can you tell?"

"I can tell. Most men would have had me naked and on the bed before now."

"I've been told that I'm not like most men."

"God! You've got that right!" she teased. "Hey, you do like girls, don't you?"

The question irritated him, but he tried not to show it. "Yeah, I like girls. I married one, didn't I?"

"What's she like, your wife?"

"Totally opposite from you!" he answered before he could help himself.

"Poor thing," she teased.

Anger flared and Barry couldn't hide it. "We won't discuss my wife," he said, too quietly. He was having to will himself to keep his cool and not blow it.

"Pardon me!" she said, seeing that his beautiful blue eyes had changed to a steel gray.

She changed the subject. "Your friend, Gary, called me a couple of days ago."

258

"Oh, yeah? Well, actually, I told him I was coming over here today. I think he was jealous." His lie was convincing.

Linda laughed. "He'll get his turn. I wanted you first, Darling. Champagne and then beer, you know."

"Gary's a first rate guy," Barry defended him.

"He's okay, I'm sure," she said, watching him speculatively. Finally, she asked, "Are you getting cold feet, Darling?"

"Me? Why, no. Why do you ask?"

"Okay, show me," she said, seductively.

Taking a deep breath, Barry pulled her into his arms roughly and began kissing her. She returned his kiss. He felt her tongue teasing his and he shivered. Encouraged, Linda ran her fingers through his dark hair and pressed her warm body even closer.

A picture of Amy flashed across his mind. He closed his eyes tighter. He remembered how worried she had been. He tried to pretend that this was Amy in his arms. He kissed Linda on her throat and then her shoulder.

Encouraged, Linda pulled him down beside her onto the couch.

Barry pulled away from her and pushed her away gently. He cleared his throat and reached for his Coke.

"Tell me, what kind of drugs can you get for me?" he asked, hoarsely.

"What?" she asked, agitated. "Now?"

"Yeah, now," he managed to say.

"You're strange, you know that?" she remarked, sitting up and arranging her negligee.

"Can you get meth or cocaine?" he asked on a hunch.

"How did you know?" she asked, surprised.

"Just a hunch. Which one?"

"Meth, all you want. You want some now? It would help you relax, Honey.

"I'm relaxed enough," he stated.

She laughed at that. "You're wound up like a snake about to strike."

"Yeah? Maybe I'm wondering how many men you've had before me," he said, baiting her.

Her eyes narrowed. "What has that got to do with us?"

"Nothing, really," he answered.

"You're right. So, why bring it up?"

"I don't know," he answered, stalling for time. He glanced at his watch. It was past one. Why didn't Amy call?

Slowly, Linda pushed him back onto the couch and laid her body across his. She began trailing her fingers through his dark hair and along his cheek. She touched his lips again with her own and ran her tongue across his lips.

"God, you're good looking!" she teased. "I wonder if Joey will be as good looking when he gets to be your age?"

"Joey probably won't be around here when he gets to be my age," Barry said. He was glad that he was taping this for him to hear.

"Why not?" Linda asked, surprised.

"He's young and doesn't know what he really wants. If he ever finds out about this.....us..., there will be hell to pay."

"I'd trade Joey for you in a heartbeat, Darling," she whispered.

Barry was thrilled that she had actually said that on tape. "Would you? What about Gary?"

"Gary? Oh, your friend. I haven't gotten to know him yet."

The phone rang loudly. Relief swept through Barry.

"Damn! Who can that be?" Linda asked, getting up to answer it.

"Let me get it!" Barry said, quickly and beat her to the phone.

Linda was surprised and watched as he picked up the

receiver.

"Hello," he said.

"Hello, Barry." It wasn't Amy's voice. It was Captain Adams. "Don't say anything, just listen. I called your house and Amy told me what was going on. I told her I'd call instead of her. Make up your story and tell Linda that you have to leave. Is everything going as planned?"

"Yeah, sure," Barry answered, "I can leave right now. You picked a heck of a time to call, you know."

The captain laughed. "That's good, Barry."

Linda was annoyed and interrupted. "Barry! You're not leaving? Who are you talking to? Who knew you were here?"

"Hold on a minute, Gary," Barry said. Then, to Linda he said, "It's Gary. A problem has come up at work and I have to leave. I'm sorry," he lied.

"Let me talk to him!" she said and grabbed the phone from Barry.

"Gary, what's going on?" she asked sweetly, "Why does Barry have to go to work now? Can't you handle whatever it is?"

The captain was surprised that Barry had put her on the phone. "The boss wants Barry, not me, Sweetheart. Sorry."

"What about you, Honey? Are you free? I have this room booked and I'll be here all by myself. Why don't you come on over?"

Barry could hardly believe his good luck. She was putting the noose around her neck.

"Me? Why, I suppose I could," the captain answered, surprised. "Well, sure! That would be great!"

"She gave him the address. I'll be waiting for you, Darling," she purred and then hung up the phone.

"You don't waste any time," Barry said, trying to hide his disgust.

"Maybe the afternoon won't be a total loss," she

pouted.

"You didn't miss me long," he stated.

She moved close to him and slipped her arms around his neck.

"You understand don't you, Darling? I have needs and you haven't fulfilled those needs. You still have time….."

He pushed her arms down gently and said, "I can't. I have to leave now. Besides, you have to get ready for Gary."

"I believe you're jealous!" she teased.

Barry wanted to laugh in her face but forced himself to stay sober.

"No, I'm not jealous. There'll be other times. I'm still interested in the meth, too."

"Look, I wouldn't do this for just anybody," she said as she took a note pad and wrote a name and number on it. "Here's a contact. Call him and tell him that I gave you his number. He'll take care of whatever you need."

"Thanks," Barry said, delighted to have the lead. He took two fifties from his wallet and laid them on the table. "This is for the room. I'm sorry I've disappointed you," he said, trying to sound convincing.

"It has been my pleasure, Darling. The waiting will just make it sweeter the next time we're together. How about one for the road?" She moved into his arms and held her lips close, waiting for his kiss. Reluctantly he kissed her, and then pushed her away.

"Good bye, Linda," he stated.

"Bye, Darling," she purred and watched from the doorway as he disappeared into the elevator outside.

Barry drew a breath of relief as he got into his car and left the Inn. He had pulled it off. It had been difficult, but it had worked. He rubbed the back of his hand across his mouth, trying to erase the thought of kissing Linda. He had never been so repulsed by anyone in his life as he was

Linda. He thought of Amy, his sweet, loving and gentle Amy. Tears misted his eyes as he thought of her. He thought of little David and felt as though his heart would burst with love for both of them. He couldn't bear it if he lost either of them.

He remembered, again, Amy's worried expression. He hoped that she would forget this ordeal and that they could move on with their lives. Surely, he had enough taped to convince Joey what he was dealing with. Hopefully, Joey would put Linda out of his life forever.

Barry arrived at home at five. He let himself in and found Amy in the kitchen.

"Barry! I didn't know you were home." She had a smudge of flour on her cheek. She was making an apple pie.

Barry took her into his arms and squeezed her so tightly that she gasped for air. He looked into her dark eyes as she gazed into his. She was afraid of what she might find there. All she saw was his love reflected there. He bent his head and kissed her, long and passionately.

"Darling," she breathed, when she was able, " are you okay?"

"I am now," he answered.

"Do you want to talk about it?" Amy asked.

"No, not now. I will later. It was an ordeal, but it worked." He pulled his shirt from his pants and began pulling the tape off the wires and recorder. Amy helped him and then tucked his shirt inside.

"I'm glad that you told the captain and he called. He is probably there by now. He'll be able to get more recorded for Joey to hear."

"Captain Adams has gone up there?" Amy asked, surprised.

"Yes, it worked out really well. Since I had an excuse to leave, he could go and set her up, too. Hopefully, we'll be rid of her once and for all."

"I hope so," Amy said, softly.

Barry wiped the flour from her cheek. "Sweetheart, today made me realize even more, how very precious you are and how much I love you."

"I love you, too, Darling." She tried to wipe the image from her mind of him in Linda's arms. He had said he would talk about it later. She was naturally curious and she knew that the heaviness in her heart was jealousy. Yet, she could not make the image disappear from her mind.

48

***

It was almost noon on Wednesday when Captain Adams came to Barry's office.

Barry had just come from the lab. He greeted the captain and asked, "Well, how did it go?"

"It was the hardest thing I ever had to do," the captain answered, truthfully.

Barry looked at him, knowingly. "I don't think I have to ask why."

"I tell you, Barry, I don't know about you, but I had to keep telling myself that I was a happily married man and I didn't want to mess that up. One thing I can say about Linda, she's persistent."

"You didn't forget that 'happily married' part, did you, Captain?" Barry grinned.

"No, but I came mighty close a time or two, I hate to admit. If my wife had been a fly on the wall, I probably wouldn't be happily married any more."

Barry chuckled in spite of the seriousness of the situation. "I think I held her at bay and she didn't really have a chance to get started on me. She even asked me if I liked girls."

"You don't mean it?" the captain exclaimed.

"Well, did you get it taped and were you able to get

out of there without her finding out about it?" Barry asked.

"Yes, I got it all. She was mad when I left, though."

"How did you get out of there?" Barry asked.

"I pretended to have a guilt complex all of a sudden and couldn't cheat on my wife. That part was true."

Barry nodded, understanding and not blaming his friend. "You know, this experience makes me have more patience with Joey. He didn't have a chance when she got her hooks into him," Barry stated.

"You're right," the captain agreed. "By the way, when do we let Joey hear the tapes?"

"As soon as we can. Are you going with me?"

"Sure, just call me and tell me when."

"I'll call Joey and see if we can go to his apartment when Linda is at work," Barry said.

49

***

Barry called Joey the next day and made plans to go see him on the weekend. He and Captain Adams copied the tapes and carried the two copies and a tape player with them.

Joey was surprised to see Captain Adams again. "You guys still on a case together?" he asked.

"You might say that, Joey," Barry answered.

"Can I get you a Coke?" he asked, grinning at Barry.

"No thanks," they answered as they sat down across from Joey.

"What you got there?" Joey asked, motioning to the tape player.

Barry looked at the captain and then at Joey. Drawing a deep breath he began, "Joey, we've brought something that I want you to listen to. Before you hear it, I want to explain why we did this."

"What are you talking about?" Joey asked, puzzled.

"Joey, it concerns 'Linda'."

"Linda? What has she got to do with it?"

"Joey, I know that you are smitten with her right now, but you don't know what you are dealing with," Barry said, meeting his brother's gaze levelly.

"Look here! I resent your coming in here and saying

things against Linda! You don't even know her! You only
saw her that one time! Wait a minute! She did say you
stopped by one day when I was at work. What's going on
here?" Joey's face was turning red and Barry recognized
his anger.

"Joey," Captain Adams said, " Both of us have seen
Linda more than that. We arranged to meet her at the Highlight Inn. She rented a room there and waited for us."

"You're lying!" Joey exclaimed.

"We set her up, Joey," the captain continued, "only,
she didn't know it. We were supposed to have sex with
her…..both of us."

"You low down cheats! I don't believe you!"

"Joey, listen," Barry pleaded. "Hear us out, please!"

Joey was on his feet, pacing. He glared at them. "I
don't have to listen to these lies!" he stammered.

"If you won't listen to us, listen to these tapes. We
wore wires, Joey and taped it all," Barry pleaded.

"I don't want to listen to any damn tapes!" he said
angrily.

Barry started the recorder and watched Joey closely.

Joey sat down heavily and lit a cigarette, his hands
trembling. The voices were distinct. Barry saw recognition
on Joey's face as he listened. Joey's face grew crimson.
Suddenly, he reached over and punched the stop button. "I
don't want to hear any more of that crap! You tricked her,
set her up!" he growled.

"Sure we did. We did it for you, Joey. So you'd see
the kind of person she is. She'll ruin you, Joey!" Barry
pleaded.

"That's a lousy trick! My own brother hitting on my
girl! Wait until I tell Amy!" he croaked.

Barry was on his feet and had Joey by the shoulders.
"You're not listening, Joey! We-set-her-up! We devised
this plan to show you what she is. If she would do this with
us, she would do it with anybody! Don't you understand,

Joey? She is a slut!"

Joey's expression was wild. "Did you let Amy hear that tape?"

"No, Joey, not yet."

"Hah! I didn't think so!"

"Joey," Captain Adams said quietly, "Both my wife and Amy know about this."

"I don't believe you!" Joey said.

"Call Amy," Barry challenged, "ask her."

Joey stared at them, defensively. "Get out, both of you! Take your damn tape with you!"

"There are two tapes, Joey. We're leaving them for you to listen to. Please use your head and listen to them after we leave," Barry said. He and the captain walked to the door.

Joey was sitting on the couch staring at the tape recorder.

At the door, Barry turned. His heart aching for his younger brother, he said, softly, "Joey, I love you. I did this for you."

"Like hell you did!" Joey grated between his teeth. "Get out!"

On the way home both Barry and Captain Adams were silent. Finally, the captain said, "I'm sorry about how that turned out back there, Barry. I think Joey will come to his senses after he listens to the tapes."

"If he listens to the tapes," Barry said, discouraged.

"He'll listen, don't worry. Wouldn't you?"

"I guess I would," he admitted.

"Just give him some time. He'll come around. Hopefully, in the meantime, he will kick Linda out of his life."

"I had hoped he would understand," Barry said, sorrowfully.

"He feels betrayed by us right now. It's a natural reaction," the captain continued. "Give him some time."

"He has the rest of his life. I just hope I'll be a part of

that life," Barry said, discouraged.

"Don't be so hard on yourself, Barry. The worse is over."

"I hope you're right."

To get Barry's mind off Joey, Captain Adams said, "Did I tell you we've got an undercover agent working on Linda's drug supplier? He has made contact with him to buy meth. As soon as the money changes hands we'll grab him."

"I'm glad to hear it," Barry said.

50

***

At home again, Barry related to Amy everything that had happened with Joey. She watched him closely as he talked and was concerned. She could see that he was deeply hurt by Joey's rejection.

When he finished talking she hugged him tenderly. "He'll come around, Darling. I'm sure of it. Just give him time to get over this."

"That's exactly what Captain Adams said," he answered. He met her gaze and with a dreaded expression on his face, asked, "Do you want to listen to a copy of the tape?"

"No," she said without hesitating, "I don't."

"You don't? Are you sure?"

"I am positive, Darling. I consider that 'evidence'. I don't intend to interfere with your work."

"This isn't exactly work, Amy."

"Captain Adams is involved and a drug dealer is involved. To me, that is work. Case closed."

Barry grinned. "You're fantastic, Sweetheart," he said, pulling her close.

51

***

A week later Barry's dad called. He told him that Joey had come by and had eaten dinner with them.

"That's great, Dad!" Barry exclaimed, encouraged.

"He told us that he had moved and had split up with his girlfriend. I have to say we were greatly relieved."

"I'm delighted to hear that, Dad."

"You talked to him, didn't you, Barry?" Mr. Reeser asked cautiously.

"Yes, Dad, I did."

"I'm glad you did. Whatever you said must have had an impact on him. I did get the impression that he wasn't too happy with you right now, however."

"How come?" Barry ventured.

"Just the way he acted when your name came up. For one thing, I invited him to go with us the next time we come see you and Amy. But, he made lame excuses."

"Don't worry about it, Dad. Whatever I said seems to have worked. That's all that matters."

"You're right, Son. By the way, your mom and I want you and Amy and the boy to come for Thanksgiving dinner. She already has the turkey and fixings."

"Sure, Dad. Don't mention we're coming, to Joey. He might not show up."

"Surely he's not that angry with you, is he, Barry?"

"Just don't mention our coming, Dad. We'll get there around ten."

"Okay, whatever you say. Surely Joey won't still be angry."

"Don't count on it, Dad," Barry said to himself as he hung up the phone.

52

***

When Thanksgiving day came Barry and Amy packed food that Amy had prepared and drove to Barry's parents' home.

His parents met them outside and helped carry things inside. Barry carried little David inside. He noticed Joey's car parked in the driveway. He wondered what kind of reception he would get from him.

As Barry entered the den he came face to face with Joey. Joey's eyes narrowed and a scowl appeared on his face. Barry set David down and immediately David ran to Joey.

"Unk Joee!" David cried, grabbing Joey around the legs and holding on tight.

"Hey, Punk!" Joey laughed, giving all his attention to David. He squatted down and gave David a hug. "I didn't know you were coming to Grandma's house today."

"We're gonna' eat ' turkie'," David said, licking his lips.

Joey laughed and hugged David tighter. He picked him up and swung him in the air. David began to giggle. Barry chuckled, watching them together.

"Come on, Punk. Let's see if we can snitch a bite of Grandma's turkey, how about that?" Joey carried David toward the kitchen, ignoring Barry's presence.

Barry's heart sank, but he was determined not to let his emotions show.

Joey made a point of avoiding Barry all afternoon. He was friendly to Amy, if somewhat reserved. He played with David, helping him build a tower with Lego blocks.

53

***

Since Barry and Amy planned to spend the night with his parents Barry went to the car to get their luggage later in the afternoon. He saw Joey go to his car for a moment and he waited for him on the porch. Joey avoided him by going around to the side door. Barry carried the luggage to his old bedroom and then went to search for Joey. He found him in Joey's room. The door was ajar, but Barry knocked as he entered.

Joey glared at him angrily. "What are you doing in here? Get out!" he said between clenched teeth.

Barry smelled liquor and realized what Joey had been doing at his car.

"Joey, don't do this to yourself. Let me help you," Barry pleaded, softly.

"Help me what? Haven't you done enough for me, big brother?" he snapped.

"I could go to an AA meeting with you. They would help you, Joey."

"Hah! Now you're saying I'm an alcoholic!"

"Aren't you, Joey?" Barry asked, sorrowfully.

"Hell no! I don't have a drinking problem! Stay out of my life. Haven't you done enough already?"

"Don't you realize that you're better off without her, Joey?"

"That was none of your damn business!" Joey grated.

"You're my brother, Joey. You'll always be my business," Barry said, hurting inside.

"Get real! I'm not a kid any more! I have my own life to live."

"I think you need some direction, Joey. You're getting mixed up with the wrong crowd."

"I ain't mixed up with 'any' crowd now, thanks to you! You put a stop to that when you played your little trick."

"Are you doing drugs, Joey? I'm warning you. If you are, the DEA will find out."

"What are you talking about?" Joey asked, paling.

"I'm sure that Linda is a user. She gave me the name of her dealer. He may have been arrested by now."

"That has nothing to do with me! I tell you, I'm not doing drugs! I don't give a rip what happens to Linda or her drug dealer!"

"I'm really glad to hear that, Joey," Barry said, wanting to believe him. "Will you let me help you with your drinking problem?"

Joey started to reply angrily but stopped himself. Suddenly, he slumped down onto the bed, burying his face in his hands. He began to sob, uncontrollably.

Barry was filled with compassion for his brother. He closed the door quietly to ensure privacy. Sitting beside Joey he put his arm around him and hugged him close. He felt Joey stiffen and then relax. When he had control of himself he drew away and seemed embarrassed that Barry had seen him cry.

"Don't be embarrassed, Joey. I cried plenty of times when David was in the hospital, remember?"

Joey nodded and wiped his nose with his handkerchief.

"Did Linda get you hooked on the booze?" Barry asked softly, hoping Joey wouldn't fly into a rage again.

Joey met his gaze, reluctantly. "I guess that was part of it," he admitted. His hands were trembling.

"Mom and Dad don't know, do they?" Barry asked.

"No!" Joey exclaimed. "You won't tell them, will you?"

"Of course not. But, you will get help, won't you, Joey?" Barry pleaded.

Joey nodded, meeting Barry's gaze. "I know I'm a wreck. I can't go on like this."

"Thank goodness it isn't too late," Barry stated. "I have been worried sick about you. Tomorrow we will check into AA meetings. You want me to go with you the first time?" he asked.

Joey thought for a moment and then replied, "No, I can do it. I'll go."

"If you change your mind, let me know," Barry said, encouragingly.

"Thanks…Barry…?"

"Yeah?"

"I'm sorry I said those mean things to you."

Barry's blue eyes were misty. "Forget it. I know you didn't mean it."

There was a soft knock at the door and Amy asked, "Are you two okay?"

"Come in, Amy," Joey called, relieved that it was Amy and not his parents.

When the door opened, little David ran ahead of Amy and bounced up onto the bed beside Joey. "I been lookin' for you, Unk Joee! Come play!"

"Uncle Joey may be tired, sport. Let's let Uncle Joey rest a while," Barry said, grabbing his son and wrestling with him on the bed. David giggled, kicked, and squealed in delight as Barry tickled him.

"I'm not tired," Joey grinned. "Give me that little

Punk!" He took David from Barry. "I'll show you how to build the biggest tower you ever saw! You'd better not knock it down, either!" he threatened and winked at Amy and Barry as he left the room with David.

Amy's gaze met Barry's.

"He's going to be okay," he answered her unasked question.

"Thank goodness!" Amy exclaimed.

Joey spent the night with his parents although he hadn't planned to earlier.

Barry could tell that he was relieved to be home with his family. He was thankful that things were looking brighter. He knew that his parents were pleased to have all of them there.

54

***

Barry was in the forensic lab one day when Captain Adams came by.

"When you get a minute I have some news to tell you," the captain said.

Barry was curious. "Sure. Give me a minute to finish here and I'll meet you in my office."

"It's almost lunch time. Let me buy your lunch," the captain suggested.

"If you insist," Barry grinned.

Barry and Captain Adams drove to a restaurant nearby and ordered lunch.

"Have you heard from Joey lately?" the captain asked.

"He called one night and said he was attending the AA meetings. He sounded excited. He said he hadn't taken a drink since the first meeting."

"I'm glad to hear that, Barry. I know you have been worried about him. The news I have to tell you is about 'Linda's' drug contact. He has been arrested for drug trafficking. He's spilling his guts, trying to cut a deal. He claims that he knows the bunch that was at Rafferty's place and he says he knows who killed Pinkerton. He says Pinkerton killed Rodney Benson."

"You're kidding! Who does he say killed

Pinkerton?"

"He won't say yet. That's his trump card he's wait-ing to play."

"I wonder if 'old Linda' knows anything about all that?" Barry asked, amazed.

"I doubt it," the captain said, grinning. "Of course one of us could go see her again and question her about it," he chuckled.

"Not on your life!" Barry exclaimed. "She can keep any information she has, as far as I am concerned."

The captain expected that reaction from Barry. "Did you ever let your wife listen to the tape, Barry?"

"I asked her about it, but she didn't want to, thank goodness."

"I didn't even consider letting my wife listen to it. She brought up the subject once and I told her that we left the tape with Joey," the captain admitted. "I threw the tape in the trash compactor after that."

"That was the best place for it. I got rid of mine and I hope Joey did too," Barry said.

***

The next time Barry saw Captain Adams was at the coffee shop a few weeks later. The captain called him and asked him to meet him there.

As they sipped their coffee the captain asked, "Have you heard the latest about Pinkerton?"

"No, what?"

"This fellow, 'Sanderson', Linda's drug dealer, finally ratted on his friends. He said the guy who killed Pinkerton was Sara Benson's brother. He says it was because of a squabble over a drug payoff. The guy has already been picked up and is in jail now."

"Finally, we have closure to all this mess that's been going on so long," Barry said, relieved.

"How is your wife and little David?" the captain asked.

"They are doing fine, Captain. David is growing like a weed and talking all the time now."

"No sign of a problem, I hope?" the captain asked, reluctantly.

"Not at all. He seems perfectly normal." Grinning, Barry added, "I'm thinking that we ought to 'order' him a little brother or sister before long."

"Well, that shouldn't be too difficult," the captain chuckled.

"Seriously," Barry continued, "I think Amy is afraid something could happen, like it did with David, if she were to have another baby."

"I can understand that. Hopefully, that will never happen again, to any child," the captain said.

"It better not happen again!" Barry exclaimed. "I talked to our lawyer last week. He is going ahead with the lawsuit. It has been long enough. The hospital is negotiating a settlement out of court."

"They don't want the publicity," the captain said.

"I would love for everyone to know about it!" Barry exclaimed. "Maybe it would help prevent it from happening to another child." After a moment, he added, "Whatever money we get from the settlement will be put in a trust fund for David's college education."

"That still doesn't compensate for what that boy went through and what you and Amy went through, Barry."

"You're right," Barry answered, feeling his heartbeat quicken, remembering.

***

After talking to Captain Adams about wanting another baby, Barry decided to speak to Amy about it that night. She was getting ready for bed after putting David to bed.

Barry was already in bed waiting for Amy. When she sat down on the bed he pulled her into his arms, gently. His blue eyes met her gaze as his lips touched hers. When she opened her eyes and gazed into his again, his eyes seemed to sparkle.

"What are you so smug about?" she asked, softly.

"I've been thinking......," he answered huskily.

"About what?"

He trailed his finger along her cheek and across her soft lips.

Suddenly, she stayed his hand and kissed his fingertips, sending a warm sensation throughout his body.

"What are you thinking of, Darling?" she whispered, seductively.

He continued his gentle caressing. Amy shivered and snuggled closer to his warm body. He kissed her tenderly, his tongue exploring her mouth, lovingly. He felt her heartbeat keeping time with his own.

Finally, between kisses, she asked, "Was this what you were thinking of, Darling?"

"Actually, I was thinking, that, this would be the perfect time to 'order' a little brother or sister for David," he suggested, hoping she would agree.

Amy hesitated only a moment. Smiling seductively, she asked, "Do you think that will be difficult?"

"I think we can handle it," Barry whispered as his lips covered hers and they began their secret journey together; the journey that they had traveled so many times before and would travel until the end of time.

ABOUT THE AUTHOR

Patsy Kirksey Ross was born at Leachville, Arkansas where she attended high school.

She later attended the University of Montevallo, Montevallo, Alabama where she studied Creative Writing and attained a BS Degree in Elementary Education.

She lives in Alabama with her husband.